FOUR DAY

G

R T
UTHOR

FOUR DAY
FLING

CHAPTER ONE
POPPY

The Morning After

I'd been in a lot of awkward situations in my life. In fact, you could almost say I was an expert in awkwardness. If it were a degree, I'd have finished it by age ten and been handed my PhD on my sweet sixteen.

Which, as history dictated, wasn't all that sweet. Mostly because I walked in on my then-boyfriend playing a pretty intense round of tonsil tennis with my twenty-seven-year-old cousin.

That was partly my fault for dating a senior who was legal to put his snake in a girl's basket who wasn't legally able to be the basket, but still.

Awkward.

Then, there was the day in third grade where I'd gotten into a very serious fight—as serious as an argument could be in third grade—with Millie Turner. Something about who was quicker on the monkey bars.

Turned out, it didn't matter. I was quicker but a hell of a lot clumsier. Halfway along, my hands slipped, and that was all she wrote.

Actually, it wasn't. What she wrote was how I ended up on my back, my dress around my waist, and my Barbie panties on show to my entire class.

I wasn't even going to get into all the things that happened between then. Starting my period while wearing white shorts in the middle of an airport... Kissing a boy on the lips in ninth grade to find out he was only going in for a hug... Finding out your parents had a genuine bias toward your perfectly put together, non-clumsy older sister who was just one week away from marrying her high school sweetheart.

Who happened to be a doctor—the youngest doctor in our state to open his own pediatric office and employ four other doctors, if you please.

I mean, who gave a shit that Daddy had bought the building? Not my parents. Not anyone in our town. Nope. Everyone loved Dr. Mark Perkins.

Even I did. Mostly because he was just a really nice freaking person—and not because he'd never told anyone he'd once walked in on me masturbating.

See?

Awk. Ward.

But, hands down, nothing was quite as awkward as the situation I faced right now.

As in, the hot guy sleeping in his bed.

He was pretty. Oh, so fucking pretty. His bedhead was the perfect, dark-brown mess of hair that spread badly across his cream pillow. Here, there, everywhere, it was all kinds of did-you-wake-up-like-that?

Ignoring that his bold, blue eyes were closed as he slept and dark-brown eyelashes fanned across obnoxiously high cheekbones, I—

Well, I had nothing, because I couldn't freaking well ignore that.

He coughed in his sleep, rolling from his side to his back. He threw one arm over his face, covering his eyes. The five o'clock shadow that coated his entire jaw seemed extra shadowy thanks to the sliver of sunlight that made it into the room through the dark-gray curtains.

God, he was beautiful. I'll-chisel-you-into-marble

kinda beautiful. The kind of beautiful that should be displayed in museums for years to come. In a hundred years, people would marvel at the statue of him the way we did the Mona Lisa today.

God, what was I doing, standing here staring at him like the idiot I was? I needed to either write the note or leave.

And, no, it wasn't a note to apologize for leaving him, it was to leave my number.

If my life was a TV sitcom, the audience would gasp at this very point. Or do that low "oooh" thing they did.

I sighed and leaned against the wall. Was I crazy? Leaving my number with a one-night stand and asking him to be my date for my sister's wedding this weekend?

Yes. I mean, I knew that. It was weird. Definitely not something a normal person did.

God. There was a hockey stick on the wall above his bed, and it was looking ever more tempting as a weapon to whack myself in the head with.

I couldn't ask a stranger to be my date. It didn't matter how desperate I was. I'd just take the stick from my mother instead, or I'd claim my non-existent date had a family emergency and couldn't make it.

I sure as hell couldn't ask Mr. Hottie McTottie with the body of a Greek god to come with me.

If I was honest with myself, my mother would take one look at him and know it wasn't real. I was nowhere near put together enough to get a guy like him.

Hell. It was seven-thirty in the morning, and I was standing, staring at him, wearing a graphic tee that proclaimed I ran on coffee, chaos, and cuss words.

I'd worn it to the bar last night, too.

That was how fancy I was.

In my defense, it was only supposed to be one drink, and it was all my best friend's fault. If my best friend, Avery, hadn't taken us to the place with a happy hour…

Well, it didn't matter now.

Unless someone invented time travel in the next two-point-five seconds, this was the situation I was stuck with.

Now how did I write this note?

"Do you often stare at people while they sleep?"

I jumped, pressing my hand to my chest. Apparently, I'd zoned out while staring at Hottie McTottie at some point during my inner monologue, and he'd woken up.

Well, shit.

Now this was awkward.

Queen of Awkward strikes again…

"Well?" He sat up in bed, lips twisting to one side. "I know you're not mute. If you were, you wouldn't have made as much noise as you did last night."

I opened my mouth, but my cheeks burned hot before I could say anything.

Hottie McTottie chuckled. "Sorry. I thought you might shoot me down, and I'm trying to get you to speak." He paused, his dark-blue eyes glancing over my shirt. "Or do you need coffee to make your mouth work?"

"What?"

"There she is." He grinned. "Your shirt. It says you run on coffee, chaos, and cuss words. I imagine you've got a few cuss words running through your head right now, and this is definitely a little chaos." He stood up, tossing the sheets aside…and giving me one hell of a look at his bare ass.

And his cock.

I blinked and looked away, blushing again. Why was I surprised? I'd been naked when I'd woken up. It stood to reason that he'd be naked, too.

"Don't worry," he said, his deep voice barely able to conceal his restrained laughter. "I put on my boxers."

"Yes. Well." I cleared my throat. "Um…"

"Sweatpants are on. Come on." He grabbed me by the shoulders and directed me toward the door. "I'll make coffee, and then you might be able to string together a sentence."

His idea had merit. Not gonna lie.

He guided me down the stairs, hands still on my shoulders, and steered me toward the kitchen. It was large and bright, with white cupboards and big-ass glass doors that let in the sunlight from the early morning sun.

I looked out at the backyard. It was…so *male*. He had a decent-sized pool just off the deck that housed an impressive barbecue area, and I was pretty sure I could see the corner of a hot tub on the other side.

"How do you take your coffee?" he asked, reaching up to the top cupboard. His back muscles flexed as he pulled down two mugs. "Cream? Sugar? Black? Or are you a latte or cappuccino girl?"

"Jesus, do you have your own personal Starbucks in here?"

"No." He looked over his shoulder with another grin. "But it made you talk."

I pursed my lips. "Cream, one sugar. Please."

"You got it, Red."

"Red? What kind of a name is that?"

"The kind I give to a redhead whose name I can't remember," he said simply, hitting the start button on his impressively big coffee machine.

Oh, thank God. It wasn't just me.

What? Those happy hour cocktails had been strong.

I knew he'd told me his name outside of Hottie McTottie. I think it started with…an E? No. He had an A-name. It was definitely an A.

"Judging by the look on your face, it's mutual." He slid a full cup of coffee across the kitchen island. "You can sit down, Red. I'm not going to kick you out."

"My name is Poppy," I said, perching on one of the black stools. "And I totally remember your name."

"All right. What's my name?"

I hesitated. "Aaron."

He shook his head, laughing. "Adam."

"What?"

"Adam. My name is Adam." He paused. "And, as pretty as Poppy is, I'll stick to Red."

"Why?"

"Because poppies are red, so it makes sense."

"Wow. How hungover are you?"

"Hungover enough that I'm glad I don't have to work," he replied, hitting the button on the machine for the second time. He turned and looked at me, then said over the sound of the machine, "So. Care to tell me why you were staring at me while I slept?"

No.

Absolutely not.

"I wasn't staring at you. Not intentionally. I was…thinking." *That was lame, Poppy. So lame.*

"Thinking. I can't say that's something girls usually do in my bedroom." He grabbed his coffee and put it on the island, leaning against the opposite side. His biceps tensed as he rested his forearms on the black marble countertop, and I flicked my attention to the veins running down his forearms.

Why did I want to lick them?

Was it the hangover?

I needed this coffee.

"Do you have many girls in your bedroom?" I asked, raising an eyebrow.

"Not particularly. That made me sound a lot more of a man whore than I am."

"Don't get me wrong, but I think you're lying."

"Why?"

"Have you looked in a mirror lately?"

Adam dropped his head and laughed. "On a daily basis," he said, meeting my eyes again. "What does that have to do with anything?"

I wiggled my finger at him. "I'm not falling for that. I'm just saying that you look like the kind of guy who thrusts his way through life, one woman at a time."

"That seems awfully judgey for a girl who can't cope without coffee."

I snorted. "If you think this shirt is bad, you should see the rest of them."

"You have a collection?"

"Some people collect, I don't know, jigsaw puzzles. I collect snarky t-shirts." I shrugged a shoulder.

"I honestly don't know anyone who collects jigsaw puzzles."

"It was a figure of speech."

"That was the best you could come up with?"

"You know," I said slowly. "I liked you a whole lot more when your face was between my legs."

Adam burst out laughing.

And, oh God, it was a glorious laugh. Like Nutella on Belgian waffles. Chocolate sauce on ice cream. Icing on cake.

Uhh. Now I was hungry.

"I didn't mind that much myself," he said, a twinkle in his eye. "But, that still doesn't explain why you were watching me sleep."

"Okay. I wasn't watching you sleep," I insisted. "I was genuinely thinking, but I can understand how waking up to a hungover redhead standing in the middle of your room, looking at you in bed, might be construed as weird."

"Well, fuck that. I was worried I'd picked up a total crazy."

"Has that happened before?"

"You don't wanna know," he muttered, taking a swig from his cup. "Why were you standing there, then?"

I clicked my tongue. "I was hoping to avoid this conversation."

Adam stared at me. "Well, I know I used a condom, so that eliminates a whole bunch of problematic scenarios."

I sighed and rolled my eyes. "Thanks for clearing that up. I didn't know what a condom was for."

His lips curved.

He had the most infectious smile. It reached his eyes every time, making them sparkle a little brighter.

It annoyed me because I wasn't in a situation to be smiling. Sure, I'd just had crazy hot sex with a hot as hell guy, but whatever.

"Look, I should probably go," I said, finishing my coffee.

"You hungry?" Adam asked, straightening up.

I stilled. "I…what?"

He moved to a floor-to-ceiling cupboard and opened the door, revealing a fridge behind it. "Are you hungry? I have stuff for omelets. You want an omelet?"

What was happening?

"Uh…sure?"

"You don't sound sure. There's bacon, tomato, ham, cheese, mushrooms…"

"I hate mushrooms. And tomatoes."

He jerked his head around. "How is that possible?"

I shrugged a shoulder. "They're slimy."

"Fair enough. Bacon omelet? With ham? Cheese?"

Seriously. What was happening?

"Okay. I guess."

He pulled a bunch of stuff out of the fridge and dumped it on the island in front of me. "Don't worry, I can cook. I'm not gonna kill you."

I stared at the myriad of ingredients on the counter. "Color me reassured."

CHAPTER TWO
POPPY

Omelets and Awkwardness

Turned out, Adam could cook.

And my tummy was very, very happy about that.

"So," he said, pushing his plate to the side. "What were you thinking about?"

I sighed, cradling my coffee cup. "I knew there was a catch to this."

"Hey, I cooked you breakfast and didn't find you completely weird for the way I woke up. Give me some credit." He grinned. "Are you done?"

I nodded.

He stood, abs tensing as he leaned over the counter and picked up my plate.

God, this wasn't fair. He was hot, had a great body, and knew how to use his very generously sized penis. Was there anything imperfect about him?

"You're staring at me again. Is that an issue you have?"

"I have a lot of issues," I said. "And they all start with my family, which is exactly why I was staring at you in the first place," I finished on a mutter.

"That sounds equal parts interesting and weird," Adam admitted, swinging a stool back under him. He sat down, mirroring my pose with how he held his cup. "Why don't you just tell me, and I'll decide how weird I really think you are?"

"Oh, boy. You're opening a whole can of worms there. I mean, who wears a shirt like this on a night out?"

I motioned to my gray shirt.

His mouth twitched as he once again glanced down. "I didn't want to mention it, but..."

I pursed my lips and hit him with a dark look.

"Kidding. I'm kidding." He held up his hands with a laugh.

I wasn't getting out of this. Hell, the man had woken up to me staring at him like I was potentially plotting his murder, then he'd cooked me breakfast.

He was obviously a nice guy, and shit—I had nothing left to lose, did I?

I was going to Rosie's wedding alone anyway, so what the hell?

"Okay." I glanced into my coffee cup. "I'm going to preface this by saying my mother is...an acquired taste for most people."

He raised an eyebrow but said nothing.

"My sister is getting married to her high school sweetheart this weekend. He's a stupidly successful doctor, and my mom is positively beside herself in joy that my sister didn't fuck it up." I paused. "And I've been told that if I show up without a date, I'm dead to her."

His left eyebrow joined his right one.

"Okay, so I'm exaggerating, but that's what she didn't say." I bit back a laugh, taking my bottom lip between my teeth. "Long story short, I've failed miserably at finding a date. So...the reason I was hovering over you like a weirdo this morning was because I was trying to figure out how I could leave you my number and explain this situation in a note without looking like... Uh, the weirdo I look like right now."

He laughed. "The note would have been weirder. Trust me."

"Really?"

"Yeah. Waking up to find that someone I'd had sex with left me a note to ask me to their sister's wedding? I'd be a little weirded out. I'd also hope that you never found me again." He snorted.

"And you weren't weirded out by me?"

"A little. But, hey. Despite that, I kinda like you, Red." He gave me a lopsided grin and tilted his head to the side. "And I get your situation. I have four sisters, and if I ever showed up to one of their weddings without a date, my mom would kill me."

"That's pretty accurate as to what's going to happen to me this weekend. With any luck, she'll ignore me entirely." I paused. "I'll probably have a better weekend if she does, if I'm honest."

Adam had his mug to his mouth, and he choked, slapping his hand over his mouth. "Jesus. I know that feeling."

"I take my kicks where I can get them where she's concerned. Especially since she'll make my life a living freaking hell after the wedding."

He coughed again, thumping his chest. "What's the deal with the wedding?"

I peered over at him. "What?"

"What's the deal? Is it a one-day thing? A weekend?"

Was he considering this? Being the date for a crazy redhead who watched him sleep?

I didn't, but it sounded more dramatic that way.

"A four-day thing," I said slowly. "It's down in Key West. Arrive Friday morning, leave Monday night. The wedding is Sunday evening."

"This Friday?"

I nodded. "It's okay. It was a ridiculous idea. I

panicked."

"Hey—I didn't say no. I was just confirming it was this weekend."

I stared at him.

No. He wasn't going to agree, was he?

"I couldn't get there Friday morning because I have a work meeting, but I can drive down after and meet you there." He rested his arms on the counter and leaned forward. "If you want me to, that is."

I blinked quickly. "You—you'd pretend to be my date for the weekend just so I'm not tortured by my mother?"

"Yes, but if the situation is ever reversed and we're both still single, I fully expect the favor to be returned."

"You're going to be my fake boyfriend?"

"Does being your fake boyfriend include real sex?"

Well, that was a scenario I hadn't considered. Judging by the night before, though…

"I'm gonna have to release stress some way, and I'm really not a runner. Plus, last night wasn't exactly terrible."

He grinned, confidence fully shining through. "I agree. Look, Red. I'm free. I can do it. Just as long as it doesn't get too awkward."

"Why would it get awkward?"

His smile faltered for the tiniest moment, and he looked at me as if he didn't understand why I was asking that question. "I'm your fake boyfriend," he said, almost as an afterthought. "And all I know about you is how to make you orgasm."

"That's solid knowledge. That's all you really need to know to make the weekend a success." I gave him my own half-grin.

"All right, Red. Let's do this."

———

"You've lost your damn mind," Avery said, pulling the cork out of the wine bottle with a little pop. "I can't believe you're doing this. Does he have a magic dick?"

Maybe.

"He's just helping me out," I said warily. "I mean, he gets something out of it, too. He gets sex."

"Oh, well, that's okay. You get your mom off your back for a weekend and regular sex." She stopped, wine bottle ready to pour. "Wait. I see your logic."

I laughed, tucking my feet beneath my butt. "It's crazy. I know it is. I don't know anything about him except that his name is Adam, he has a really nice house, he has a magic dick, and he makes a mean omelet."

Straight-faced, she met my eyes and said, "Marry him."

"Avery—"

"I'm serious. Omelets are hard, girl. I don't think I've ever made an omelet that hasn't ended up as scrambled eggs."

"You burn toast."

"I did that one time, and that was because my dumbass brother turned the dial-up. You know that." She finished pouring the second glass of wine and handed it to me. "I'm just worried about you. You know what your mom's like."

"Exactly. That's why I'm glad I have a date."

"A date you don't know."

"I know him quite well," I said. "I know how to

make him come."

"Oh, well, slap my ass and call me Suzy—that's the kind of info your mom wants to know!"

I paused. "She might stop asking questions if that's what I come out with."

"She'll call her local priest and send you in to confess your sins!"

"Lies. It'll be an exorcism."

"Which, ironically, she needs on occasion," Avery mused.

"On occasion?"

"Hey, she's still your mom. I'm just being real about it."

"Being real would be comparing her to the devil himself. Or herself. Has anyone ever confirmed Satan's gender?" I twirled my glass.

Avery shook her head. "Stop trying to distract from the matter at hand. Your date being someone you don't know from Adam."

"Good thing my name isn't Eve, then."

"Poppy."

I sighed. "Avery."

"Have you actually thought this through? I mean, from beginning to end, all the implications, your mom from the second you walk in until the second you leave?"

No. Not at all.

"She's going to wonder why you haven't mentioned him to her. She's going to ask where you met, how long you've dated, what his job is, how rich his family is—"

"And I'll give her the same old reply that money isn't everything."

"Says the girl from money."

"Who lives with her best friend and works at the

Cheesecake Factory," I reminded her. "My parents have money. I do not."

She let go of a sigh. "Point well made. But, still. She's going to ask you all kinds of questions before you have a chance to figure out any answers, and you just know she's going to bombard him the second he arrives. Don't you remember senior prom?"

"As a rule, I try to forget it."

"She stood at the end of your driveway for thirty minutes until Percy Hamilton got here, only to interrogate the poor bastard over his family's financial situation and what his intentions were with you. You were eighteen."

"And, if I remember correctly," I said slowly. "He was so fed up with her by the time she got to the intentions thing that he told her he intended to take my non-existent virginity."

Avery snorted into her glass. "I thought she was going to shit a cow. A legit cow. She was furious, but she had to let you go."

"And that was exactly why Percy didn't get laid that night," I reminded her. "I was eighteen and she took away my car keys."

"Has it ever occurred to you that your mom is a control freak?"

"Every single day since I was old enough to understand what such a thing was." I nodded solemnly. "Which is why I think I might be able to get away with taking someone who is basically a stranger to the wedding."

"I don't see your logic at all."

I sat up straight, running my fingers through my hair. My elbow propped up on the back of the sofa, and I rested my head on my hand. "Think about it. It's

Rosie's *wedding*. She'll be so caught up in making sure nothing goes wrong, that she'll forget about Adam pretty quick."

"You underestimate your mother."

"I'm an optimist."

"Your t-shirt has three wine glasses. Two are half-full and labeled optimist and pessimist, and the third is empty and labeled realist. You're the realist, Pop. The only thing you've ever been optimistic about is how much cheese sauce you'll get on your fries."

"Well, if there was ever anything to be optimistic about, it's that." I grinned. "I think I'll be okay. We live an hour away from our hometown. My parents can't possibly know who he is, and we don't talk enough for them to be concerned about whether or not I have a boyfriend. Besides, Mom hasn't even asked me. I think she just believed me when I said I had a date."

"That's because you told her disbelief against your daughter was a sin, and she's so menopausal that she believed you."

"She manipulated puberty. Menopause is my toy."

"I don't think it works like that."

"Probably not, but the notion of it is charming."

Avery snorted. "You need to stop watching British sitcoms. You're starting to talk ridiculous."

"Look, just because I have an obsession with The Crown and you keep using your ex's subscription for Friends doesn't make me ridiculous," I told her. "At least use Greg's passwords for something decent. Like ordering midget porn to his apartment building."

She paused, tucking her dark hair behind her ear. "Could I do that?"

"I would," I said. "But I'm an asshole."

"He did cheat on me." She genuinely stopped and considered it. "Where would I find midget porn?"

"I'll send you a link."

"You know where to—" She froze. "No. You subscribed your mother to it?"

"No. Rosie did. I just found the subscription," I said. "I'm not that evil."

"What did she ever do to Rosie?"

"I don't know. I never asked. I never considered that she'd have been a bigger pain in the ass to Rosie than me."

"Well," Avery said. "That is a very valid point. And I will consider the midget porn thing. Are you sure you don't need me to come this weekend?"

I wanted my best friend and roommate at the wedding. She had a standing invite based upon the time she could get off work. In other words: my parents didn't want to upset her parents since basically, our entire lives were intertwined, and my mom freaking loved Avery.

"Aves, if you can get off work, even for Sunday, you know you have a chair," I reminded her.

"I'm not asking that. I'm asking if you need me. That's something different. Do you need me?"

I nodded before I could change my mind. "But only if you can get away."

She winked. "I'm sure I can figure something out."

CHAPTER THREE
POPPY

Family and Fuck This

WELCOME TO KEY WEST.
I didn't feel very welcome. The sign was bright and beautiful, sure. Friendly and touristy, but I wanted to be anywhere other than here.

It didn't really matter that I'd seen that sign forty-five minutes ago. The roads all looked the same, and it was a miracle that they still did with all the tourists who drove up and down them every single day.

I already knew how this weekend would go. My nephew would make havoc rain down at every given opportunity. Grandpa would pull out some random story from his back pocket and tell everyone about it whether they wanted to hear it or not. My control-freak sister would go full Bridezilla. My mother would go all demon Queen and strike the fear of God into anyone who dared speak out of place.

And my dad? Well, he'd likely slip a glass of whiskey into the bathroom on a semi-regular basis.

I'd join him. That was the only way to cope with my freaking family.

I sighed as the giant resort my sister had booked for the wedding came into view. I wasn't even on the resort property yet, but I could already tell I was a fish out of water.

No doubt both my mom and sister would be dressed to the nines like decent ladies. I was dressed in a shirt with a rooster and the caption, "What the cluck?"

and ripped jean shorts.

God, I should have gotten a stomach bug. Faked it. Because this situation was only going to get worse when Adam showed up later this afternoon.

Fact was, what Avery had said to me made perfect sense, and I'd spent the last few days wondering what in the hell I was doing.

I didn't know Adam from, well...Adam. I didn't know anything about him. Sure, I knew that he had a body that would make a room full of women cry and a pretty magic cock—and one hell of a tongue.

But that didn't change the fact that I didn't know anything about him as a person. I didn't know where he was born or if he moved or grew up there. What did he do for work? Did he graduate from college? What was his major? Did he have any hobbies? Who was he, really?

How the hell did I get through this without my eagle-eyed mother figuring out what I'd done? Then, no matter what happened, I was in big trouble. For lying, trickery—God only knew what kind of shit she'd pull out of her hat.

Ugh. This was just going to be hell on Earth, wasn't it?

Why was I asking that? I knew that. I knew that this weekend would be hell the second Rosie had announced she was engaged and had set a date and booked the venue. Quite literally all in the same breath.

I'd moved out of Key West to see my family as little as possible. You can imagine how delighted I'd been to hear that I had to spend four days with them.

Now, as I pulled into the expansive parking lot that would rapidly fill up with my sister's guests, those four days had begun.

I turned off the engine and sat for a while. With

any luck, I'd be able to check into my room and dump my suitcase before running into any of my family.

Actually, my dad would be okay. He'd smuggle me to the bar and give me a shot of liquid courage to get through this weekend.

Hell, I needed the whole bottle.

Ugh. Double ugh. Triple ugh.

Knock knock.

I jumped at the knock right next to my head, whacking my hand on the gearstick in the process. Jerking my head around, I literally bit back a groan at the sight of my mother's face pressed against my window.

She tapped one baby-pink nail on the glass and wiggled it in a motion that told me my game was up, and it was time to open the window.

I pressed the button to unwind it. "Hi, Mom."

"Poppy!" She practically put her head through the window and tucked her chestnut-dyed hair behind her ear. "Why are you sitting out here in the parking lot?"

"I just got here," I lied. If by "just" I meant twenty minutes, then sure.

"No, you haven't. I saw your car pull in twenty minutes ago."

"Were you watching?"

"Of course. You said you'd be here around eleven, and it's eleven-thirty."

Great. I should have known.

"Why are you sitting in the parking lot?" she repeated, smacking her light-pink lips together and shooting me a piercing gaze courtesy of her dark-blue eyes. "Are you delaying coming inside? For your own sister's wedding?"

Jesus. I wasn't even out of the car yet, and my inner black sheep was already showing.

"No. I have a headache. I took some ibuprofen and I was waiting for it to kick in before going inside." Another lie, but this time, a little more believable.

Mom squinted. "You don't look like you have a headache."

I stared at her. "They have visible symptoms now?"

"Migraines do."

"I don't have a migraine. I have a headache. They're entirely different."

"Excellent. Well, twenty minutes should be long enough for your pills to kick in, so come on. We have things to do." She stepped back from the car and opened the door.

That told me.

I grabbed my purse from the passenger seat and got out. "We? What do I have to do?"

"You're the maid of honor. You have to ensure your sister has everything she needs."

I almost choked on my own spit. "You want me to be her slave for the weekend?"

"No. But, you need to organize the bridesmaids, ensure the flowers are delivered to the right room on Sunday afternoon, make sure the bartenders on the beach bar don't mess up the cocktails. Oh, and you also need to try their proposed special cocktails and pick two to be served at the reception."

Okay. I could get on board with the last option. "Do I have to pay for the cocktails?"

Mom paused by the trunk of my car. "That's what you're concerned about?"

"This place charges fifteen bucks a cocktail. I'm a waitress. Of course I'm concerned about it." What? I wasn't going to beat around the bush.

She sighed. "No, you do not have to pay for them. But you are not to get drunk. Oh, and, also—keep an eye on your father. I already stole a whiskey bottle from his suitcase."

"He knows how to handle family gatherings," I said under my breath as I opened the trunk.

"What was that?"

"Nothing, Mom." I hauled out my case.

"Poppy, where's your bridesmaid dress?" Mom's eyes widened.

Oh, good. Rosie hadn't told her.

"It's here. In Rosie's suite. Where it's supposed to be."

She grabbed my wrist. "No, no. The last thing I heard, bridesmaids were bringing their dresses. Did you forget it?"

"Chill out, Mom," my sister called. "It's in my room." She bounded down the stairs leading to the resort building and over to my car, her honey-blonde hair flowing behind her. "Hey, you!" She enveloped me in a big, tight hug.

I hugged her back. We had a great relationship. Mostly because we only saw each other on occasion. No doubt we'd hate each other if we saw each other every day—we were too alike.

"Mom, seriously, chill," Rosie said, letting me go and touching her arm. "I went up to Orlando to find my dress, remember? We picked the bridesmaids' dresses then, and I had them ship them all down to me. Poppy's stayed so she could have her final fitting. It was here waiting when I checked in on Tuesday. I swear."

Mom sniffed. "Someone could have told me. And I'm still bitter I wasn't invited to the dress party."

"And I said I was sorry, but it was the only time

all the girls could get together to make the trip. If you hadn't been on the cruise, you know you would have been there." Rosie slid a wink in my direction.

That was a heavy dose of bullshit. We'd deliberately planned the dress party to coincide with my parents' cruise.

I didn't need to explain why.

I closed the trunk and pulled out the handle of my suitcase. "Can I check in before we descend into drama, please?"

"There's no drama here," Mom sniffed, looking every bit as annoyed as she sounded.

"Yes. Let's get you checked in." Rosie grabbed my arm and tugged me toward the steps. "Now."

I couldn't agree more.

———

"This is your room," Rosie said, tapping the sensor with the keycard. "I made sure our families got the best ones, so it's actually more of a mini-suite." She pushed open the door, revealing a huge room with floor-to-ceiling windows that looked out onto the beach.

"Holy—"

My sister grinned.

There was a TV and a sofa, and an open door led to a giant bedroom with giant patio doors that led out to a balcony.

"So, your room," Rosie said. "There's an en-suite and a walk-in closet just off the bedroom. The phone is on the bedside table. They do room service twenty-four-seven for when you're avoiding Mom—"

"You get me."

"—Just set up your card at the main desk and

they'll charge it all to that, okay?"

I nodded. "Sounds good." I wheeled my case into the bedroom. "How is everything going?"

"It was going well until Mom showed up." She sighed and perched on the arm of the sofa. "I swear, I'm going to be Bridezilla in the next twenty-four hours if she doesn't chill the fuck out."

"Oh, God. I was afraid that would happen."

Rosie shook her head. "Don't. You'd think it was her wedding. She's constantly trying to tweak things, and she forced me and Mark to have dinner with her last night." She met my eyes. "It was torture. Pure torture. I texted Celia and made her fake Rory being sick just so I could get away."

"And you left Mark with them?"

"Look. I've grown up with her picking. He's marrying into it. Think of it like a warm-up."

Cruel. So cruel.

"Then, this morning, she showed up at our suite when we were having breakfast. She freaked out that you were showing up today without your plus one, and because you were showing up alone, she's certain your plus one will desert you and not come." She ran her hand through her hair. "He is coming, isn't he?"

"He said he was." I shrugged. "I can't reach up to Orlando and drag him down here, can I?"

"Oh God."

"He'll be here, okay? Don't worry. I promise."

Rosie stood and clasped my hands. "Phew. Okay. Will you call me when he arrives? I want to meet him."

"Of course." I smiled. "Do you need me to do anything?"

She shook her head. "Mom has your weekend itinerary. I'll text Dad and see if he can get it from her to bring up to you, but if not, you can get it tonight. All you need to do is get your plus one here and show up in the Palm Ballroom for tonight's pre-wedding reception, okay?"

A pre-wedding reception? Whose wedding was I attending—my sister's or a British royal's?

"Got it. What time?"

"Seven on the dot. Six-thirty would be even better."

"I'll be there at six," I smiled wryly.

"You are the best!" She hugged me again. "Okay, I have to go find Celia and Rory. I promised her she could spend the afternoon on the beach since she'll have Rory all night."

Ah, yes. Their live-in cleaner-slash-nanny who was the most adorable woman. Not to mention she was from Alabama and made the best peach cobbler I'd ever tasted.

"Okay. No problem. I think Adam should be here in time for the party, but I can text him and check."

"Okay, good. Cool. Awesome." She took a deep breath. "This is the most peace I've had since yesterday morning."

With that, she gave my hand one last squeeze and left me alone in the suite.

I pulled my phone out of my purse and texted Adam.

Me: Hey. Do you know what time you'll be here?

His response came much quicker than I thought it would.

Adam: I was just about to text you. My meeting got canceled, so I left early. I'll be there around four. Is that good?

Oh, thank God.
One: he'd be here in time for the party.
Two: he was still coming.

Me: Perfect. See you then!
Adam: See you then, Red.

CHAPTER FOUR
POPPY

Friday Night Frights

Adam: I'm in the parking lot. Which room are you in?

I texted him back the room and floor number and tossed my phone on the sofa. Butterflies fluttered through my stomach, and when I pressed my hands against my tummy, I realized I was nervous as hell.

I was insane. Truly, truly insane. Why did I ever think asking a one-night stand to be my weekend date was a good idea?

And why the hell was I nervous to see him? And why right this second, knowing he was here? I hadn't felt this way all day. Granted, I'd spent the entire day on the beach with my nephew, Rory, and Rosie, but still.

Ughhh.

Every second that passed felt like a nightmare. Where was he? Was he on the elevator? Down the hall? Downstairs? Still in his car?

Three knocks sounded at the door. I jumped and stared at it for a minute before moving to open it.

He was just as handsome as I remembered him. That dark hair, that stubbled jaw, those bright eyes...

"Hey," he said, voice dipping at the end of the word.

"Hi." I smiled, my cheeks flushing a little, and opened the door completely wide. "Come in."

"Thanks." He stepped into the room and glanced around. "Nice. Great view, too."

"Definitely. I think my sister is buttering me up for having to deal with our mom," I said, grabbing my water off the table in the middle of the room. "The bedroom is through there. There's a walk-in closet if you want to unpack."

"Got it." He pulled a slate-gray case into the bedroom. "Hey, Red. Do they do room service? I need a shower and I'm starving."

"Yeah, they do. Want the menu?"

"I got it." He strolled back into the room, pulling his shirt over his head. "Sorry. I'm sweaty."

Yeah. Well. If only being sweaty made him look a lot less worse, because from where I stood, sweaty or not, he was hot as hell with his tight abs and rippled muscles.

"Don't worry about it. It's not like I haven't seen it before."

Adam glanced up from the menu to shoot me a sexy half-grin. "True. Are you hungry?"

Actually, I was.

I nodded.

"Do you mind ordering while I take a shower?"

"No," I said. "I don't mind. What do you want?"

"I'll have the bacon cheeseburger with a Pepsi," he replied, handing me the menu. "Give me fifteen minutes."

I took the menu, nodding and smiling. He disappeared into the bathroom, and I blew out a long breath.

Well, that hadn't been too awkward. Except for that second where he ripped his shirt off.

I scanned the menu, quickly deciding that the bacon cheeseburger and Pepsi sounded perfect and called through to room service to place the order. The sound of the shower running filled the room, and I dropped onto the sofa with my water. I picked up my phone and texted Rosie that Adam was here, so she could stop freaking out, and sighed.

First things first: when Adam got out of the shower, we needed to figure out the things my mother was going to ask. If we were going to pass him off as my boyfriend, the very basics needed to be nailed down before it could go horribly wrong.

My mother was like a bloodhound. She could sniff out the tiniest lie if you didn't cover your tracks adequately enough.

The shower stopped running, and I tapped my fingers against the soft material that covered the sofa cushion next to me. How did I bring it up? Did I just go straight to the point, or mention it gently?

"So," came Adam's voice. "Have you given any thought about how we convince your family we have a real relationship?"

I turned my head, then froze.

Uhhh.

He was standing in the doorway. Tall. Tanned. Muscular. And wet.

Very, very wet.

His dark hair hung over his forehead, dripping water onto his shoulders where the droplets trailed over his chest. I saw one even trickle right over his abs and into the fluffy white towel he had secured at his waist.

"Red? You listening?"

I jerked my attention from his waist back up to his face. His lips were twisted in a knowing smile, and he wiped his face with another towel.

"I'm listening," I said. "You asked how we're going to convince my family this weekend isn't a ruse."

"Oh, good. You retained the information. I thought it might have gotten lost somewhere between my shoulders and my cock."

I glared at him. "I'm regretting this already."

"Don't. I'll remind you later why this is a very good idea." He winked. "Well? Do you have any ideas?"

"Yes, but, honestly? Please put on some pants. If the person who brings our dinner is a woman, you'll have her fainting in the hall."

He stared at me for a second, then burst into laughter and turned back to the room. He emerged again two minutes later, this time wearing light gray sweatpants.

"All right," he said, sitting with me on the sofa. "What's the plan?"

"For you to wear more clothes so I stop getting distracted," I muttered, ignoring his quiet snort. "I think we need to agree on the most basic things: where we met, when we met, and how serious the stage of our relationship is."

Adam nodded and scratched his jaw. "Well, I vote we stick to the truth where possible. We met in a bar, so let's actually use that."

"I agree. But when?"

"Let's say a few months ago. That's vague enough to make our relationship serious enough that you'd bring me to a wedding, but not necessarily needed to bring me up in conversation with your family."

"You're good at this. Have you done it before?"

"No. Believe it or not, I'm not in the habit of accompanying random, hot women to family weddings."

I blushed at him referring to me as "hot." Damn it. He was charming. "Okay, so, we met in a bar a few months ago and just recently stepped toward being more serious. How does that sound?"

He nodded. "I think that's good. We should be able to deflect any others. The key is to not be split up, and if we are, find each other to fill any gaps. Agreed?"

I took a mouthful of water and returned his nod. "Agreed. Failing that, we pay someone to cause a distraction so we can run away."

His grin made his eyes sparkle. "I saw those heels in the bedroom. Do you think you'll be able to run in them?"

Shit. "Absolutely fucking not."

"Don't worry, Red. I got you. I'll throw you over my shoulder and we'll run into the sunset."

He looked so damn serious I couldn't help but laugh. Of course, that made him break the serious persona he had on, and he laughed, too. "No, but seriously, if you can't run, I'll handle it."

"You have my full confidence," I managed to eke out between giggles.

He got up at the sound of two knocks and a call of, "Room service!" He pulled open the door and shot the poor young woman on the other side of it a dazzling grin. "Thanks. I can take this in. Don't worry about it. Do you have the check?"

Wordlessly, she handed him a slim leather wallet and a pen. Adam opened it and scribbled on the bottom with a flourish.

"There you go. Thanks." He smiled once again, pulled the tray inside, and shut the door on the poor thing.

"Well, that was smooth," I said. "And they were supposed to charge it to my card. It's on file."

Adam shrugged. "I set up my card on my way up. They didn't question it."

"What? You're here doing me a favor. I can at least buy you room service."

"Hey, I get something out of it, too. Fake boyfriend, real sex. Remember?"

I did remember.

"And if there's real sex, you need sustenance, and I'm happy to pay for it. So…" He pushed the tray right in front of me. "Eat up, Red. You'll need it to get through the party…And for what I have planned for you later."

"What—what you have planned?"

He grinned and picked up his burger.

Oh, man.

I should have ordered a shot of vodka with this Pepsi.

"Are you ready to do this?"

I looked at Adam. He was dressed in a white shirt, sleeves rolled to his elbows. His black pants were perfectly tailored to fit him like a glove, and even his black shoes were so shiny that, if I got close enough, I'd probably be able to see my reflection in them.

Aside from the obvious? No. No, I wasn't ready. I regretted telling Rosie I'd be there at six. Nobody else would be there to distract my family from the fact I was bringing a super hot guy as my date.

Hell, I needed distracting from that. I'd already seen his ass in those pants.

Never mind two people meeting eyes across a crowded room—I'd be searching out his ass to find him.

I just wanted to…you know. Reach out and pinch it. Like a crab. Pinch, pinch, pinch.

"Red. Pay attention." Adam clapped his hands sharply.

"Oh my God, if you want me to focus, get ugly or something!" I snapped, smoothing out my tight-fitting dress.

He laughed. "Right. This from the woman who has my cock twitching right now."

"It's not the only thing that's twitching." I moved uncomfortably. "I'm not a fancy-dress kind of person. I prefer t-shirts that make my mom feel awkward."

"Is that why there's a t-shirt in the closet that says, 'I'm sorry, I'll try to stop swearing,' followed by a claim it's a lie and someone can fuck off?"

I nodded solemnly. "I was going to wear it to breakfast tomorrow, then change into the one that says, 'I'm allergic to stupidity, I break out in sarcasm.'"

"What is that? A warning to anyone who talks to you?"

"All my t-shirts are. Including the one that claims I'm winging it, and the other that says, 'Not today, Satan.'"

"Is that one for your mom?"

"No, but it's about to be." I smiled. "Thanks. That'll really piss her off."

He snorted and walked over to me. "You're welcome. Shall we try this conversation again? Are you ready?"

"Uh, no."

"I figured. You look like you're about to walk to your death."

"I might as well be. If my mom figures out that we're faking this, I'll never hear the end of it. She'll mention it at my future birthdays, my wedding, my funeral."

"She won't figure it out." Adam ran his hands up my arms. "I promise. We'll pretend the fuck out of this relationship."

I peered up at him. "This would be so much easier if we knew anything about the other person beyond how good they are in bed."

"It was your crazy idea, Red. Now you have to deal with it."

"I didn't expect you to agree to attend a stranger's sister's wedding."

"Neither did I." He chuckled. "Come on. Four days. How hard could it be?"

"You are not prepared for my family, Adam."

His chuckle quieted, and he twisted his lips. "Maybe not, but by the sounds of it, you're not either, and you know them."

"Get ready for the crazy."

"I'm ready. But, first..." He dipped his head, bringing his face close to mine.

I took a short, sharp breath, my eyes fluttering closed right as his lips touched mine.

It was better than I remembered.

The kiss was firm, but his lips were soft. Warm and slow, he kissed me thoroughly, sliding one hand into my loose curls and cupping the back of my head.

My heart thundered against my ribs.

"There," Adam murmured, lips barely a breath from mine. "Now we can go."

I nodded. "We can go."

He pulled away and darted his gaze over my mouth. "No lipstick smudges. You're all good."

"Thank God for that," I muttered under my breath, following him toward the door.

His shoulders silently shook as he guided me out

of the room with a hand on my back. A shiver ran down my spine, and I did the worst possible job at hiding it if the fact his laughter when from silent to...not so silent...was any indication.

We made our way to the elevator and waited in silence. It was awkward—at least for me. Adam didn't seem to be bothered about it at all. He was totally relaxed. A little too relaxed if you asked me.

Not that anybody did, but I was in the terrible habit of giving my opinion anyway.

We stepped into the thankfully empty elevator. My phone buzzed inside my clutch, and I dug it out as Adam hit the button for the second floor where the Palm Ballroom was.

Rosie: I'm going to kill her
Me: I'm going back to my room
Rosie: COME AND SAVE ME FFS

I sighed.

"What's up?" Adam asked, sliding his gaze to me.

"My sister texted me begging me to come save her, which means my mom is all sunshine and fucking rainbows," I replied. "Can't wait."

"I should cheer her up, right? Wasn't she expecting you alone?"

"She fully expected you not to show up," I agreed. "So, you're right. You should cheer her up for a good, oh, fifteen minutes."

He quirked a brow as the doors pinged open. "You're not terrifying me at all, Red."

"I warned you," I reminded him as he guided me out of the elevator, too.

His hand was so gentle against the small of my

back. That didn't stop the tingles that ran across my skin without him even touching it.

I held my clutch against my stomach as I turned us in the direction of the ballroom. It wasn't hard to find. Mark's family had booked out the entire resort for the weekend, but there were still white and baby pink signs that pointed guests in the direction of the ballroom.

Since there was nobody else arriving yet—because we were early as I'd promised—we were completely alone in the outside area.

"Ready?" I asked Adam.

"Yep. Are you?"

"I wasn't ready five minutes ago. You think that shit changed in the last five minutes?"

He laughed, pulling me closer into his side. "Come on. If we get through the first hour of being fake boyfriend and girlfriend, we've got this. Sixty minutes. We can do it."

"Man, you're so perky. I might have to break up with you." I shook my head. "You're totally gonna ruin my hating people persona."

"Is that the one you put out with your shirts?"

"Yes. Embrace it or RIP to our totally real relationship."

He pressed his face into the side of my head as we walked into the ballroom.

I couldn't lie. It was decorated beautifully. Pearlescent white and baby pink balloons adorned each table, each four-balloon bouquet sprouting from the top of a white and pink flower arrangement.

If it wasn't already obvious, the color scheme for the wedding was white and baby pink.

Long story short, it was perfect. Everything from

the napkins to the lights above the bar had been changed.

It was like a fairytale. Seriously. My sister's vision was unreal.

If I had to have a pre-wedding reception party, it'd consist of nachos and dips and *Friends With Benefits* blaring on the big screen. And me, alone, in my bed, with nobody else.

I was not my sister.

Not even close.

"Poppy! Finally!" My mom came rushing over to us.

We were barely in the goddamn room.

"Where have you been? We need you to help set up!"

I did a double-take. "I told Rosie six. She never told me she needed help, or I'd have been here."

"Well, thank goodness you're finally here. And you're not alone." Surprise briefly crossed her face. "Miranda Dunn. Poppy's mom. And you are?"

I glanced at Adam. I think he finally "got" why we clashed. And it'd been sixty fucking seconds.

"Adam. It's a pleasure, ma'am." He ignored her offered handshake and, instead, took her hand and kissed her fingers.

Mom put her hand to her chest. "Handsome and he has manners," she said to me, then turned back to Adam. "You look familiar. Have we met before?"

"I'm pretty sure I'd remember if we had." He shot her a charming grin.

"Huh," Mom said. "You are really familiar to me. Maybe I know a family member? What's your last name?"

That was an excellent question.

Adam opened his mouth to speak, but he was interrupted by my father.

"Adam Winters! As I live and breathe." Dad grabbed his hand and shook it enthusiastically. "What are you—Poppy? You brought Adam Winters to your sister's wedding?"

I was missing something.

Something big.

"I, er," I started.

"Adam Winters!" Mom clapped her hands. "Of course! I told you I knew your face!"

Adam grinned.

I glanced at him. My chest was tight. What was going on? What was I missing?

"My grandson is going to go crazy. Wait there! Mark!" Dad yelled, spinning in circles. "Mark! Get Rory!"

"Dad? Why are you yelling?" Rosie asked. "Rory's here with me. What's going on?"

I wanted to know that, too.

She looked up and saw Adam. "Well, shit."

Adam laughed.

"Rosie! Your language!" Mom scolded her.

I looked down at my six-year-old nephew who was staring at Adam like he'd just met his hero. You know, how I imagine I'd look if I ever met Channing Tatum.

Adam crouched down so he was eye-to-eye with Rory. "Hey, buddy. It's Rory, right?"

Rory nodded, completely dumbstruck.

"I'm Adam." He held out his hand, but Rory was frozen in place. "How you doin'?"

Rory opened his mouth, but instead of speaking, he burst into tears.

45

My mouth opened as I stared at the situation in front of me.

Seriously.

What.

Was.

Happening?

"Uhh," Adam said, standing up. "Sorry?"

Rosie hugged Rory to her leg and grinned at Adam. "Don't be. He loves you. Once he's gotten over the shock, he'll probably follow you around all weekend."

Seriously!

"I'll be waiting when he is." Adam touched my back again with a smile.

"What's going on?" Mark said, joining the group and adjusting his tie. "Why is Rory crying? Sam, did you scare him again?"

Dad chuckled. "No. He just met his hero."

Mark looked around the group until his eyes landed on Adam. "Adam Winters! Well, hell. What a pleasure." They shook hands. "Poppy? You brought Adam Winters?"

I did the only thing I could.

I nodded.

Mark shook his head in disbelief. "Is this our wedding present? Kidding!" He laughed.

I met Rosie's eyes. I was going to hyperventilate if somebody didn't get me out of this situation.

"Honey, can you take Rory? Now we're all introduced, I really need Poppy to help me with something," she said, extracting a now-calm Rory from her right leg.

"What do you need her help with?" Mom asked, looking between me and her.

"Something!" She grabbed my arm and dragged me away. Mom's eyes narrowed as we left the ballroom.

Oh God.

She knew.

She knew I didn't know.

I was so, so screwed.

CHAPTER FIVE
POPPY

What The Cluck and a Hockey Puck

"What's wrong?" Rosie said in a low voice.

"What is happening?" I breathed, pressing my hands against my stomach. "Why does everyone know who he is?"

Her lips parted, and she stared at me. "Wait. Are you telling me you *don't* know who he is?"

I rubbed my hand across my forehead. "Jesus, no."

"I'm so confused."

"He's not my boyfriend," I whispered. "We met last weekend, I slept with him, and asked him to come with me to your wedding and he agreed."

"What?" Rosie paused, then laughed. "Okay, we're gonna come back to that, but again: You don't know who he is?"

"I have no fucking idea! Oh my God. What's going on?"

"Okay, first, you need to calm down." She grabbed my upper arms and looked me in the eye. "Remember when I was in labor and you talked me through the breathing?"

I nodded, my breath hitching.

"Breathe. And breathe. And breathe." She did that for a few more seconds until my breathing was under control once again. "Okay?"

"I'm good. Sorry. I panicked."

"That is the general reason for a panic attack," she said. "Adam Winters is a star forward for the

Orlando Storms."

"I don't know what that means."

She sighed. "He's a famous as fuck hockey player. He's both Dad's and Mark's favorite player on the team and he's Rory's freaking idol. He's the reason Rory is learning how to play. He wants to *be* Adam when he's older. Do you understand that?"

Oh.

Oh, shit.

Yes. I understood that.

"Oh, fuck," I whispered. "This just went from bad to worse."

"Why?"

"Because Mom is going to think I did this deliberately to upstage you, and I can't tell her that I didn't know who he was!"

"Ohhhh," Rosie breathed out. "Oh, shit. Okay, don't worry. We can handle this. I can talk her down."

"How? How do we talk me out of this situation?"

"I'll tell her she didn't give you a choice. You're seeing him, so you had to bring him, because you couldn't come alone."

"Okay. Jesus. This is a shitshow."

"What's going on?" Mark asked, touching both of our shoulders. "Your mom is about to have a cow in there."

Rosie glanced at me.

"Rosie, no!" I begged.

"Somebody brought the most famous hockey player in the country to the wedding and didn't know who he was." She grinned at him.

"What?" Mark looked at me, fighting laughter. "Poppy—no. She's lying."

"Ohhh!" I covered my face. "It's true. Damn it. I

slept with him last weekend and asked him to be my date. I had no idea who he was until ten minutes ago."

He didn't even try to hide his laughter.

"Don't laugh at me! This is a disaster!"

"Oh, Pops." He wrapped me in a hug, and I pouted at my sister. "Only you could do this."

"Mom can't find out," Rosie said. "And also if she tries to claim that Poppy did it to overshadow the wedding, we have to twist it back on her, okay?"

Mark released me and gave her a thumb up. "Tell me what to do and I'll do it."

"Keep her away from me," I muttered. "Where's the bar?"

"Hey," Adam said, sliding onto the chair next to me. "You hiding from your mom?"

"As a rule, yes." I took a big gulp of my wine. "So, this has been fun and not at all awkward."

He looked down and chuckled. "Not at all."

I sighed and turned my head to meet his eyes. "Why didn't you tell me who you are?"

"You never asked," he replied simply. "And for the first time in a long time, I was with someone who didn't look at me and see what I was."

"You knew I didn't know who you are?"

"Yeah. That was obvious when we met. Your friend, too. You were the only women in the general area who weren't trying to get my attention in that bar, and when I approached you, I realized that you really didn't know who I was." He paused, twisting his beer bottle around. "Of course, had I have known I'd be coming here and walking into a family of hockey fanatics, I'd have given you the heads up."

"And I would have really appreciated that." I dropped my head and laughed. "Oh, my God. This is insane. I'm sorry you're here."

"I'm not. Your family is great. Your mom's a little bit of a loose cannon—"

"A little bit?" I looked at him. "She's lost her marbles!"

He laughed, leaning closer. "I'm trying to be nice."

"Just say it as it is. You might have noticed that my family tends to say what they think."

"I figured that out when your dad told me I'm a fucking amazing player, but I need to stop wasting chances a spider could take."

"Oh, God," I muttered.

Adam laughed and touched my back. "Don't worry, Red. He's right."

"Oh, Goddddd," I muttered again. "I want to die."

"There's no need to be so dramatic. It's fine. On the bright side, we didn't have to handle the whole, "How did you two meet?" scenario."

"Not yet," I corrected him. "But the worst is yet to come."

"Why?"

"My grandfather gets here tomorrow. He's the worst of us all. He has a story for every family function and he'll talk your ear off."

"It's a good thing I'm a patient listener." He grinned.

"It's too late for me, but you can still leave." I finished my wine. "My mom is undoubtedly going to say I deliberately brought you as my date to upstage my sister."

"Which you couldn't have possibly done, because you had no idea who I was."

"Adam. I can't tell her that. I lose in every scenario."

He looked at me for a minute, then laughed.

"This isn't funny."

"It's ridiculous. I have a feeling this weekend might be the most fun I've had in ages," he said.

"Really? Being in a room where everyone knows who you are is fun to you?"

"Well, it's part of my job."

"I mean here right now."

He turned his entire body until he was facing me and leaned in. "Actually, nobody has recognized me at all. Only your family. For the most part, unless anyone here is a fan, they won't know who I am."

"Like me."

He grinned. "Like you, Red."

I blushed and pushed hair behind my ear. "I hope so. If too many people fangirl over you, my mom is going to kill me."

"Should I set up a table in the corner if it happens? Send people in groups?"

"No. Pick me up, and we run, just like you promised."

"Deal. Where are we running to?"

"Anywhere that my mother isn't." I snorted.

Rosie slipped into the other chair. "Okay," she said, leaning over to both of us. "I think I convinced Mom you didn't do this to upstage me. I heard her mention it to Dad who promptly told her to shut up and jumped in there. Then she got pissed at me for talking to her instead of entertaining my guests." She gave me a grimace and pinched her fingers. "I'm this close to going Bridezilla on her."

"Rosie. Shouldn't you be entertaining your guests?" Mom appeared out of nowhere and gripped the back of a chair.

"We were just clearing something up," Rosie said.

"Like what?"

"She's not sure about one of the cocktails," I lied. "I told her I'll do the cocktails tomorrow at lunch, so she doesn't have to worry."

Mom looked at us suspiciously. "Which cocktail was she worried about?"

Ah, shit.

"Does it matter? It's Poppy's jobs to handle the cocktails," Rosie said.

"Thank God," I muttered.

"What was that?" Mom shot daggers at me with her eyes.,

"I coughed."

"Hmm." She scanned us all with one quick flick of her gaze and let go of the chair. "Rosie, Mark's parents are looking for you. They have a gift for Rory in their room and don't know what you'd like them to do with it."

My sister shot me a look and stood up.

"It's also time for the speeches after that. Poppy?"

"Yes?"

"Is your speech ready?"

"What speech? I don't have a speech. I have to say something at the wedding, but not now."

Mom stared at me. "You're scheduled for a speech tonight."

Through gritted teeth, I said, "Then unschedule

me."

"Are you going to upset your sister by not doing what you should be?"

I folded my arms and sat back in my chair. She wasn't going to guilt me into this. Not a chance in hell. Nobody told me about speeches at this party, and I wasn't going to stand up there and look like an idiot.

No way.

Mom sighed. "Fine. No speech. But I expect you to pay full attention."

"Mom, this is a wedding, not a math class."

She looked like she was going to say something, but instead clicked her tongue and turned to Rosie. "Come on."

Rosie wiggled her fingers and followed Mom through the tables.

I let go of a heavy breath, rested my elbows on the table, then buried my face in my heads. "Fuck me."

Adam laughed, rubbing his hand down my back. "Need a drink?"

I nodded.

I needed ten.

———•••———

I snatched my sister's hand before she got wrapped up in another conversation with a guest. "Hey. I wanted to let you know that we're leaving."

She glanced at the dainty watch on her wrist. "You are?"

"Yeah, three of Mark's cousins recognized Adam, and in the way only teen boys could, made a fuss. He stole the bartender's pens, took selfies, and signed napkins. I think it's probably better if we leave before someone notices he's getting a lot of attention."

She smirked. "I agree. Okay. We have to meet with the priest in the morning, but you're ready for the rehearsal dinner, right?"

"Six-thirty, right here," I said.

"Okay." She hugged me, and I darted out of the ballroom before my mother saw me and tried to stop me.

Adam was waiting for me. "Did you manage to escape the mothership?"

I bit back a laugh and nodded. "Like a ninja."

"Quick. Let's go before anyone else recognizes me today." He grabbed my hand and gave it a tug.

"Whoa, careful. I can't run in these heels. And no, that isn't an invitation for you to haul me off like a caveman."

"Take them off, then. I'm on borrowed time. All it takes is one more crazy hockey fan from your family to up and leave that party, and I'm screwed. And if I'm screwed..." He raised one eyebrow.

I took off my shoes. "Where are we going?" I asked when he dragged me into the elevator and pressed the down button.

"To the beach. It's quiet out there."

"It's also quiet in our room."

"I know. But if I take you up there right now, it won't be quiet for long." He shot me a gaze. "And after what happened earlier, I think we probably need to get to know each other a little more."

Well, there was a logic I couldn't deny. There was no doubt that my mom would start her bombardment of questions the second she had a minute and found us alone. If I had another deer-in-headlights moment like I had tonight, I was done for.

"That's a very good idea."

The elevator doors pinged open, and luckily for us, the lobby was deserted. Mostly because everyone was still at my sister's pre-wedding reception, but still. We made our way out to the front of the hotel and down the path that led to the private beach.

"There's nobody here," Adam said as we stepped into the sand. "Did your sister hire out the entire resort or something?"

"Actually, she did," I confirmed, shaking my head. "Mark's family is filthy rich, and mine isn't exactly poor. Not to mention that Mark himself makes a fuck ton of money."

"What does your sister do?"

"She looks pretty," I muttered. "She says she's going back to school to do a business and marketing course, but we've been waiting for that for two years."

"In other words, she's getting married, will claim she's going to school, and miraculously get pregnant again."

I pointed at him as we sat down. "We have a pool going about when she goes back to school, and that was my answer."

"Can I get in on that?" He undid a button of his shirt and leaned back on his hands.

"No. I need that five hundred bucks more than you do." I paused. "Also, I don't think I actually have a hundred bucks spare to pay my share, so, come on Mark's sperm." I crossed my fingers.

He laughed. "I'll lend my support to Mark's sperm, so you don't have to pay a hundred bucks. But, hey—since it's also my vote, if it happens, I'll pay your share."

I rolled my eyes. "Thanks. Charity is so hot."

Another laugh. "Think of it as we're a team in our choice."

"That sounds better."

"So, I have a question." Adam rolled his head to the side and looked at me. "If your family has money, why don't you have a spare hundred dollars?"

I sighed and leaned back on my elbows. "Because," I said, looking at him, "I'm a waitress at the Cheesecake Factory."

His lips pulled right up.

"What are you smiling about?"

"I just really like cheesecake." He fought a laugh. "So, my next question. If they have money, why are you a waitress at the Cheesecake Factory?"

"Because I did one year studying law and decided that being lorded over by my mother in both my personal and professional life would drive me to jump off a cliff by my twenty-fifth birthday. As you can see, I passed that without my death," I said. "My dad is a hotshot lawyer, and my mom is a paralegal. That's the family business. Until they snuff it, I'm serving cheesecake to people who probably shouldn't be eating a whole lot of it."

"I want to say that sucks, but you made that choice, so…good for you."

"It's not all bad. Sometimes, I get to take the leftover cheesecake home. Which was why I had to lose ten pounds before this wedding," I muttered.

"Really? You had to lose ten pounds? Where did you lose them?"

"Somewhere in the middle of DisneyWorld. Although, if that were the case, they'd have found me again."

Adam chuckled. "True story. I have to stay away

during the season, or that place messes up my entire diet."

"You go to DisneyWorld?"

"Four sisters. One is married, one engaged long-term, and two nieces and a nephew. I take the kids. They go for the magic, I go for the food, and I get major uncle and brother points. Everyone wins."

"I really need to steal Rory more often."

"Does your family live in Orlando?"

I shook my head. "My parents split their time between Miami, where the law firm is based, and Key West. They're old enough now that they can work part-time for the most part. And Rosie and Mark live in Fort Lauderdale."

"Where were you born?"

"Hey, you're asking an awful lot of questions for someone who wasn't embarrassed earlier today."

His eyes sparkled. "Fine. You go. Ask me whatever you want. I'm an open book."

"Okay." I pretended to think. "Why didn't you tell me you were an uber-famous hockey player?"

"I told you that already."

"I know. I just wanted you to know that I'll never let you live that down."

He nodded slowly. "Point taken. I'll do better next time."

"Damn right you will. Okay, where were *you* born?"

"In Orlando," he said, eyes still on mine.

"How old are you?"

"Twenty-eight. Twenty-nine in October."

"What made you want to play hockey?"

"Ooh." He tilted his head to the side. "I don't really know. My family has always been big lovers of it, and both my grandad and my dad played it in school, but my dad kind of petered it out in college when he realized he wasn't really good enough to make the major leagues."

"But you knew you were?"

"I got on the ice when I was four for the first time. It was an easy thing to become obsessed with, you know? My dad would take me to all the home games for the Storms, and I guess I just felt at home on the ice. I was the worst teenager ever. I didn't party or go wild. I had great grades and it meant I could get a scholarship to college for hockey."

"Woah."

"That sounded like a shocked whoa."

"Kinda. Remember that I know nothing about any sport. Not a single one. Except that baseball pants are God's gift to women."

He laughed, dropping his head back.

"I'm just saying," I fought my own laughter, "That it's crazy. My sister said you were a star forward, but I don't know what that is."

"Uhh…"

"Wait, do *you* know what that is?" I teased.

He reached over and nudged me. "I'm trying to explain it in a way you'll understand."

"Gee, thanks."

"You're welcome." He winked. "I'm an attacking player. So, it's my job to score, pretty much."

"Oh. How the hell was that hard to explain?"

"You think baseball pants are God's gift to women. First, that's me. And second, they have to wear cups, so that impedes access."

"I'm gonna skip over the bit where you think you're God's gift to women and agree with you on the cup thing," I said. "So, this might sound stupid, but have you won anything?"

"In hockey?"

"No, in football."

He side-eyed me. "I wouldn't take that sarcasm if you weren't so cute."

"Great. I went from being hot earlier to now being lumped in with newborn kittens and bunny rabbits."

He laughed again, and goosebumps dotted my arms. "Yes, I've won things. How can you live in Orlando and know nothing about any kind of sport?"

"The same way city people live in the country and know nothing about cleaning out chickens," I retorted. "I don't care about it much, so I don't know anything about it."

"Wow. So, you're dating a hockey player and you don't care what he does."

"Fake dating."

"Same difference."

"If I'm fake-dating you, I should probably know what you've won. You know, so I don't look like a freaking moron if anyone asks me," I finished dryly.

Adam sighed. "Boy, I'm really never living that down, am I? You weren't kidding there, Red."

"I never lie. I'm incapable of it. Unless you're my mother."

"This entire weekend is a lie."

I paused. "Look, if you're gonna be technical about things, this relationship just isn't gonna work, hockey boy."

"Really? That's what you're gonna call me? Hockey boy?"

"You call me red because my name is Poppy, and

my hair is red. Both lame reasons."

He sat up and held up his hands. "Okay, okay. I won the Dave Tyler Junior Player of the Year Award when I was seventeen, and since going pro with the Storms, I've won the Stanley Cup three times."

I stared dumbly at him. "See, I thought that would help, but...no."

"You don't even know what the Stanley Cup is?"

"Aside from the fact my disinterest in sport is already firmly established...Do I look like the kind of girl who follows hockey?"

He turned and looked at me. From head to toe, his gaze took in every inch of my body, and I did my best not to react like it was bothering me.

Because it was. His gaze was too slow and too careful to not bother me.

"No, you don't. Not at all."

I swallowed and dropped my gaze for a second. "Right, so explain these awards and cups and things to me. Before someone mentions it and I—"

"Look like an idiot. Yeah, I know." His lips curved to one side and he reached out, gently pushing hair from my face. "The Dave Tyler Junior award is given to the best American-born player in Junior Hockey. I quit after that so I could focus on college."

"And the Stanley Cup?"

"The top prize in the national league. The one everyone wants to win."

"And you've done it three times?"

"In six years."

"Wow. Even I know that's impressive." I smacked my lips together. "Do you think that's enough get-to-know-you for one night?"

"Depends. What do we do now?"

I pulled my phone from my clutch and glanced at the time. Ten-thirty. "I have to be up early. I have to taste-test cocktails and pick three to be served at the wedding, and I'm doing that at lunch, so…" I closed my clutch back up, securing it with the clasp.

"So…" Adam muttered, reaching over to me. His hand slid into my curls and he cupped the back of my head.

"So." My breath hitched because I knew exactly what was going to happen.

The King of Kissing was about to kiss me.

And he did. His lips covered mine, and shivers ran down my spine at the exact same moment. I lifted one hand to the side of his neck and slowly fell back so I was lying flat on the sand.

Adam flicked his tongue against the seam of my lips. He leaned his upper body right over me, kissing me deeper as I parted my lip. His tongue toyed with mine, and sparks of lust shot right between my legs.

I just wanted him to carry on. I wanted to stay in this little bubble on the beach, with his hand in my hair and his lips on mine. With this other hand traveling down my body and over the curve of my hip as mine both cupped his neck.

He tasted of whiskey and coke, and he smelled like my next big mistake.

His fingers dug into my ass as the kiss deepened even further—hotter, more desperate, more needy.

"Oh, my goodness!"

I jerked away from Adam at the sound of my mother's voice.

Of course.

Of. Fucking. Course.

This was the story of my life, wasn't it?

I looked up to see Mom looking at us. "Um. Hi, Mom?"

"I was—never mind!" she turned on her heel and walked back to the hotel as quickly as she could, barely even stopping to make sure the heels of her Jimmy Choos didn't sink into the grass if she missed one of the stones that made up the path between the hotel and the beach.

"That was awkward," I muttered, rolling away from Adam.

"You think it's awkward for you? My cock is trying to escape my pants. That's awkward." He sat up and looked at me. "Ah. Yeah. You have a little…" He scratched at the side of his mouth.

I wiped the side of my mouth and pulled away some smudged lipstick. "Did I get it?"

He nodded. "Come on. It'll all be off soon enough anyway." He helped me up from the sand, grabbed my shoes, and laced his fingers through mine.

I knew exactly where this was going. And I wasn't even mad.

CHAPTER SIX
POPPY

Cocktales and Cocktails

Adam tapped the card against the sensor. It beeped bright green, and he pushed the door open. His hand was still firmly linked through mine, and he pulled me inside. My body was against his and our lips were together before the door had even clicked shut.

He tossed the keycard onto the sofa and, with his hands on my hips, lead me into the bedroom. I broke the kiss to drop my clutch on the TV unit, but it only lasted seconds.

Adam's fingers splayed across my lower back. I wound mine in the collar of his shirt as he kissed me, dipping me back just slightly. His tongue once again teased mine, the kiss deepening and going straight to the heat we'd had when we'd been interrupted.

I wanted to wind my fingers in his hair, but I also wanted his shirt off. It was quite the conundrum, but when one of his hands crept up my back and clasped hold of my zipper, my choice was made.

My fingers went to his buttons. I undid two, and as he unzipped my dress, his fingertips brushed against my skin, leaving me tingling wherever he'd touched me.

My heart was beating double-time, and my clit throbbed like crazy.

I wanted him.

All the buttons undone, I tugged his shirt out of his pants. He reached up to pull the straps off my shoulders at the same time I moved to push his shirt down, and we had a weird minute of push and pull that ended with us both laughing.

Adam shrugged off his shirt and threw it to the floor. He kissed me as he hooked his fingers beneath my straps and slid them over my shoulders and down my arms.

We spun, and he kicked off his shoes, pushing me down onto the bed. I bounced on the soft, downy cover, but I barely had a second to think about just how soft it was before Adam pushed me right down to my back and leaned over me.

He kissed me thoroughly before his lips trailed over my jaw. He kissed down my neck, taking my dress down my body as he went. He stood, pulling it all the way down my legs, and left it to join his shirt on the floor.

He explored my body with both his hands and his mouth. From my collarbone to my naked chest and over my nipples to the waistband of my underwear. He was relentless and methodical, kissing every inch and touching even more.

He pulled my underwear to the side, his mouth almost trailing the path of it as he pulled it. It took him no time at all to find my clit with his tongue and get to work. He played it like magic, knowing exactly how to tease and toy to get me to cum. It circled and spiraled and flicked until my hips were bucking beneath him and I could barely breathe as the orgasm took hold of my body.

He loved it, holding my pussy in his mouth until I was limp in his hands.

Then, he stood, tossing his underwear to the side. The condom came out of nowhere—I couldn't fucking see, he'd damn well blinded me with that orgasm—and he parted my legs as if he were meant to be between them.

The head of his cock rubbed my clit a few times before he finally pushed inside me. It was relief of the most devilish kind—perfect yet torturous at the same time. I didn't know what he had in store for me, but I still wanted it.

Wanted him.

He didn't hold back. His hands slid up my body until they were positioned either side of my head and mine were wrapped firmly around his neck.

He fucked me deep and hard, driven by nothing but desire. My pussy clenched around his hard cock, and every second made me hotter and more anxious for the orgasm I knew was coming.

My heart pounded, lungs tightening as I tried to get control on my breathing. I grasped at him as if he were an anchor to the Earth as the pleasure built in me. With each steady stroke of his cock, I came closer to the edge until I couldn't take it anymore.

I gave in to the hot flush of pleasure that flooded my body. The orgasm hit me hard, dangerously so, and my body arched and writhed in response to it.

The strength he held me with said his orgasm had hit him just as hard as mine. We rode it out together until we both collapsed in a limp heap.

He was good—so fucking good. My vagina honestly wanted to cry and weep and bow to his penis. That was just the facts of it.

I nudged him off me after a minute or so. Hot sex or not, a girl needed to wipe and get panties. And pee. That was real life, and while pornstars might have gone to sleep like that, I was no pornstar and the camera wasn't about to shut off on me.

I made my way to the bathroom to clean up and

put in here yesterday afternoon. My hair was the weird mix of both natural and fake ginger-slash-orange. An ombre, almost. My natural color at the roots and a lighter, brighter orange at the ends. It drove my mother insane, but the brightness reflected me far better than the darker, copper-ginger ever could.

I squeezed a healthy dollop of shampoo into my hands and rubbed them together. Somehow, I managed to get it onto my head without actually punching Adam in the face and lathered it up. I rinsed and reached for the conditioner.

This time, I wasn't so lucky.

My elbow connected with his jaw.

"Fuck!" He stepped back from me.

"I told you!" I said, turning as I ran the conditioner through my hair. "I warned you I'd hit you."

"No, you said you'd punch me in the face." He worked his jaw side-to-side. "Not elbow me in the fucking jaw."

"Whatever. You knew you'd get hit. Ugh." I turned, so my head was under the water and rinsed the conditioner out. Somewhere in the middle of rinsing it, I spun back around and tilted my head back so it all washed out.

When my hair ran clean, I turned back around to Adam. His hair was soaped, and he gripped my hands.

"Turn around," he muttered, grabbing my sponge from the tiny plastic shelf.

"I can clean myself."

"Sure, you can, but shut up." He soaped up the sponge and turned me, then ran the sponge up and down my arm. Hot, soapy water covered my skin as he pulled me back from the shower flow and rubbed the sponge over my back. It moved over my shoulders and down my other arm slowly.

It was weird. Nobody had ever done this for me—at least since I was six. But there was something so weirdly sexy about Adam using the sponge to explore my body.

Hmm. Sexy.

Did he want shower sex?

God. I wasn't a sex in the shower girl. I was a slip-on-the-soap in the shower girl.

Hell, who said I needed soap?

"Uh, Adam?"

"Yeah?"

"We're not going to have sex in the shower, are we?"

Adam stilled, then spun me around and pulled me forward a step so I wouldn't get pelted in the face with water. "Why?" he said, eyebrow raised. "Are you offering?"

I shook my head. "No. I'm telling you that if you try it, I'm going to hit you in the face again."

"Don't shatter my dreams, Red."

I sighed. "Not because you didn't listen, idiot. But because I can slip on carpet. Do you understand that?"

"I understand." He grabbed my shoulders and slowly spun us around so his back was under the water. "Sorry. I'm cold. You can slip on carpet?"

"Now I'm cold!" I pushed open the door and snatched a towel off the heated rail. "Yes. I wasn't even wearing rollerblades. Wow, that makes me sound like a useless adult."

He laughed, rinsing all the soap from his body before turning off the shower. He stepped out onto the floor with me and looked down. "Should you be standing on a tiled floor there? I mean, I know first aid, but in the interest of your safety…"

I tugged off a second towel to wrap my hair in. "If I go down, I'm taking you with me."

"There's no way you could drag me down to the floor with you."

"I didn't say I'd take your entire body." I looked pointedly at his cock. Then, I turned and flipped my hair over so I could wrap it up.

"Well, in that case, let me get a towel and I'll carry you into the bedroom. I'd prefer if you didn't put my cock out of commission."

"Why?" I straightened and paused. "Actually, I mean, I know why. I don't know why I asked that. I need coffee."

Adam laughed and tucked his towel around his waist. He stepped behind me and touched his hands to my waist. "Come on, Red. Let's get you from here to the carpet in the bedroom without you taking out my penis."

"I'm perfectly capable of wa-ahh!" My foot went out from under me. My heart jumped into my throat. My entire life flashed before my eyes in a haze of cheesecakes and inappropriate shirts.

And my ass never hit the floor.

I clamped my hands over my eyes. The hard body I was pressed against shook, and laughter rumbled against my ear.

"Perfectly capable of it, huh?" Adam murmured, lips brushing my ear. His arm was locked around my waist tightly, and he showed no sign of letting go.

"I would have been if you hadn't mentioned about looking after your cock. It's all your fault."

"Sure, blame the thing that had you screaming into a pillow last night."

"It'd have me screaming bloody murder if my ass

had hit that tiled floor." I stepped onto the plush carpet and looked at him. "I'd thank you for saving my life if you hadn't been the cause of my almost-death."

"I see the dramatics run in your family."

"I'm merely preparing you for today. The entire day will be spent with my family. Are you excited?"

Adam finally let me go fully and walked over to the closet doors. He peered at me sideways. "Oh, yeah. I can't wait. Isn't your grandpa coming today?"

I glanced at the clock on the wall. "Just after lunch. Thank God my orders are to test all the cocktails."

"All the cocktails? How many are there?"

"Six. I have to narrow to three."

"Sounds fun. Need a hand?"

"Wanna have lunch with my mother?" I asked wryly. "Do you think she honestly trusts me to leave me alone to do such an important job?"

He gripped the knot that kept his towel in place and pulled open the closet door, looking over at me. "Seriously? She can't even let you do cocktails?"

I sat on the edge of the bed and stared at him. "Here's how today is gonna go. My mom is gonna freak out like a fly around shit until my grandpa arrives here safely. When he gets here, he's going to tell everyone he meets about some eccentrically wild story from his crazy life. That, in turn, will drive my sister to insanity, because while Mark's parents are used to him, everybody else is not. Something will inevitably go wrong, because that's how it works in this family. Rosie will go Bridezilla—she's already on the verge—and then, Mom will freak out because she's freaking out. My dad will keep a small flask of whiskey tucked somewhere on his person, and I will sneak to a small secluded corner of the hotel and steal that flask from him."

Adam blinked at me. "Can I have a family emergency? I know I said I could handle it, but after meeting your mother... In the nicest possible way, she can be worse?"

"Oh, hockey boy. You have no idea."

CHAPTER SEVEN
POPPY

Life's a Beach... Then You Meet One

"All right," Adam said, holding up a piece of melon. "What happens between now and the cocktail extravaganza at lunch?"

"Well," I started. "For one, we need to get you a disguise. I have no idea who that teenage girl was, but I'd like her to return my eardrum."

"She didn't scream that loud."

I ripped a croissant in two and hit him with a glare. "Adam, she screamed so high at one point that only dogs could hear her. And those dogs were in Europe."

"At least we were outside?"

"You'd just gone for a run. God knows why you did that after showering—"

"I planned to go before, but, well, you were naked."

"Not an excuse," I said. "Because by the time you got back, I was hungry."

"You could eat without me."

"Not without anyone screaming at you like they're thirteen-year-old girls meeting Taylor freakin' Swift."

He tilted his head to the side. "To be fair, she's kinda hot."

"That's not the point here."

He held out his hands. "It's not my fault I'm a handsome, famous, rich hockey player."

I blinked at him. "Unless someone held a gun to your head and made you be a handsome, famous, rich hockey player, then uh, yeah, it is."

"I hate to agree with you, but you're right. I chose everything but the handsome part. I got lucky with that."

"Ugh. I'm going to follow sports from now on to make sure I never, ever find myself getting a wedding date over omelets again," I muttered, then tore off a bite of croissant.

"I'm an excellent wedding date."

I swallowed the pastry and dropped the final bite on my plate. "Since you got here, you've been fawned over by my father, my nephew, my brother-in-law to be, my sister, three cousins, and now a teenage girl I've never seen in my life."

"To be fair," Adam said, picking up his cup of coffee, "I've also been fawned over by you."

"I don't fawn over people. I'm not a fan of anything."

"Except graphic t-shirts."

"This is a tank top, and it's more of a public service announcement."

"It says 'Not today, Satan.'"

"What part of "my mother is here" do you not understand?"

He choked on his coffee. Actually choked. He had to put down his mug and thump his fist against his chest.

"Sorry. I didn't mean to kill you," I told him. "But it is payback for the bathroom thing this morning."

"What bathroom thing?" the sharp question came from—go on, guess—my mother.

Adam coughed again, leaning away from her.

Pussy.

"He got out of the shower and left the floor soaking wet," I lied smoothly, picking up the piece of croissant I'd discarded a second ago. "I almost died."

Mom rolled her eyes. "There's no need to be so dramatic, Poppy."

"That's what I said," Adam managed to scratch out. "I caught her. She was fine. She wasn't close to injury, never mind death."

I sniffed. "That's what you think."

Mom's dark blue eyes flitted between us. "Late breakfast?"

She was like a dog with a bone. A big, granite-made bone that needed diamond to chip it.

"Yes," I said. "Adam had to work out, and we said we'd have breakfast together since I have to do wedding stuff the rest of the day."

"Makes sense. Have you seen your sister? Or your father? He's supposed to pick up your grandfather, and I have something to ask Rosie."

"You know you can text her, right?"

"Poppy."

"Mom."

Adam glanced at me.

I leaned back in the seat so the letters on my shirt were fully visible.

Mom's gaze dropped to it. "Must you wear such ridiculous shirts?"

"They're cool and comfortable." I folded my arms across my chest. "No, I haven't seen either of them. If I do, I'll let them know you're looking for them."

She nodded. "Good. I'm off to speak with the wedding planner. There's an issue with the table plan."

"Rosie did the table plan."

"Well, I think the planner messed with it. I have to speak with her."

The table plan was the one thing my sister refused to allow anyone to have any input in, so that conversation was going to go fucking fabulously.

"Well, all right," I said wearily.

Mom turned her attention from me to Adam. After a second of silence, she said, "Can I expect to see you for lunch, Adam?"

He wiped the corner of his mouth with his napkin and sat up straight. "Absolutely. I'd love to get to know Poppy's family a little more. You seem like a fascinating bunch."

Excuse me. I need to go vomit.

Mom's frustrated expression faltered. "And I can't wait to hear more about the boyfriend I never knew she had."

Fuck a duck dead.

"I don't have to tell you everything, Mom."

"We haven't known each other that long," Adam added before Mom could reply. "Honestly, I wasn't sure I could come this weekend due to work obligations, so that's probably why she never told you. I'm sure she didn't want to upset you by changing everything at the last minute."

Damn. He was good.

Almost too good.

As proven by the fact Mom's eyes briefly narrowed at him before she shook it off. "That makes sense," she said, lying through the skin of her damn teeth.

You know how I knew that?

She'd been too suspicious before. You just didn't drop an idea because a hot guy grinned at you.

All right, maybe I did, but my mother didn't. And the button to my pants was probably way looser than hers was.

Hopefully, anyway.

"So, lunch. I'll meet you at the beach bar. They serve food there, and I'll be able to help you with the cocktails," Mom said, turning to me.

I raised my coffee cup in a toast. "See you then, Mom." *Satan. Whatever.*

"Looking forward to it." Adam shot her the most devastatingly handsome grin I'd ever seen.

Seriously.

All the panties on women within a ten-mile radius?

Poof.

Gone.

Just like that.

Eat your heart out, David Copperfield. I bet you couldn't do that.

Mom's cheeks heated, and she actually looked flustered for a second. "Great. Awesome. Fantastic."

My eyebrows shot up, and she glanced at me before turning and flouncing away.

Adam chuckled.

"Did you just flirt with my mom?" I asked him, putting my cup down with a clang.

He shook his head. "I charmed her."

"Same difference. The last time she got that flustered was at a Pink Floyd concert, and if my dad didn't have photographic evidence, I'd swear he was lying."

"I'm not Pink Floyd." He laughed. "I figure it doesn't do any harm to get her to like me."

"What? Like you'll still be my boyfriend this time

next week?"

"No. But unless you want her to catch you out in your lie…"

I pointed a crispy rasher of bacon at him. "Don't go there. I don't want to play that game. I'm already flirting with the stakes as it is."

"This isn't poker, Red."

"No? It may as well be. My sister and future brother-in-law know this relationship is a sham. My mom is virtually Sherlock with a pair of breasts, and the moment my dad questions this? I'm done for. So yes, yes. This is poker. This is Dunn Family Poker, and the only person getting poked in this is me."

Slowly, his lips curved into the widest, sexiest smile I'd ever seen. "I'm trying to take that as you mean it, but I admit, I'm struggling like fuck."

What?

I stared at him and then, it dawned.

He was *technically* poking me, too.

Oh, God.

"I don't want to have this conversation," I mumbled, reaching for my coffee cup. "It's too early for it."

"No, it was too early to discuss how you could slip on dry land, never mind in the shower."

I rolled my eyes. "Whatever. Are you going to do the cocktails with me or just lunch?"

"I'll do both."

"Why? So you can sweeten up my mom?"

"No, because I'm your boyfriend and I should spend the whole weekend with you." He didn't move a muscle—his lips didn't even freakin' twitch.

"I don't know how you just said that with a straight face."

He cough-snorted. "Neither do I, but it's pretty convincing, huh?"

"If I didn't know you were more full of shit than a pig farm, sure."

Adam reached over, grinning, and snatched the last piece of bacon from my plate.

"You know," I said, mimicking his previous straight face. "That's the fastest way to get your ass dumped."

"You won't dump me. I'm a rich, handsome, famous hockey player, remember?"

I slid my gaze toward the three teenagers sitting two tables away from us. Adam followed my eyes, shooting them all a smile. The boys both grinned back before they whispered to each other, and the girl blushed before she picked up her phone.

I sighed. "Actually, I think that's the perfect reason to dump you."

"Yeah, well, you'd actually have to be dating me first."

I threw a clean napkin at him. "Shut up."

Rosie: I HAVE HAD ENOUGH.

"Oh no," I said, lifting up my sunglasses to see the screen properly.

"What?" Adam turned his head toward me, using his arm to block out the sun.

"Remember how my mom said she needed to speak to Rosie about the seating plan?"

"Yes…"

"Bridezilla has woken."

He rolled over onto his stomach like I was and leaned over onto my towel, tilting my phone. "How do the words, "I have had enough" equal Bridezilla?"

"It's probably not too much of a stretch to imagine that we have completely different temperaments."

"What? You mean she's not fiery and sarcastic and borderline bitchy like you?"

"Do you *want* me to bite you during a blow job?"

"Depends. How hard will you bite? I don't mind a little teeth, but there's definitely a line."

I glared at him under the rim of my glasses as my phone buzzed in my hand.

Rosie: I MEAN IT POPPY. I'M GOING TO KILL HER.

"Oh, no," I said. "She's still all-capsing me."

"Is that a word?"

"My docile, patient, tolerant sister is all-capsing me how she wants to kill my mother. And you're worried about whether capsing is a word?"

"It's a real concern."

"Hockey boy, you're one more sentence from being on my shit list," I warned him.

"I'm not on your shit list? You've thrown some serious snark my way this morning, Red."

"That's my generally delightful personality. You'll have to pretend you like it since you're my boyfriend and are determined to sweeten my mother up."

"No offense, Red, but you're not gonna do that anytime soon."

"Of course I'm not. My relationship with my mother is based upon mutual tolerance and a somewhat unhealthy love of peanuts. I can't be both nutty and sweet, Adam."

"I have no idea how to respond to that."

"You do what all good boyfriends do. You smile and nod like you understand, then grab my ass."

He smiled at me, nodded, then reached out and grabbed my ass. He smacked it, too.

He learned fast.

I nodded once. "Better. You're learning."

"I'm learning?"

"Yes. You're learning. I like my boyfriends to be slightly possessive assholes so I can tell them off. That's how I get my kicks."

"I don't know if you're fucking with me now or not."

"She fucks with everyone. *That* is how she gets her kicks," my sister snapped, walking up to us. "Why aren't you answering my texts?"

My eyes widened, and I immediately dropped my sunglasses.

"Why are you hiding your eyes?"

"Sun's in them," I lied.

"The sun is behind you."

"It's reflecting off your watch. Who are you? The sunglasses police?"

"Poppy! This is serious!" She dropped onto the sand in front of me. "Did she tell you that she changed my seating plan?"

I locked my phone and put it into the flimsy material that made up my preferred beach purse. It wasn't expensive, but the lining prevented sand getting in it, and since my screen was a tiny bit cracked... It spoke for itself.

"She told me she was looking for the wedding

planner," I admitted wearily.

"You didn't stop her?"

"Hey! I'm not a sumo wrestler. I told her you handled the seating plan personally and it was nothing to do with the planner, but she didn't care."

"Great." Rosie ran a hand through her hair and dropped her head forehead. "Poppy, do you understand how much of a mess this is? She's meddling in things she has no business meddling in!"

I wanted to quote Harry Potter, but I decided not to. I didn't think it would go down well.

"I understand," I replied. "But really, what can I do? Stop her from finding the wedding planner?"

"Yes!"

"I was eating my breakfast!"

"And food is more important than my wedding?"

"When I'm starving and have been made to wait for this guy to take a run and shower? Yeah. Sorry, Ro. Nothing is more important than food."

Adam cleared his throat. "In my defense, I didn't make you wait."

"You shut up." I pointed my finger in his face. "You're on my side."

My sister groaned and flipped her hair as she sat up. "You're supposed to be on my side."

"No, he's my fake date. He can't be on both our sides."

"Poppy!"

"Rosie!"

"You have to do something about our mother!"

I stared at her for a second. "I can hire a hitman."

Adam choked on the mouthful of water he'd just taken.

"I don't want her dead," Rosie said.

"Just...sedated."

"You could get her drunk," Adam suggested.

Rosie's eyes lit up.

"No!" I scrambled and sat up on my towel. "No. I'm not getting her drunk. No way in hell am I doing that."

Rosie grabbed my hands and leaned forward. "Pleeeease, Pops. Please. I need her to go away for a few hours. She's driving me crazy."

I looked her dead in the eye and said, "You're driving me crazy."

"So? Get Mom drunk, then I'll stop being crazy."

"I witnessed your sweet sixteen. I should have known to be sick the weekend of your wedding."

She pouted. "You'd never miss my wedding."

"I don't know. If this is the start of it and it's going to carry on like this, I'm going to get food poisoning tonight."

Rosie reached forward and grabbed my ear the way she used to when we were kids. Hard and tight and, kinda twisty. "You get food poisoning and I will finish you! I will bury you alive!"

"Ah! Ah! Ahhh! Get off my ear, you bitch!" I wrestled her hand off my ear and cupped it. "Fine. No food poisoning. I'll be there. The devoted sister. I'll sing your praises—"

"Please don't actually sing."

I shook my head. "No. I don't want to break the windows."

"You can't be that bad," Adam said.

"Ah," Rosie sighed. "Spoken like a true fake boyfriend."

He cough-laughed. "Careful. We're trying very hard to keep the fake thing a secret. Don't give it up."

Rosie's head swung side to side as she looked around. "There's nobody around. Stop being so panicky. You'll give up the ghost. Like the time Poppy tried to convince our parents the used condom in her room wasn't her losing her virginity."

Adam slid me an amused glance. His lips tugged to one side and one of his dark brows quirked. "That's a story I haven't heard."

"Okay, first," I said, holding a finger. "That is so not true. My virginity was disappointing. We're talking ninety-seconds disappointing. I don't even think I felt it. And the condom was not mine." I finished by staring at Rosie.

She rolled her eyes. "I was a wild one. I didn't do it on her bed, and she was still a virgin then, but it was fun watching her work her way out of that."

Adam's expression didn't falter. He still smirked at me.

"Stop looking at me like that," I snapped.

"No."

"Why not?"

"I'm just thinking how unlucky the guy who stole your virginity was."

I glared at him.

My sister swiped my bottle of cold water and took a sip, her eyes flitting between us both.

"I mean—fuck. That came out wrong."

I snatched the bottle from Rosie. "Ya think?"

Rosie's phone rang. She grabbed it and silenced it, then looked back at us.

"Don't you need to answer that?" I said.

"No. Not until he's talked himself out of this. This will be his defining moment as your totally real boyfriend."

Good God. I needed to get out of here.

Adam coughed into his hand and sat up. "I don't feel comfortable clarifying this in front you, Rosie."

"Why? I'm not a virgin. I pushed a human out of my vagina in front of a room full of people. You can't embarrass me."

He rubbed his hand over his stubbled jaw, finishing with one swipe of his thumb over his full lower lip. "All right." His eyes slid to me, his hand still cupping his jaw, thumb still positioned dangerously close to his mouth. "He missed out because he'll never know how damn good you are at sucking cock."

My jaw dropped open.

So did Rosie's.

"I—" She paused, scooting back on the sand. "I need to, um, hide from Mom. Okay. Bye now." With her cheeks bright red, she scrambled up and ran across the hot, soft sand until she was out of our earshot.

I smacked Adam's arm. "Why the fuck did you say that? You have no idea about my cock-sucking abilities!"

"I know." He grinned, eyes dancing with laughter. "But she doesn't know that I don't know. And it got rid of her, didn't it?"

"Yes, but—but—" I sputtered. "That's not the point!"

"It is. Look at this way. She came here to convince you to distract your mom. You didn't agree. I got you out of jail."

"I—" I had nothing to say to that.

"See?" He held out his hands and shrugged. "It worked. You didn't promise her anything, so you're not obligated to anything except keeping your mom amused during the cocktail tasting session."

"You...are a genius."

"I captained a team of men to the Stanley Cup last season," he said simply. "And I grew up with four sisters and didn't die."

"I have more respect for the latter. I grew up with one and we almost killed each other at least a dozen times."

"In total? That's pretty good."

"No. A month. I almost started a fire when I left her curling iron on while she slept."

"Why would you do that?"

"She stole my journal. I burned her favorite bear in the process."

"How are you still best friends?"

I shrugged. "Hormones."

"Fair enough." He paused. "But I still got your ass out of jail. Now, you owe me."

"You don't have a lot of time to cash in whatever it is that I owe you. You're on a timer, remember?"

"I know." His lips quirked to the side, and he stole the water the same way my sister had and took a mouthful before he capped it and stuck the bottle back in the sand. "I figure you'll make it up to me."

I eyed him for a second, then moved onto my knees on the hot sand between our towels. My toes dug until they found the colder, wetter sand, and my hand cupped the back of his neck so I could kiss him.

My lips found his as if they had a radar. It was easy. Too easy. Too simple for my mouth to find his and kiss him. As if my lips were made to find his.

Adam gripped my hip, pulling me closer, sliding his other hand up my back. My left hand fell to his left leg, my nails digging into his tanned thigh.

I teased my tongue against his lips, teasing him,

begging him to let me into his mouth. He did, answering my deep kiss with the same vigor I attacked him with.

Sparks danced across my skin, and maybe it was the hot sun beating down on us, or maybe it was the way his fingers spread across my bare back, but not a second of it felt wrong.

Not a second felt fake.

It felt real.

Very, very real.

I dragged my teeth across his lower lip and pulled back, moving to my towel.

"Good answer," Adam muttered, adjusting his shorts as he lay back down.

"I know," I said, making sure my sunglasses were in place. "If I can do that to your mouth with my tongue, imagine what I can do to your cock."

His rough groan was all I needed.

So was the way he tugged at his waistband as he rolled onto his stomach.

I glanced at him, biting the inside of my cheek.

I guess he just learned a valuable lesson about fucking with a redhead.

Spoiler: You don't fuck with a redhead.

CHAPTER EIGHT
POPPY

Redheads and Devilheads

I always wondered what I'd look like as a Funkopop. Random, I know, but I wondered if they'd ever accurately capture my boobs. I wasn't exactly a Pamela Anderson, but if anything ever needed immortalizing, it was my boobs.

God only knew nobody wanted my attitude to be infinite.

Not even I wanted that.

However, my attitude was what was going to get me through this damn wedding. My grandpa had landed and was, at my dad's last phone call, yelling at the airport workers to find out where his suitcase was.

Fifty bucks said it was on the baggage carousel.

In fact, I'd wager a hundred. I was just that sure. Mostly because I knew the drill. Last Christmas, I'd been the one tasked with getting him from the airport and delivering him safely to my parents' house.

Guess what? He'd yelled at the airport people, and I'd found his baggage exactly where it should have been. On the carousel, making its way around.

Now, I sighed and brushed my curls around to one side, over my shoulder, and stared into the mirror. To braid or not to braid? That really was the question. To topknot or not to topknot? That was the other one.

Did I risk them getting uber frizzy at the hottest part of the day or did I get proactive and knot them up before my hair could decide for me?

I blew out another breath and flipped my head

89

forward, then gathered my thick hair up. Straightening my back, I teased my bangs out of the mass and tied my hair up loosely. Another hair tie swept the ponytail into a topknot that was beautifully messy.

Huh.

I bet I couldn't do that again if I tried.

"Ready?" Adam strolled out of the bedroom, playing with the button on his shorts.

"For lunch with my mother?" I turned and stared at him, expressionless. "I'm thrilled."

He laughed and adjusted the short sleeve of his white shirt. "It's what—an hour? Then she'll be back snapping at your sister's ankles. Surely you can give Rosie a break for sixty whole minutes."

"Oh no. I've done that guilt trip my entire life. I'm not getting it from my fake boyfriend, too." I waggled my finger at him before turning back to the mirror to finish my makeup. "And yes, I can give her a break, but it doesn't mean I need to be happy about it."

"Do you ever get along?"

"Yes. When I'm in Orlando and she's in Key West."

"I mean when you're together."

"In the same room together, or having a conversation together?"

"Now you're just being awkward, Red."

I brushed a final stroke of mascara over each of my eyes, then stopped, wand in hand, and met his eyes in the reflection of the mirror. "Given how you ended up here, I would have thought you knew that awkward was my default mode."

"That was cute-awkward. This is attitude-awkward."

"How do you know there's a difference?"

He pointed at himself. "Four sisters. I grew up with attitude-awkward. I could recognize it blindfolded with hands cuffed behind my back from two hundred miles away."

"Wow. Someone's cocky."

"I thought we established that the night we met."

My cheeks flushed. Damn it. Why did I have to blush like an idiot? Oh, that's right. I was a redhead and so pale I was a distant relative of Casper the Friendly Ghost, which meant you could see my blushing a mile off.

"You're adorable when you blush." Adam grinned.

"Thank God," I drawled. "That was my life goal. Be adorable. Now, I can get it in neon lights over my bed."

"Will they be black to match your soul?"

"Red, actually."

"To match your hair?"

"No. Red to match your blood when I murder you in your sleep." I put the wand back in the tube and put it in my makeup bag.

"I'll keep it in mind. And hide all the sharp objects."

I turned, leaning against the sink. "Who said I needed a sharp object?"

"You're right." He walked over to me, trapping me against the counter with his body. His fingertips grazed my knuckles as his hands clamped onto the counter and gave me no means of escape. "Hockey pucks are deadly. I've seen them slam into people more times than you can imagine."

"I always told my parents, sports are dangerous."

"Is that why you don't follow them?"

"No. I don't follow them because I literally do *not* care about them."

He blinked at me for a second before his lips curled and laughter burst from him. His forehead rested on my shoulder, and his entire body shook with his amusement at my words.

"Did I make a joke I don't understand?" I asked, moving as if I could look at his face.

"No," he chuckled, straightening and looking at me. "Your honesty is so refreshing. Every time it comes up, it makes me believe a little bit more, that you really have no idea."

"Are you saying I lied?"

"Don't twist my words."

"Shit. I hate it when people catch me on that." I paused. "I have no idea. I thought the Stanley Cup was football until I met you. I don't know what to call it when you score. A goal? A try? A point?"

Adam scratched his stubbled chin. "Wow. You really are completely sport-ignorant, aren't you?"

"You're a smart man to put 'sport' in front of 'ignorant.'"

"You're a redhead and you're getting ready to have lunch with your mother, who you don't get along with. I can honestly tell you I have no intentions of making you angry. I would also like to get out of this lunch in one piece, preferably with my sanity intact."

Tilting my head to the side, I raised my hand to his cheek. *Ah. Spiky.* Why was that hot?

"Oh, honey," I said slowly. "You think you're going to leave this weekend with any sanity at all. That's so cute."

"Did you just call me honey?"

"Would you prefer I reverted to Hockey Boy?"

"No, actually. I wouldn't."

"All right. Hockey Boy it is." I kissed his cheek and, with one quick shove of his arm, made my escape. I slid my feet into my flip-flops with a giggle and grabbed my phone and purse from the bed.

Adam sighed behind me. "You know what you are?"

"A pain in the ass? Sarcasm personified? Queen of Sass?"

"Yes, yes, and yes," he replied. "You're also the internet troll everyone assumes is a twenty-something gamer living in his mom's basement."

"That might be the nicest compliment anyone's ever given me."

"Don't get excited. It wasn't a compliment."

"Then you need better insults, because five-year-olds at recess have you beat. *Hockey Boy.*" Another grin and I twirled into the main room of the suite. "Come on. My grandpa will be here after lunch, then you'll really see how crazy my family is."

"It gets worse?"

"Oh, yeah. You ain't seen nothin' yet."

Adam pulled the door open and held it for me to walk through. "You know, if it weren't for the sex, I might be regretting this entire weekend right about now."

"You know, if it weren't for the sex, I would definitely be regretting this entire weekend," I replied. "Come on. Let's go. Satan can only last so long on the surface before she gets too cold and has to go back underground."

"How the hell did you survive past your teenage years?"

"Avoided my mother as much as possible and left

for college the minute I was able."

"Write a guide for teens on surviving those seven horrible years. You'll make millions."

I hit the button for the elevator and glanced over at him. "Noted. But I'm putting your name on it to make those millions."

"Do I get royalties?"

"I'll give you a blow job for every thousand dollars I make."

"What if I ever get married?" Adam placed his hand on the side of the elevator opening so the doors wouldn't shut.

Shrugging, I stepped into the mirrored box. "Then we'll have to draw up a contract about this and your future wife will have to be in full agreement. If not, then you'll have to take whatever the going rate is for a blow job."

He leaned against the side, sticking his hands in his pockets. His lips quirked to the side. "Do you know what the going rate is?"

Blinking quickly, I did my best to look offended. "What are you trying to say, sir?"

"Nothing. It was merely a question. Nothing insinuated," he said quickly.

I grinned. "Okay, first, stop panicking. It'll take more than that offend me."

"I wasn't panicking."

"Liar," I said as the doors swooshed open. "I could smell your panic from here."

"What are you? A wild animal?"

I glanced over my shoulder. "If you really want to find out, you can buy me tequila."

His eyes flashed with something, and he placed his hand on the small of my back. "I'll lose a little sanity for that," he said, guiding me toward the main lobby.

Eyes were on us—on him—the second we stepped into it. I didn't recognize the little boy who was staring at him like he'd just seen God in real life, but I knew exactly what was about to happen.

The little boy grabbed hold of his mom's dress and tugged. She bent down, fussing at him, and he pointed in Adam's direction. He was bouncing on the balls of his feet, and I swear, I could feel his excitement.

He looked exactly how my nephew had the night before.

Adam hadn't noticed. He was happy to guide me toward the door, and I dipped my head. Something tugged in my stomach—guilt, regret, just the general feeling of being wrong.

A glance to the side showed me why.

We'd walked right past him. Adam still had tunnel-vision to the main doors, and the little boy, while excited, stopped. Every step we took closer to the door meant his shoulders dropped a little more.

If that was my nephew, and I were the woman standing next to him, would I let them keep walking?

No. I'd go out on a limb and see if I could do something.

I faltered in my step, reaching my hand onto Adam's chest to stop him.

"What's up?" he asked, dipping his head.

"There's a little boy over there," I said softly. "He knows who you are. He wants to meet you."

He slowly turned his head in the direction of the little boy who'd commanded my attention. Now, he was shyly hiding behind his mom's leg, as if meeting his hero was too much for him.

"Poppy—"

I said nothing. I wriggled free of his hold and walked to the little guy. My eyes met his mom's, and with a smile, I kneeled down in front of him. "Hey, buddy. Are you here for Rosie's wedding?"

Clutching his mom's dress tighter, he nodded.

"Wanna know a secret?"

Another nod.

"I'm Rosie's sister. And that guy? That's Adam West."

"From da Stowms?" he whispered.

I leaned right into him. "Yes. Don't tell anyone, okay? I'll bring him over here if you promise to keep it secret."

He nodded so enthusiastically I thought his head might fly off.

"What's your name, buddy?"

"Adam," he whispered.

Oh. My heart.

"Okay, hold on." I pressed a finger to my lips and stood. My flip-flops thundered against the tiled floor as I crossed back to Adam.

"What are you doing?" Adult Adam whispered.

I linked my fingers through his. "You're his hero," I whispered right back.

"We'll be late for lunch with your mom," he reminded me.

"I don't care. He needs you." I dragged him across the floor to where Little Adam was standing, starstruck.

I mean, I kinda got it. I'd be the same if a naked Channing Tatum showed up in my bedroom, you know?

"Adam, this is Adam," I said, releasing Adult Adam's hand. "He's a big fan of yours."

Adult Adam dropped to his knees. "Hi there,

Adam. That's a great name. Did you know that?"

Little Adam nodded. "My dad said he named me after your dad."

Eh?

"He has good taste," Adult Adam replied. "Are you here to see Rosie and Marcus get married?"

The little one nodded again. "I love Uncle Marcus," he said.

Ah. Clarification. Wonderful.

"Marcus' sister-in-law," Little Adam's mom said, touching my arm. "Jerica."

"Poppy. Rosie's sister," I replied softly, touching her hand.

"Thank you," she whispered. "Adam West is his Iron Man."

Adam laughed at something her son had said. Little Adam threw back his head, clutching his stomach, laughing as though every single one of his dreams had come true.

I swallowed hard. "He's amazing. I think he's spent more time with guests than he has with me." I rolled my eyes.

She laughed, touching my arm. "I'd say that's a sign of a good man, but that's probably debatable right now to you."

I looked back at Adam giving her little boy a high five, and there was nothing debatable about it. "No. He is. He's a good man."

Jerica nudged me with her elbow. "You got a good one. Don't let him go."

I smiled, but I didn't say anything. He was my fake boyfriend, after all. But I knew it—he was a good man, and that was all there was to it.

"Adam, baby, we need to go and check in," Jerica

said softly, approaching the two Adams. "I'm sure we'll see Mr. Winters again this weekend."

"Your mom is right," Adam said. "I'll see you at the wedding!"

Little Adam nodded, grinning widely. "Okay. You promise?"

My Adam nodded. "Sure. I promise."

"That was cute," I said, turning onto the sloping stairs that led to the beach.

"It was?" Adam reached over and cupped my elbow when I almost tripped on a little crack in one of the steps.

"Thanks." I smiled at him. "Yes, it was cute. You made his day. How can that not be cute?"

"Is this like when I tell you that you're cute or adorable and you don't like it?"

"No. Because I'm neither cute or adorable, but you interacting with little Adam actually was cute. Like a line-up of fluffy kittens interspersed with ducklings cute."

"Wouldn't the kittens chase the ducklings and try to eat them?"

I stopped at the bottom of the stairs and turned to him. "Are you trying to hurt me?"

Laughing, he wrapped one arm around my shoulders and hugged me against him. "I'm sorry. The kittens and the ducklings played with a little ball of wool and lived happily ever after."

"Why would ducklings be playing with wool?"

"Why would you line up ducklings and kittens?"

"Because it's my explanation and I can use

whatever imagery I like," I replied. "It's like asking J.K. Rowling why Ron got annoyed at Dean for dating Ginny but didn't bat an eyelid about Harry doing it. Personally, I think she needed to be more consistent in his emotions, but I wouldn't question her on it. Why do you need to question my comparison for cuteness?"

Adam opened his mouth as if he was going to respond to that, but he quickly shut it and shook his head.

I see he was understanding why I once made my mom roll her eyes so hard she gave herself a migraine and had to lie down.

I was a delight.

"Okay, so what I did was cute. Great. That's how I want to be seen. The guy who does cute things," Adam said with a sigh.

"Then don't do cute things," I told him, grinning. "It's really all your own fault."

He rolled his eyes, squeezing me again gently. Obviously, he'd come to his senses and had decided to give up arguing with me. Not to mention that I could see the tiki-style beach bar and my mom was already sitting at a table with four rattan-style chairs.

The bar wasn't anything fancy, but it was definitely somewhere I could imagine being the heart and soul of a warm evening on the beach. It was all made out of wood, and the sloping roof was coated in palm tree leaves, giving it an exotic feel.

Large, colorful lights were attached to the edge of it, although they weren't turned on right now, I imagined they looked beautiful in the dark. The bar jutted out enough for someone to sit and eat—not that I would sit at the bar.

The seats were swings.

Could you imagine sitting at that bar after one too many cocktails and trying to sit still? It wasn't going to happen. Hell, it probably wasn't going to happen for me stone cold sober.

Adam caught where I was looking. "You're trying to figure out how long you'd last on one of those swings, aren't you?"

"Can you read my mind?"

"No. I was thinking the same thing." His lips twitched. "Fifty bucks says three margaritas and you're on your ass."

"Fifty bucks says one glass of water and I'm on my ass, and that's pushing it," I muttered. "All right. Here we go. Let's survive this."

"You say it like we're going down to burn in hell."

"We are, and I'm taking you with me."

Another squeeze. This time, a reassuring one. "Come on. We got this."

I was glad he was so confident. I was shitting my pants. My mother had an eye like a hawk and her mind was as sharp as my tongue was. You could sedate her and tell her a lie and she'd wake up knowing you were lying.

Being so close to her for at least an hour was not going to be a good thing. She'd spend the next sixty minutes examining us to make sure our relationship was what we were saying it was.

Since it wasn't, that was problematic. If she knew I was faking, I'd never hear the end of it. Birthdays. Christmases. Christenings. Weddings.

Hell, she'd put it on my gravestone.

Here lies Poppy Dunn. She was a big fat liar, liar, pants on fire who faked a boyfriend.

I glanced up at my mom. She picked up a large plastic cup and sipped through the bright red straw that was inside it.

Then, she saw my t-shirt.

"I want to be where the people aren't," read my nice, bright, turquoise tank top.

Mom frowned.

Adam looked at my shirt. "Maybe you should have worn a dress."

"And miss the look on her face? Never."

He shook his head. "And you think she's the one who'll drag us to hell."

I jabbed my elbow into his side.

I'd remember that.

CHAPTER NINE
POPPY

Drinks and Disasters

"Mom. Did we keep you waiting long?" I asked, being perfectly sweet.

"Yes," she said, pinching the arm of her sunglasses and lifting them so I could get the full hit of the ire that burned in her eyes. "You're late."

"That's my fault, Mrs. Dunn," Adam stepped forward. "I'm sorry. One of Mark's cousins saw us in the lobby, and her son is a fan. I stopped to say hello."

Mom touched her hand to her chest. "Oh! That was lovely of you. Why don't you both sit down? I'll get the first cocktail brought over for us to try."

I took a deep breath and reached for my chair, but Adam beat me to it. He pulled it out, the bottoms of the legs scratching against the patio we were on.

Mom caught it, raising an eyebrow, but she didn't say anything.

"Thank you," I said softly, taking my seat.

Adam positioned himself between us. A wise choice. The women in my family had been known to kick each other under the table on occasion.

Mom sat up straight and waved in the direction of the bar. "Rosie asked them for three light pink cocktails to match the theme of the wedding, and we have to pick one out of the three. The first we're trying is a rhubarb and ginger gin cocktail."

"Rhubarb? In a cocktail? At a wedding?" It escaped me before I could engage my brain. "Really?"

She sighed. "I know. I raised the same concern.

Gin is rather an acquired taste, not one I'm sure I possess."

"They put rhubarb in a cocktail and the gin is what you're worried about?"

"It might be nice," Adam said in an obvious attempt to defuse the situation. "The weirdest things make sense sometimes. Like pineapple on pizza."

Mom shook her head. "Pineapple on pizza never makes sense."

With a grimace, I nodded.

"Why are you smiling like that? Is it because you're agreeing with me?"

I pretended to look around at the bar. "Are the cocktails ready yet?"

Mom smiled and looked at Adam. "Pineapple on pizza is about the only thing we agree on. That and the shortness of her temper."

"Really? You agree about your temper?" Adam turned to me.

I shrugged. "I have a hot temper. It's not my fault. It's the redhead in me. My temper strikes like a match."

"And burns like a house fire," Mom continued.

"If prison suits didn't clash with my hair, I'd probably be a murderer."

"They're orange. They blend with your hair," Adam said, frowning.

Mom shook her head. "She wore orange once. She looked like a human bowl of fruit."

That was sadly true.

I sighed. "That was a rough day."

Adam looked at me and tilted his head. "So that's really your natural hair color?"

"You didn't know that?" Mom asked.

"We've never discussed her hair," he said honestly.

"Yes." I jumped in before it could go any deeper into what we had and hadn't spoken about. "The bottom isn't, but the top is," I explained, referring to the ombre effect I had that took my hair from dark ginger to a lighter, brighter color. "Keeps it fresh. I like it."

"You never discussed it?" Mom continued with her interrogation.

Great. Now she had a bee in her bonnet. I saw the glint in her eye. She was a bloodhound and she'd picked up the scent of absolute bullshit.

"Do you discuss your hair with Dad?" I shot back.

She paused. "Well, no."

"There you go then."

Right on cue, the server appeared with a silver tray. Three small glasses that resembled stemless wine glasses sat on it, filled with a light pink liquid, a handful of ice cubes, and a weird swirly pink thing that I was afraid was real rhubarb.

I was already skeptical, and now I was ready to veto this drink just on its look.

"Rhubarb and ginger gin cocktail," the server said, lowering the tray to the table. One by one, he picked up the glasses and set them on woven coasters in front of each of us. "And your menus." Folded, laminated menus were then placed in front of us.

"Thank you," Mom said. "Could we have some bread, please?"

"Absolutely, ma'am. I'll get that for you now."

"Thank you." She opened the menu, effectively dismissing him, and Adam glanced at me.

It lasted only the briefest of seconds before he

returned his attention right to the glass.

His expression could only be described as one thing.

Regret.

"Are you all right?" I asked him.

"Yeah. I'm just considering how I'd never live it down if any of my teammates ever saw me drinking pink cocktails." He frowned. "I don't think I will, even they don't see me."

"You're doing it for the greater good," I told him chirpily. "And a lunch date might stop random teen girls screaming at you."

"That happened one time," he reminded me, holding up a finger. "And it was not my fault."

"Teen girls screamed at you?" Mom asked, picking up the cocktail before quickly putting it down. "Do we need to send out a note asking people to control their children?"

I choked on my own saliva. "What is this? A freaking zoo? Mom, you can't do that!"

"Well, if you hadn't had brought a famous sports star as your date..."

And this was why my mother and I did not do lunch dates.

"I didn't do it deliberately." I shifted in my seat. *Oh, if only she knew how true that was!* "It's not like I set out to sabotage a wedding or anything. Hell, I didn't even know who he was when we met."

That's right. I was going to toe the line of truth as closely as I could. The fewer lies I told, the less chance I had of being caught with my pants on fire.

And nobody wanted their pants to be on fire. If my pants were on fire, my vagina would be at risk, and man was that a useful thing to have around and fully functioning.

Especially if the person who could, you know, do something with the vagina was Adam Winters.

Luckily for me, right at that point, the server saved my ginger ass once again.

"Here's the bread basket you requested, Mrs. Dunn." He put a wicker basket full of sliced bread in the center of the table, along with three small plates, knives, and a small dish full of butter. "Did you look at your menus or taste your drinks?"

"Yes, I know what I'd like to order," I lied, opening my menu for the first time. Skimming it with my eyes and pretending like I knew what I was looking for, I ran my finger across the menu. "I'll have the salmon with sweet potato fries. Thank you." I folded it and handed it to him.

Adam's eyes widened like I'd told him a puck was coming at his nose. "I'll uh, I'll have the steak."

"Which steak, sir?" the server asked.

"Rump. Rare." He snapped the menu shut and handed it to the server.

Mom, however, looked marginally amused. "I'll have a Caesar salad with chicken, thank you. Dressing on the side."

With that, he was dismissed. Even if he did open his mouth to ask about something else—probably our cocktails. I didn't blame him. Mom was terrifying at the best of times. Horrific at the worst.

"So," Mom said, taking a napkin from the table. Without looking at us, she folded it and set it on her lap. "Where did you meet?"

"In a bar," Adam answered honestly. "She was the only woman in the general vicinity who didn't look at me like I was a meal ticket. Turned out, she had no idea who I was." He peered over at me, lips twitching into a smile.

Okay, wow. We really were going to skirt the truth here.

I picked up my drink and looked at Mom. "It's true. He could have been that guy who plays for that Spanish team and I still wouldn't have recognized him."

"Which guy?" Mom asked, frowning.

"I don't know," I replied. "If I knew, I'd have said his name."

"Ronaldo?" Adam jumped in, saving my ass.

"That guy. Isn't he in Portugal? Why did I think he played in Spain?"

"He does play in Spain." He was visibly trying not to laugh at me at this point. "He's Portuguese, so he plays for Portugal, but his club team is Real Madrid."

I looked at Mom again and shrugged. "There you go. All I knew was that he was hot with his shirt off."

Mom sighed. "You really didn't know who he was?" She motioned to Adam. "Even I knew who he was when I saw him."

"When have you ever seen me watch sports?"

"You were awfully interested in baseball as a teenager."

"Yes. They wear tight pants. Every teenage girl is interested in baseball, and it's not for the sport." I rolled my eyes and took a sip from the drink.

I didn't know if it was the gin, the rhubarb, or the ginger, but this drink needed to die in a fucking house fire.

"Eh! Ack! Oh no!" I sputtered and put the drink on the table, wincing as a shiver took hold of my entire body. "Oh no. Make it go away."

Adam burst out laughing, while Mom simply

sighed at my theatrics.

"Poppy, it cannot be that bad," she said, picking up her glass and bringing it to her face. She swilled it in the glass, sniffing it.

Good lord. It was a cocktail, not a vintage wine.

Mom took a sip. Instantly, her face contorted into the picture of absolute disgust, and when she set the glass down, I swear, she almost looked mildly offended that she'd dared put it in her mouth.

"Oh, dear Lord," she gasped.

Adam shrugged and looked at his glass. "I like it."

"You're outvoted," I quickly said as Mom waved her hand for the bartender.

Oh no.

My eyes widened, and Adam's foot nudged mine under the table. Our eyes met for a brief second, and he raised his eyebrows.

No bartender came.

Mom took a deep breath and grabbed all three glasses with some extreme skill.

All right, not extreme, but a move so slick I'd drop it them all if I tried.

"What is she doing?" Adam whispered, leaning over to me and resting his arm on my chair, his eyes on my mom taking the drinks to the bar.

I turned, peering over at her. "Well, if I know her, and I do—"

"I would hope so."

I shot him a quick glare. "She's about to tear one of those poor guys a new asshole for daring to serve her something so vile."

"But...the cocktails were requested."

"Yeah," I said, meeting his eyes. "That doesn't mean she'll be reasonable about it. Have you learned nothing since you got here?"

"Well, between the fact you didn't know who I was, your sister's issue with the seating plan, and now your mom with the cocktails… I think I'm getting there, actually. I'm seeing unreasonable as a female family trait."

I blinked at him. "If your face wasn't so pretty, I'd punch you in it."

He grinned, twirling some of my hair around his finger. "No, you wouldn't."

"Are you sure? I'm pretty good with my right hand."

One of his eyebrows quirked up. "I know."

"That's not—I didn't. I mean." I took a deep breath and glared at him. "Stop fucking with me."

"I could, but I know you'll fuck with me the second you get, so…"

Mom came back seconds later and took her seat. "They won't serve that again," she noted. "Pink lemonade margaritas next."

Well, that sounded better than the gin shit we'd been given, that was for sure.

Mom refolded her napkin and set it back on her lap before smiling at us both. "So, talk me through your relationship. I'm surprised you never told me about him, Poppy."

We'd already covered this.

"Like Adam said before, him being here was last minute. I didn't want to tell you that I was seeing anyone. We were keeping it to ourselves."

"Media attention and stuff like that," Adam interjected. "I'm followed occasionally, and these past few months have been bad with the sports tabloids while I was in new contract negotiations."

I stayed quiet. So far, so good. I hoped.

"I hoped they'd leave me alone after the team announced I'd signed another, but they saw me having dinner with my sister a couple weeks later and spun a story about a 'mystery girl.'" He snorted. "After that, I was the one who said to keep it quiet to protect Poppy."

He was good.

He was very good.

Even if the story was a little dicey—I mean, what if he'd been seen with real mystery girls? What if my parents knew that?

Right at that point, our next round of cocktails arrived, distracting Mom from responding. She narrowed her eyes and as she asked him a question, Adam nudged me under the table and winked at me.

He was a hell of a lot more confident that I felt. Even now.

CHAPTER TEN
ADAM

Lust and Lies

Poppy bit the inside of her lip and glanced down.

She was worried. I got it. I was fucking worried, too. I was the one sitting here, opposite the sharpest woman I'd ever met, lying through my damn teeth.

I didn't even have a plan. I was making it up as I went along, praying like fuck it was a plausible story. One of my teammates had kept his relationship secret for that exact reason a couple of years ago.

I didn't care if she thought I was lying. I just wanted her to believe Poppy was being honest.

She wasn't, but that was beside the point. We'd been sitting here for all of ten minutes and I understood entirely why Poppy needed a fake date.

Why I'd agreed to be it… The jury was still out. It'd been an impulse, something to fill a free weekend.

Or maybe it'd been those fucking beautiful brown eyes of hers. Maybe even the adorably shy smile her lips curved into whenever our eyes met.

Whatever it was, I'd agreed, and I hadn't been prepared for it at all. Neither of us had.

And I got the impression that she still didn't forgive me for not telling her who I was.

"Pink lemonade margaritas with sugar," the guy said as he set three glasses down in front of us.

"This place is completely private, isn't it?" I double-checked with the bartender.

He blinked, recognition flashing in his eyes. He gave me a brisk nod. "Yes, sir. Anyone caught trespassing is detained by security until the police arrive."

"Good. Thank you."

He nodded again. "Your food should be out soon."

"Thank you," Poppy's mom said, dismissing him.

She was efficient at that. I needed some fucking tips at getting rid of people on occasion…

"Are you worried about your privacy?" she asked, turning her sharp gaze on me.

"It just occurred to me that there are an awful lot of people here who know who I am," I said slowly. "And all it takes is one social media post, and we could have a problem."

"What? Your teammates will see photos of you drinking pink cocktails?" Poppy smirked. "Oh, the shame."

I would be lying if I said the thought hadn't crossed my mind. "That'll be the least of my worries if they bring their long-lens cameras and your ass is plastered all over the internets."

She paused, then shrugged. "I squat for this ass."

"Poppy!" Her mom pressed her hand to her chest. "My goodness!"

"It's true! And unless your name is Chris Hemsworth, my ass is all I'm gonna squat for."

I made a mental note to change my name… Or buy a cardboard mask of his face, just to see if she'd make good on that promise.

Her mom cut her a dark look then turned to me, a hint of compassion in her eyes. "I can ask security to keep an extra eye out, if you'd like."

"I don't want a big deal made out of it, but I'd

hate Rosie's wedding to be ruined because of a few nosey bastards."

She nodded sharply. "Let me see the bartender and see if I can call the manager and ask him to come down." She picked up the margarita and sipped. "This is good. I like it." She took another big mouthful and got up, leaving the glass almost a third empty on the table.

Poppy looked at the glass, back at her mom's retreating back, then to me. "You said that on purpose, didn't you? To get rid of her."

I picked up the margarita glass. "What makes you say that?"

"Because she's gone," she said matter-of-factly, her gaze just as calculating as her mom's had been.

She said her mom had the eyes of a hawk, but she had them, too. And the biggest problem with Poppy Dunn was that she didn't miss a damn thing.

"Maybe it was to give us a break from interrogation," I admitted, "But after I said what I did…" I put the glass down without touching it and ran my hand down my face.

Poppy frowned.

Reaching over, I pushed some hair from her face, letting my fingertips trail across her soft skin. She met my eyes, and uncertainty shone at me.

"It's a thing, Red." I sighed, dropping my head. "I wish it weren't, but it is. There are a whole bunch of teens here, and if teens love anything, it's fucking social media," I finished on a mutter.

"I didn't think of that."

"Why would you? You had no reason to." My lips tugged to the side. "I also don't want anything to happen to your sister's wedding. She seemed stressed enough this morning without me being an issue for her."

I also don't want you wrapped up in anything you don't need to be.

Poppy's lips pursed as if she knew there was something I wasn't saying. Her gaze darted back and forth across my face. She was figuring out if I was hiding something from her—like I was—and I knew she'd figure it out.

She plucked a straw from the holder in the middle of the table and put it into her glass. Leaning forward, she made sure her hair was out of the way and took the straw between her lips.

My eyes dropped to her mouth.

Fuck. I'd never wanted to be a plastic straw so much in my life.

Her eyes slid to me as she released the straw. "You want a photograph so you can keep staring even when I'm not here?"

"Depends what the photo is of."

"Me giving you the finger," she muttered.

I laughed, leaning right back in my chair. "Probably the easiest photo to get of you."

Proving me right, she flipped me the bird and took another big drink. "By the way, I know you stopped yourself from saying something a minute ago, and by the end of the weekend, I'll get it out of you."

I picked up my margarita and shrugged a shoulder. "You can try."

"So you're admitting it?"

"Lying doesn't do me any good now, does it?"

"I don't care," she said. "You'll tell me. I'll annoy the hell out of you until you do."

"Do what?" her mom said as she joined us again at the table. "What are you doing?"

"Admitting that he was more interested in me

than I was in him when we first met," Poppy said without batting an eyelid. "It's a point of contention."

"Even if it were true, I'd never admit it," I said, picking it up immediately. "God knows what you'd do with that info."

"Hire Banksy to put it on the wall on the side of your house," she quipped.

"Can you do that? That's on my property which would mean I'd own it. That's money right there."

Poppy opened her mouth, something flashing through her eyes. She kept that expression for a moment before she decided against arguing with me. Snapping her lips shut, she grasped hold of her glass and leaned back in her chair, eyeing me with annoyance.

I grinned at her. Then, to rub salt in the wound, lifted my glass to her.

Her mom looked between us both, eyes flitting back and forth for a good few seconds. Then, she picked up her own glass, looked at me, smiled, and raised hers.

Well, well, well.

I just got the approval from her mom—one I didn't need.

But, strangely, I was fucking happy to have it.

"That was torture," Poppy said, dropping onto the sand. "And you! You traitor." She shoved me the second my ass hit the sand. "You enjoyed yourself!"

I reached behind my head and pulled my shirt off with one tug. "What?"

"You enjoyed yourself!" she said.

To my stomach.

"Do *you* want a picture of me?" I pulled out her

line from lunch.

"Ugh! You're insufferable!" Following my movement, she pulled her tank top off and tossed it over me to join my shirt.

Her bikini top was white, showing off a weird pink-golden color to her skin, and she swept her hair around to one side, exposing the side of her neck.

She jerked to look at me. "Now who needs another fucking picture?"

I held up my hands. "Just because I got along with your mom…"

"This is not because she now adores you!"

"Adores me, eh?"

"She hugged you longer than she hugged me!"

"That's because I was nice to her," I reminded her. "You were, well, a human cactus."

Poppy rolled her eyes and lay down, pulling her sunglasses from the top of her head to cover her eyes. "And you're the worst fake boyfriend ever."

"Hey, you know that isn't true." I knocked my foot against hers. "If I was a bad one, I wouldn't be friends with your mom."

"That's the point, dumbass." She rolled onto her side, propping herself up on her elbow, and pulled down her glasses to look me in the eye. "She likes you. Now, when this weekend is done, I'm going to have to field questions about you until I can come up with a viable reason for why the hell I'd break up with someone like you."

"Someone like me? Want to elaborate?"

"No." She dropped her glasses back in place and herself back onto her back.

I rolled onto my stomach. "Oh, come on. Even I know you're gonna field her calls and avoid her when this weekend is done. You'll avoid it until you absolutely have to, then tell her you didn't want to tell her we'd broken up."

"Oh yeah? And what excuse am I going to give her, Einstein?"

"I dunno, Red. Make me out to be an asshole. Say I cheated on you or something."

She snorted. "Please. Look at your damn abs. You couldn't cheat on a diet. You don't get abs like that from cheating on a diet."

"Actually, I'm great at that. There's a reason I'm at the gym before you even wake up. It's because I have a minor addiction to sugar."

"Oh, yeah, I mean, you look it. I've never seen you not eating sugar."

Laughing, I rested back on my elbows. "You laugh. When my eldest sister was pregnant, she craved Cheesecake Factory cheesecakes. One day, when her husband was away working, I went to get her one to take her the next day. I had to go back the following day to get another because I ate the entire thing by myself."

"You're so full of shit," Poppy muttered.

"Believe it or not, Red, it's the truth."

"Sure. It's the truth." She made air quotes.

I shook my head and turned my face into the sun. She wasn't going to believe me, and I wasn't going to fight her for it. She was stubborn and headstrong—I'd learned that much.

Yet, in a weird way, it made her attractive. She wasn't afraid to say what she thought, and she wasn't afraid to stand up for what she believed in.

And let me tell you—groupies were a thing. They weren't just for rock stars. They were for everyone with a bit of money and media star, and I'd come across more than a few of them who were interested in me for what I was, not who I was.

I hadn't lied when I'd told Poppy that.

When she'd waltzed into my life at that bar, she'd been a breath of fresh air. I'd be lying if I said that hadn't been attractive to me. It had been. It was a rarity and something I'd relished.

Not that I'd ever expected to find her at the end of my bed, staring at me the next morning. And I sure as hell hadn't expected her to explain that she needed a date for this wedding.

But she had, and I was here, and I was starting to get uncomfortable.

Not because of her stern mother. Not because everyone here knew who I was when she hadn't. Not because of the crazy grandfather I had yet to meet.

But because I knew one thing to be very fucking true.

Poppy Dunn, with her red hair and her brown eyes and her smartass mouth, was someone I could see myself falling for.

"So. What are you not telling me?" she asked.

"Not telling you?"

"Earlier. When you spoke about the media. There was something you never said to me." She raised one arm above her head, bending it at the elbow, calm as you fuckin' please.

Dropping my head back, I said, "I have no idea what you're talking about."

"Sure, you don't. I'll believe that when, oh, that's right. I won't."

"You've got such a mouth on you."

"Don't get into the discussion of my mouth again. We've already had this conversation once, and if you need a reminder, then you don't deserve to know what my mouth can do."

I didn't need a reminder. I could well imagine it. Not that I was in a position to be imagining it while lying on the beach in a pair of shorts, but there I was, imagining it.

Wondering what it'd feel like to have her kneeling between my legs, her hand wrapped around the base of my cock while she played with the top with her mouth.

I adjusted my shorts, shifting uncomfortably on the sand. Poppy's head turned the slightest amount, so she'd caught my movement. If the turn of her head wasn't enough, the curve of her pouty, bright pink lips gave it away.

She'd be shit at poker. I knew that much.

"Look at me like that again, Red, and I'm gonna kiss the smirk off your lips."

She snorted. "You wish."

"Don't test me."

"You don't scare me."

"I don't need to scare you, but I already know that your self-control is running low."

Poppy propped herself up on one elbow and glared at me over the top of her glasses. She was lying there in her bikini, fingers pinched on the arm of her sunglasses—well, it was hard to take her seriously.

"And what do you know about my self-control, hockey boy?"

I rolled onto my side and kept my gaze on hers. "I know I could run my finger up the inside of your thigh and you'd squirm."

"Of course I would. That's a ticklish area."

"I know could lean in and not even kiss your neck and you'd start breathing heavily, and that if I did kiss you, your nails would be digging into my skin."

"If you're trying to turn me on, it's not working." She replaced her glasses and dropped down again. "All you're doing is making me want to take a nap, honestly. That lunch was stressful."

"And that's how you're going to cope with it? By napping?"

"Isn't that how everybody deals with stress? By sleeping and pretending it doesn't really exist?"

Slowly, I shook my head. "No, Red. Most people, I don't know. I work out."

"Yeah, well, that sounds like too much exercise for me." She sniffed. "I'd rather nap, then eat a pint of ice cream and deal with it tomorrow."

"That would be more beneficial if your mom wasn't here today." I chuckled. "Come on. It wasn't as bad as you're making out and you know it."

She sniffed, rolling onto her stomach. "I can't talk to you when you're being this unreasonable."

Laughing, I reached over her. With a big tug, I pulled her onto her back once more and straddled her, pinning her in this position. I didn't need her to remove her glasses to know that she was glaring at me as if I'd just kicked her puppy.

"I'm unreasonable?" I asked, running my hands down her arms. My fingers toyed with her palms until I slipped them between hers. "You're the one making a fuss out of absolutely nothing."

"Absolutely nothing? We barely escaped through the skin of our teeth."

"Maybe in Poppyville. In the real world, she believed everything we said and drank three of those margaritas." I quirked one eyebrow. "You're just annoyed because she likes me. You all but admitted it a few minutes ago."

"Fine. I'm annoyed she likes you. But not just because I have to fake break up with you. I'm not used to her liking my boyfriends. Real or otherwise."

"Boyfriends? You mean more than one person has put up with your drama for real?"

"If you weren't sitting on me I'd kick you in the balls," she threatened, wiggling beneath me.

My dick twitched. "I'd stop moving if I were you."

"No." She wriggled harder.

With a jerk, I pulled her with me as I rolled onto my back. She squealed, and as she came down on top of me, I wrapped my arms around her back, our hands still clasped.

"I am not comfortable!" she snapped.

"Neither was I when you were wriggling under my cock," I retorted.

"So, you're going to dislocate my shoulders?"

"No. I'm just going to keep you here until you understand that I told you to stop wriggling for a reason."

I swear she rolled her eyes.

"I know why you told me to stop, hockey boy," she drawled. "I can feel it pressing against my stomach. It's not exactly a blink-and-you'll-miss-it penis, is it?"

I bit back a laugh. "That's the strangest way anyone has ever told me I have a big cock."

"I didn't say it was big. I said it wasn't small." She paused. "For all you know, I was calling it mediocre."

She was so full of shit, but damn, that sharp wit would kill me one day.

"All right, Red. Why don't you put your money where your mouth is and we'll go back to our room so I can show you just how mediocre it is when your pussy is wet and you're begging me for more?"

Poppy squirmed, and I felt her legs clench together. "Actually, you know what, I remember promising Rosie I'd help her do something today."

She forced her way out of my grip, and I smirked, letting my hands fall to the sides.

"You did, huh?"

She nodded. "Yeah, uh, something about that table plan Mom was interfering with."

I sat up as she reached for her tank top and grabbed it. "And you just remembered."

"Uh-huh. I'm forgetful. Forget everything. What can I say?" She tugged the shirt over her head and went to move.

I snatched her wrist and tugged her back to me. She squeaked out a weird sound, and I slipped my fingers into her hair and round the back of her head.

And kissed her.

Her nails instantly dug into my thigh as she leaned into me. She tasted of tequila and strawberries and ice cream and smelled like the sea. It was an addictive combination.

Or maybe it was just her who was addictive.

I released her with a graze of my teeth over her lower lip. "Forget that," I murmured.

She opened her mouth, then stopped, shook her head, and scrambled up to her feet. The sand moved beneath her, almost making her trip, and I had to laugh into my hand, so she didn't turn around and hit me.

Which, let's face it, was probably something she'd do.

I watched her go, flicking her fiery hair over her shoulder. She glanced back, blushing when she realized

I'd caught her looking, and jerked her gaze away just in time to avoid tripping over the bottom step.

Helping Rosie my ass.

All she was doing was helping herself keep her pants on—and my cock hard.

I rolled to my front, shifting my hips so my throbbing, hard cock wasn't totally flat against the sand, and buried my face in my arms.

This was turning out to be a long weekend.

CHAPTER ELEVEN
POPPY

Clits and Clucks

I rubbed my hand down my face with one hand and set my glasses on top of my head with the other.

Oh. My. God.

Adam Winters was going to kill me.

It wouldn't be my mother after all. Maybe my gravestone wouldn't read that I was a liar. Maybe it would read that a red-hot hockey player made my clitoris explode with lust and that was how I died.

I mean, as long as I orgasmed first, I wasn't against it.

Now, I'd lied to escape his sex God ways, and I was screwed. After seeing Rosie earlier, I did not want to be in the presence of the female equivalent to Godzilla. Unlike me, she was able to hold her temper.

Unfortunately, just like me, when she let it fly, it was a doozy, and everyone needed to evacuate the immediate area.

I tucked hair behind my ear and wandered through the lobby. I didn't know if I was expecting her to pop out from behind a wall or something, but she didn't. Leaning against the concierge's desk, I pulled my phone out of my pocket and texted her.

Her response was a little too quick for my liking.

Rosie: Ballroom from last night. Done w lunch?

Me:...Yes

Rosie: Come here before I murder someone

Oh, goodie.

I clutched my phone tightly in case, you know, I needed to use it as a weapon or something. You never knew with her. Once, when I'd forgotten to turn off her curling iron and burned a hole in her favorite shirt, I'd had to use a tape dispenser to get her out of my room.

That was the fifth time I'd burned something from not turning it off. In hindsight, it wasn't totally unreasonable for her to hit me with it or to ban me from using it in the future.

She could have let it cool down before she hit me, though…

I stepped out of the elevator and headed for the room the other side of the hall. Mark was standing outside, phone to his ear, hand on his forehead.

"Hold on. I'll call you back," he said into the phone. "Pop, where's your mom?"

"Judging by the margaritas at lunch and the giggle at the bartender, I'm going to say in bed," I said slowly. "Why?"

He sighed heavily. "That was your dad. Apparently, your grandfather had a Bloody Mary on the plane."

"Oh no."

"Yes. Long story short, he started stripping in the car on the way home until your dad agreed to take him to a strip club for a dance."

"Not again," I groaned. "We specifically told the airline not to give him alcohol when we booked his seat. People pick gluten-free, we pick alcohol-free."

Grimacing, he nodded. "He had a dance, and now he won't leave. Your mom isn't answering her phone, and your dad is panicking."

Why was this always left up to me? I was the youngest. And why had I let my mother drink at lunch knowing this shit was happening?

I held my hand out for his phone.

He unlocked it and handed it to me.

Bringing up the last call, I dialed my father's number.

"Mark. Did you find her?"

"Dad, it's me. Poppy. Put Grandpa on the phone." I sighed.

"Pops? Where's your mom?"

"Too much sun at lunch," I lied. "She's got a headache and is lying down."

"Cocktail tasting went well, then," he replied with a chuckle.

"Yeah, watch her on those tomorrow. Grandpa?"

"Give me a second." There was a rustling, followed by muffled club-style music. I couldn't make out what happened next, but after a minute or so, silence cut through the line and Dad said, "Here."

"Grandpa?" I asked.

"Pops! Why are you calling me? Am I in trouble?" Grandpa's gruff voice was weirdly playful and filled me with warmth.

"Yes, you are!" I said firmly. "This is your granddaughter's wedding, and you're messing around in strip clubs! What did we tell you about Bloody Mary's on the plane? You can't be trusted, and this is why! Rosie's devastated you're not here, and Mom is about to have a cow, so you get yourself in that car and you come home right now!"

There was a moment of silence, then, "Your mother is always having a cow."

"Grandpa!"

"All right, all right, firecracker. We're leaving now."

"And you're coming straight here. I'll see you soon."

I heard a faint "Bugger!" right before I cut the call. I'd caught his loophole, and he had no choice but to behave himself and come here.

"Done," I said to Mark. "Here."

He took the phone and blinked at me. "You're scarily like your mother sometimes."

I pointed at him. "Say that again and I'll slice your balls off with a butter knife."

He put one hand over his groin and gave me a thumb up with the other.

"Is Rosie in the ballroom?"

Another grimace. He was so out of his element. "Yep. And someone let her bitch flag fly."

"I told you to burn it." I sighed.

"Something to do with the catering. Apparently, I wasn't helping, so I was sent away." He snorted. "Figured I'd get Rory and head down to the beach. And stay far, far away from my lovely wife-to-be."

Now it was me who snorted. "I think Adam is still down there. He didn't show any signs of moving when I left. You should see if you can find him."

"You want me to hang out with your fake boyfriend?"

I held up my hands. "Look, if Chrissy Teigen was here as someone's fake girlfriend, I wouldn't care about the fake thing. I'd be down there asking her how to write bomb-ass Instagram captions and the art of trolling on Twitter."

"I think you just need an account to do that,

Pop."

"Whatever. He's Rory's hero, and after Monday, I'll never see him again. Make the most of it for him." I paused. "And you, you big kid."

His eyes sparkled with laughter. "Right. Sure. Monday."

"What does that mean?"

"Nothing." He dipped and kissed my cheek. "Try and make sure Rosie doesn't kill anyone, would you?"

"Been doing that for twenty-four years," I muttered, turning away from him to the ballroom.

It was nowhere near as crazy as it was last night. The centerpieces were still in place, but all the balloons had disappeared. A top table had now been set up, and I shuddered at the idea of being up there in front of everyone.

Rosie was standing by the bar with a man wearing a sharp suit and shiny shoes.

Well, I say Rosie was standing. The man was standing. She was pacing, and she looked like she was ready to go all Hulk or something.

"Hey. I found you," I said, interrupting her pacing. "What's up?"

My sister stopped, took a deep breath, and closed her eyes. They snapped open a second later after a heavy exhale and she said, "They've run out of chicken."

I stared at her.

"Poppy! Why are you staring at me? There's no chicken!"

Apparently, silence wasn't the right answer.

"Why isn't there any chicken?" I asked.

"Because they've run out!" she shrieked.

I turned to Mr. Suit. "How can you run out of chicken? They're not exactly an endangered species."

He opened his mouth to respond, but she beat him to it. "Some supplier issue! They'll be delayed!"

"Can't you use another?" I asked him as if he'd answered.

"Apparently not!" Rosie ran her hands through her hair.

I spun and looked at her. "Are you the manager?"

"I'm just saying what I know!"

"Okay, Bridezilla." I stepped toward her, grasping her gently at the tops of her arms. "Mark is taking Rory to the beach. Why don't you go back to your room and lie down for half an hour? Mom had a couple too many margaritas at lunch, so you'll have some time to chill out without her causing problems."

"But I—"

"And I will help this nice man find a few chickens to shoot and pluck, okay?"

"Right. Like you could pluck a chicken. You can't even pluck your eyebrows," she muttered.

"Rosie!" I snapped my fingers in front of her. "Figure of speech. Take yourself up to your room and lie down before you give yourself a migraine."

She hovered, looking like she'd argue, but after a minute gave in. Her shoulders deflated, and she dropped her chin so she was looking at the ground. "Okay, fine." She pulled a big file off the bar and handed it to me. "This is yours. For now. It has everything you need. The wedding planner is around and needs final confirmation on the table plan." She whipped open the front and slammed her fist against the first page. "This is my plan. It does not change. You're stubborn, Pops. You dig your heels in if she's changed anything."

"Uh...I think that was a compliment, so sure."

"And you find me chicken!" Rosie said, jabbing

her finger in the direction of Mr. Suit. One last glance at us both and she left the ballroom, taking all the tension with her.

Mr. Suit breathed out a huge sigh of relief.

"Sorry about her. She's a bit uptight," I said brightly. "I, however, am much more pleasant to deal with."

His eyes darted to my shirt. His lips barely twitched, but amusement definitely flashed in his eyes for a second. "Thank God for that, because that's not the only problem."

I groaned. "Hit me."

———•••———

I slammed my car door shut, pressing the button on the key a little too vigorously. "Fucking chicken. Fucking strawberries. Fucking wedding," I muttered to myself. "I'm not a fucking personal shopper for a wedding venue that can't cater for chicken and strawberries."

I clutched the receipts tightly in my hand. I never wanted to see another grocery store again. I was gonna do it all online from now. I'd been to every damn store in Key West to get as many strawberries as I could.

I swear, by the time I entered the last Publix, there was a security guard following the weird redhead buying everyone's strawberries.

And I was over them.

Strawberries, that was. Not Publix. They'd provided me the aspirin I needed for my damn headache from this day.

The bright side was that I knew Grandpa was safely locked in his room—for now—my mom was waking up from her tequila-induced nap, and rumor had it that Celia had slipped my sister something by telling her it was paracetamol, and she'd been sleeping for the last hour.

I wished someone would slip me something. Like a shot of vodka.

I asked for the Mr. Suit at the desk. Using his real name, of course. But Mr. Suit sounded better in my head.

"Ms. Dunn." Resting his hand on my elbow, he pulled me aside. "Did you get the strawberries?"

"Cleared the entire place out of them," I told him. "And as soon as you reimburse me, you can have them from my trunk." I held the receipts out to him.

He unfolded them, eyes flitting back and forth frantically as he added up each total. "Three hundred dollars on strawberries?"

"Do you want my sister to find out about this?"

His spine straightened. "No, no, of course not. Will you take a check?"

"You told me cash." I folded my arms. I needed that money to pay my damn rent. "But I'll accept a bank transfer."

"Very well, very well. Cash, I can do." He waved me into the main office. There was a small safe in the corner, and I raised my eyebrows as he prodded in a code.

That didn't seem very safe to me, but what did I know?

I just wanted my money back.

I waited patiently for him to count out three hundred dollars and secure it in a brown envelope.

Why the hell did I feel like I was executing a drug deal?

"Thank you," I said, taking the envelope. "Can you have someone come out with some crates? My car is full."

"Of course. Ten minutes." He nodded, signaling that I should leave.

I did just that and almost walked right into Adam.

"Whoa, Red. Careful." He touched my arms and looked down at me with a smile. "Where've you been? Drug deal?"

"Shit. You caught me." I rolled my eyes. "No, I had to go on a mission. Walk to my car with me?" I started walking before he could say no.

"Like a secret mission?" he asked, catching up with me.

"I wish. It would have been more fun with a cape and a mask." I sighed. "Remember how I fake-remembered to help Rosie earlier?"

He side-eyed me. "Oh, that was fake? I couldn't tell."

I nudged him with my elbow. "Well, turned out, there was a real issue. The hotel has run out of chicken."

"How does a hotel run out of chicken?"

"Something to do with a supplier. Anyway, I sent Rosie to bed because she was this close to having a heart attack." I pinched my finger and thumb together to show him just how close. "And the guy tells me they are also about to run out of strawberries."

Adam rubbed his hand over his stubbled jaw. "I think I can see where this is going."

"Right. So, I told him he had until I got back to find a new chicken supplier and get it here first thing tomorrow morning, and I'd go on a strawberry hunt."

"Don't say it."

"Yep. I've spent the last hour or so looking like a

crazy woman, and…" I unlocked my car and popped the trunk. "Voila. If you need strawberries in Key West, you're shit outta luck, because I bought them all."

"How many strawberries do you need?"

"Three hundred dollars' worth."

"Are you serious?"

I turned to face him. "Do I look like I'm joking?"

"No. I'm just wondering why the hell three hundred dollars' worth of strawberries is necessary."

Leaning against the side of my car, I said, "Because I'm petty as fuck, and they needed a lesson taught to them."

"That…weirdly makes sense to me. I can see my sisters doing the same thing to me one day."

I grinned. "Then don't make this mistake."

"Noted. Are they coming to get them?"

"No, they're staying in my car until they're ready for them."

"Poppy." He drew closer to me, cupping my chin. His thumb stroked the curve of my lower lip as he dipped his head, bringing his mouth closer to mine. "Stop running your mouth."

"Or what?"

"Or I'll make you."

"You can try."

In hindsight, challenging him like that was a bad idea.

Gripping my hip, he pulled me right against him, bringing his lips to mine for God knows how many times today. I didn't care—kissing him was like flying. Everything else melted away when Adam held my body against his and our lips came together.

He cupped the back of my neck, his other arm clamping around my lower back. My hands fisted in his shirt, grabbing the collar of the polo as I leaned into him.

Something inside me—my heart, my soul, whatever—sighed. And no part of me had any business sighing at anything when he kissed me.

Some kisses were fairytale ones. Heart-thumping, foot-popping, soul-sighing kisses.

I'd always imagined mine would on a first date or under a sunset or after the 'L' word.

But, no. My fairytale kiss, my heart-thumping, foot-popping, soul-sighing kiss, was standing in a parking lot next to a car full of three hundred dollars' worth of strawberries, with a guy who was kissing me to shut my smartass mouth up.

I didn't want to think about how much more appropriate that was for me than something romantic.

A throat cleared behind us, and before I'd even turned, my cheeks were burning.

The young guy who'd obviously cleared his throat shifted. "The, uh—Mr. Smith sent us to get the strawberries."

I swallowed, stepping away from Adam. "Right there. Please take them before they get fried."

Adam covered his mouth with his hand, dipping his head. His shoulders gave away his light chuckle, and I jabbed him with my elbow.

That was all his fault.

We waited in silence until the team of porters had moved all the strawberries into crates and into their wheelie-things. It took them a good fifteen minutes, and I hoped like hell they had a decent fridge to keep them cool.

They thanked me and left. I slammed the trunk shut and locked my car, the beep sounding extra loud in the silence of the parking lot.

"That was awkward," Adam announced, grinning.

"Story of my life," I muttered, stuffing my keys into my ass pocket. "Did Mark find you earlier?"

He nodded. "Rory talked my ear off for forty-five minutes before Mark finally convinced him to get ice cream."

"He picked you over ice cream?" I raised my eyebrows. "Wow. He must really love you."

Shifting, he answered, "Yeah, I sometimes have that effect on kids."

"Aw, now what's awkward?"

"I just... Yeah." He rolled his shoulder, reaching behind to rub the back of his neck. A tiny smile played on his lips. "I don't see myself the way Rory does. I just play hockey 'cause I love it, Red. I don't do it to be some kind of superhero."

"It just comes with the territory, right?" I leaned back against the car.

"Sometimes. I still don't believe I'm a hero."

"Tell that to my dad."

"Exactly my point."

I smiled at him. I couldn't pretend to get it, because I didn't. I would never understand how he viewed his world because it was so very different from mine. Sure, I didn't care about what he was.

I had no reason to care. Not really. Not personally.

"All right. Enough of that." He clapped his hands and wiped them on his shorts. "What time is the dinner tonight?"

"Six-thirty. So I need to be there for at least five-thirty."

He pulled his phone out of his pocket. "All right...So, what you're saying is we have time to go up to

135

our room and finish what we started earlier."

"No. I have to find the wedding planner since my sister is drugged and asleep."

Adam looked at me, face void of all expression. "If I hadn't seen her so anxious this morning, that would seriously concern me."

"You're not concerned?"

"No."

"Good. Now, how do you feel about serial killers?" I asked, glancing over my shoulder as I walked away.

"Documentaries or being friends with them?"

"You know a serial killer?" Oh, man, I sounded way too excited.

He drew level with me and frowned. "Pretty sure a guy I went to school with killed three or four people when he was in college."

I grabbed his arm, stopping us both in the middle of the parking lot. "Oh my God. Tell me everything."

"Of course," he muttered, sliding my hand down to his. "Most girls want me for my money, but you're interested because I know a serial killer."

"Not true. I was originally interested because you were hot. Now, I'm interested because you know a serial killer."

He linked his fingers through mine and sighed. "All right. Get this wedding planner stuff out of the way—because that will take forever—then I'll tell you about him."

"That's the sexiest thing you've ever said to me."

CHAPTER TWELVE
POPPY

Sex and Serial Killers

"So, he posed as a handyman and killed them?"

Adam nodded. "I think so. That's what I remember, anyway. He got caught when he was on campus and posed as the handyman there. He didn't realize the girl's roommate was in, too, and he got caught. I'm pretty sure she hit him over the head with a lamp."

I snorted, my cold water going up my nose. "I'm sorry—it's not funny, but that's just the lamp thing is why I keep a lamp by the side of my bed."

"In case someone tries to murder you in your sleep?"

"No, in case a stranger wants to spoon."

"A lamp wouldn't be much good if they want to shoot you," Adam pointed out. "Unless it's bulletproof and they shoot at the lamp."

"Well, yeah, but—" I didn't actually have a response for that. "Shut up."

Oh, look. I did.

He laughed, finishing his ice water.

"I don't need a babysitter, Miranda. I'm perfectly capable of finding the bar on my own," came my grandfather's rough tones from the other side of the restaurant.

"That's exactly why I'm here, Dad. To stop you from finding it!" Mom replied through what sounded like gritted teeth.

"Oh no," I whispered.

Adam glanced over. "Your grandpa?"

I nodded.

"Too late!" He cackled. The clonk-clonk of his stick against the floor had me sitting up straight. "Pop-pop!"

Oh, no.

Adam stifled a laugh.

I didn't stifle a glare.

"Grandpa. I see you made it here in one piece." I hopped off the stool and kissed his old, wrinkled cheek.

"No thanks to your parents," he mumbled, resting his cane against the bar and hauling himself onto the stool I'd just vacated.

Adam slipped off his and motioned for me to take his. I waved him away, but he pushed me to it, so I had no choice.

"I like him," Grandpa said. "He's got manners."

"Unlike you," Mom said, finally catching up with the wily old man. "Stealing your granddaughter's seat!"

"She got up for me. Isn't that right, Pop-pop?" He winked at me.

I shrugged a shoulder as I sat on Adam's stool. "Sure. We can go with that."

"Introduce me to your friend," Grandpa demanded. "I'm Grandpa." He stuck out his age-spotted hand.

"Adam," Adam replied, shaking it.

"And he's her boyfriend," Mom interjected.

Give me strength. Or vodka.

They were the same thing, right?

Grandpa's eyes narrowed, and he stared intently at Adam. "I know you from somewhere."

Here we go again.

"Do you report the news?" he asked.

Adam shook his head. "No, sir. I play hockey."

"Hockey?" Grandpa looked him up and down. "I don't believe you."

This was going well.

"Are you sure?" he continued.

"Yes, sir," Adam replied. "I play for the Orlando Storms."

Grandpa pinched the arm of his glasses and peered at Adam over them. "Didn't they win the Jeremy Cup this year?"

"The Stanley Cup, sir."

"Why do you keep calling me sir? I'm not a knight."

Help. Help. Is there an escape route?

Mom clearly felt the same because she pinched the bridge of her nose.

"I was just being polite," Adam said.

Grandpa barked a laugh and pointed at him. "I know! I'm fucking with you!"

"Oh, Jesus," Mom muttered.

"What does an old man need to do to get a drink around here?" Grandpa leaned right onto the bar. "Hellloooo?"

Mom stepped forward and pulled him away. "Dad, no. You're not drinking alcohol."

"I just want a coffee!"

"Then we'll go to the on-site coffee shop," she replied.

"No, no," he said. "Hello, my fine lady! I'd like a Bloody Mary, please!"

"He'll have it without the Mary," Mom said quickly. "Virgin. No alcohol."

Grandpa rolled his eyes and looked at Adam.

139

"You see this shit, boy? I raised her. Wiped her little ass when she was a baby."

"Dad!"

"Didn't say a thing when I put her bras in the laundry. Didn't shoot any boyfriends in high school. I was the model father, and here I am, in my old age, and I can't even get a Bloody Mary!"

"I'm not putting up with this today. I have to handle last minute things for dinner tonight. Poppy, you'll have to deal with your grandfather." Mom patted my shoulder and turned away.

I sputtered. "Wait. What? No, Mom!" I ran the few steps to her. "No, Mom. I'm not doing it. I've dealt with two meltdowns from Rosie, kept you out of the way at lunch, drugged Rosie, argued with a man about a lack of chicken, and driven all over the Key for fucking strawberries. I'm not babysitting, too!"

Sighing as if she knew all of that, she patted my hand and extracted it from her arm. "Honey, I have things to do."

"So do I! If I'm late for dinner, Rosie's going to kill me!"

"I simply have to be on time. I don't have the time to make sure he controls himself."

"Fine." I jabbed my finger at her. "But when I'm not there at five-thirty, I'm blaming you."

She said nothing. She turned, and in typical Mom fashion, disappeared out of the bar.

Of course, she did. I should have known that I'd be stuck babysitting at one point this weekend. Grandpa—God love his soul—was one hell of a man, but he was also at the age where he believed he could get away with anything.

Unfortunately for him, he still had a few too

many of his faculties about him for that just yet. Maybe in five years, but for now... No.

"Okay?" Adam asked, looking at me with concern as I rejoined them at the bar.

"Fine." I gave him a tight smile and turned to the girl behind the bar. "Can I have a vodka with cranberry juice, please?"

"Sure." She turned to do that, and I sat down on the stool.

"Psst, Pop-pop," Grandpa whispered, holding up his hand. "This is both Bloody and Mary."

Awesome.

"And I still don't believe your boyfriend plays hockey. He's too skinny for that," he continued. "Aren't they big old bastards who tackle you down?"

I rubbed two fingers against my temple. "You're thinking of football, Grandpa."

He narrowed his eyes and looked away. "Nope. I'm thinking of hockey."

"You're thinking of football," I repeated.

Not to mention there was nothing skinny about Adam. Not his arms. Not his legs. Not his waist. Not his cock. Nothing.

Not even his pinky finger.

Adam leaned into me and wrapped an arm around my waist. Warmth spread through me where his thumb slipped beneath the hem of my shirt and drew tiny circles on my skin.

"Are you sure?" Grandpa asked, a twinkle in his eye.

I took the vodka-cranberry from the bartender with a grateful smile. "I'm sure." Then I wrapped my lips around the straw and I drink-drink-drinked.

Drank? Drunk?

You know, I didn't care. I didn't need to be grammatically correct inside my head.

I needed to be drunk, though. I knew that much.

"So, son. You play hockey. You ever won anything?" Grandpa asked Adam.

He glanced at me, hiding a smile. "Yes, sir. The Stanley Cup went to my team this year."

"What's that? The World Cup of hockey?"

Adam paused for a second. "I guess that's one way of looking at it."

"You won a gold medal?"

"Ah, no. Maybe one day."

"Then it ain't the World Cup of hockey, is it?"

"Grandpa, hockey doesn't have a World Cup. That's soccer." I put my glass down.

"Well," Adam said slowly. "Technically, there is a Hockey World Cup, but it's field hockey. Not ice hockey."

I picked my glass back up and pinched the straw, looking at him. "There's more than one type of hockey?"

"There's more than one type of football, depending who you ask," Grandpa offered.

"Yes. There's American football where you use your hands, then soccer football where they use their feet," I muttered, drinking again.

One of these wasn't going to be enough, was it?

"Oh, enough. I know what hockey and football and soccer are," Grandpa says. "I also know who your boyfriend is. He plays hockey for the Orlando Storms."

"He told you that!"

"So? I still know!" He stuck his tongue out at me. "Adam, son, let me tell you about the time I was stationed in the Netherlands with the Army."

Jesus, no.

No.

No.

Nobody needed these stories.

Grandpa clutched his glass of Bloody Mary and leaned toward him. "Are you familiar with the Red Light District?"

I waved to the barmaid and, ignoring the straw, swallowed the last of my vodka. "Can I get another? Please?"

"I have," Adam said warily.

"Well, do I have a story for you. It was back in, oh, I don't remember, but there was this lady. Hot as a heatwave in Florida," Grandpa said. "And she came to us and she said, "Fellas, I've got a treat for you!" We were young and thought she meant a damn beer or something, so we followed her and—"

"Thank you!" I exclaimed to the girl who put the drink in front of me.

Adam squeezed my hip.

I drank.

And Grandpa?

He carried on telling the story of how he and his friends got lured to a brothel in Amsterdam.

I was done.

So. Done.

I stepped off the main stage into Adam's waiting arms. I'd gotten away with any kind of speech, but I'd been forced to greet every single fucking guest to this damn pre-wedding dinner.

And I'd had more than two vodkas during Grandpa's story time this afternoon.

Thus, I'd been on water during the entire rehearsal dinner.

"This is the longest wedding I've ever been to," I said into his chest.

He chuckled, his whole body shaking. "Have you ever been to a wedding?"

"Only as a reception guest. Otherwise, no." I turned my face to the side, resting my cheek against him. "Have you?"

"Yes. And you are correct. This is the longest wedding I've ever been to," he replied. "Although that might have been your grandfather."

I groaned, wrapping my arms around his waist. It was all for show for my family, but I wasn't going to deny that being wrapped around him koala bear style wasn't nice.

"He's unreal," I said. "I told you. He's insane. He thinks everyone wants to know about his life. Be thankful you didn't hear about his pensioner swing parties."

"What?"

"Oh, yeah. After my grandma died, he was lonely, so joined a bingo club. Turned out bingo was a front for old-people swingers."

"That's…interesting."

"Mhmm. Keep holding onto me. It'll stop anyone else talking to me, okay?"

He tightened his arms around me, bringing his lips to the top of my head. "Duly noted. Your mother is looking at us."

"Of course, she is. She's imagining our wedding right now," I scoffed.

"So, a time where Bloody Marys aren't on the menu for your grandpa."

"Exactly that. And my mom doesn't get to choose cocktails. And nobody knows who you are or any embarrassing stories about my childhood, of which there are plenty."

"We're eloping then," Adam said.

"Absolutely. If we ever get fake married, eloping is the only way to do it." I pulled back and tilted my head to meet his eyes. "How else will we be able to convince everyone we actually did it?"

He laughed, dropping his forehead to mine. "Well, there is that. Eloping sounds good. Where would we go? Vegas? That Gretna place in Scotland?"

"I do like Scotland. They don't wear underpants under their kilts."

"Oooh." He blew out a long breath. "I don't know if I could do that, Red."

"We can negotiate. How do you feel about going pantless under a kilt when we're married?"

"Are you also commando?"

"Only after the wedding. You can't pick and choose, hockey boy. That's not how this works."

He mock-sighed, his entire body moving with the exhale. "I suppose we can make that work."

"I like when you agree with me. It makes the vodka I snuck at the table a lot more reasonable."

Leaning back, he met my eyes. "You were drinking up there?"

"Did you hear my mother's speech?"

"I did. I didn't see you drinking."

I tutted him. "Vodka. Water. And a lemon. A la Rihanna."

"What?"

"Never mind." I tucked myself back into his body. "I needed it to stay sane. I need another. Are you finally understanding my family?"

Adam stroked my lower back with his fingertips. "Slowly. Your aunt Jean asked me if I was into older women, and if I change my mind, to call her."

"Sounds like her."

"Then, your uncle Peter asked me if the Storms would win against this season, and apparently, "I hope so, sir," wasn't the answer he wanted."

"He's a gambler. You should have given him your guess for a team."

"My guess is the Storms. I'm in the team."

"That's cocky."

"I know. He didn't accept that answer either."

I laughed, moving to his side. I didn't release his shirt, keeping my fingers tucked into it as much as I could. He never loosened his grip on me, holding me firmly against his side.

I hated how normal it felt to be against him. Hated how good it felt to have him by my side, holding me, tucking me into his body.

It wasn't supposed to feel anything close to this good.

"Wanna sit?" he asked into my ear.

I nodded, allowing him to pull me over to the closest empty table. He pulled my chair out for me. I sat, and the second he brought his chair to mine, his arm was around me against.

I leaned into him. He didn't seem to mind at all. His fingers drew lazy circles on my bare upper arm, while his other hand sat happily on the table until he had to motion for a server to come over to get us a drink.

I didn't say a word as he ordered me a vodka cranberry and him a beer. I had drunk enough water today that it didn't make much of a difference, and I'd been to enough family gatherings like this to know that it was a necessity.

Dad slid into the chair next to me. "Save me, Pop," he said without looking at me.

"Am I fucking Batwoman today or something?" I asked him.

"No, honey, but my flask is out of whiskey," he replied.

I tapped my fingers against the table. "How big is it?"

He showed me a baby-sized one.

"I'll fill it if you bring a bigger one tomorrow. I've already done Grandpa duty once."

Dad made a face. "My poor girl. All right. You slip me a whiskey, and I'll slip you one tomorrow after your speech."

"Done." I held one hand out flat on the table.

He tapped it with his in our form of a deal. "I'll be back in five." He got up as smoothly as he came. Seconds later, our server returned, and I asked her for my dad's preferred drink before she left.

"I feel like that's a habit with you two," Adam said, picking up his beer.

Slowly, I nodded. "We survive these events knowing that we're there for one another. I buy whiskey, he's there in the hall when I can't take my mom anymore. He'll still pull a shotgun on anyone who hurts me because I'm his little girl, but he'll booze me like the adult I am, because we both get the shit end of the deal in this family."

"So if you break up with me because I cheat on you, he's gonna shoot me?"

"God, no." Rosie sat two seats away from me. "He only pulled a shotgun once, and that was because he found a pregnancy test in my bathroom that belonged to our cousin."

True story.

"How are you doing?" I asked her.

She twirled a wine glass between her fingers. "Can I tell you something? I'm so done with this shit."

I blinked.

Adam held me a little tighter.

Rosie leaned in. "This fancy stuff? I didn't want it, Pops. Me and Mark have Rory. We're a family. This is just a piece of paper."

She'd had too much champagne.

I knew that straight away.

"I don't want a big wedding. I want to marry him. But no. Our moms said big wedding where there's no chicken and my sister has to run around for strawberries and there are so many parties that Fashion Week feels inadequate."

Adam glanced at me.

"Ro, why don't you come to the bathroom with me?" I stood up, rounding to her. "Ad, make sure Dad gets his...water, okay?"

"It's fucking whiskey," Rosie muttered.

"Okay, his whiskey," I agreed.

"It's cute when you call him Ad," my sister carried on.

"And we're going!" I looped my arm through hers and, after shooting Mark an ok sign with my fingers, took her into the bathroom closest to the ballroom.

I pushed the main door shut behind me, closing out the noise of the music that pounded through the ballroom.

Rosie leaned against the counter. Her pale pink nails contrasted with the black marble. Her other hand swept her bangs to the side, and she looked at me, fear and panic shining in her warm brown eyes.

"I'm scared," she said softly. "All of this, Pop. And for what? Mom to change plans I didn't want? Chicken to disappear? You to chase strawberries around Key West?"

Shit. She knew about that.

"Yes, I know," she said, reading my mind. "I can't even be mad because you did that for me. This wedding is too big, it's too much, and I can't do this."

"You can." I stepped forward and grabbed her hands. "I love you, Ro, and you can do this. You already are. Who gives a shit if there's chicken or strawberries? You're here for Mark, and he's here for you. You're here to get married and if someone has to eat beef instead of chicken or have carrots or something then tough shit. Order McDonalds."

She laughed, bringing a hand to her mouth.

I pulled her into me. "You're getting married, not putting on a fucking state fair, even if Grandpa is this close to setting up a booth and charging ten cents for a story about his time in the Red Light District."

More laughing, this time into my shoulder.

Crying, too. I felt the wetness of a tear as it dripped to my shoulder.

"You can elope, you know," I said, hugging her and staring at the tiles. "You've probably got time to get to Vegas and back by now. Depending on flights and delays and shit."

She laughed.

The door opened.

I dropped her like hot coal and rammed my body against the door. "Sorry, this one is occupied!"

"It's Mark!"

"It's still occupied! I'll call you!" I yelled. "Go away!"

"Poppy, I swear, I'll—"

"Do nothing because I'm holding your future wife hostage!"

He shuffled. "I'll tell all future dates about the time you accidentally tweeted a photo of your boobs."

"It's probably already saved on the Internet. Go ahead."

Rosie laughed into her hands.

"Are you done?" I asked him. "I'm being a good sister in here and you're killing my vibe."

"Is that a sex toy?"

"Why don't I shove it up your ass so you can find out?"

Rosie gave up hiding it at that point. She collapsed against the wall, laughing like someone invisible was tickling her.

She was ticklish. It was a real analogy. You so much as wiggled a feather in her direction and she keeled over.

"If I didn't love you like my sister, I'll kill you in your sleep," Mark shouted.

"Is that how you talk to your son's aunt? Wash your mouth out with soap!"

Rosie intervened at this point. "Honey, it's fine. I just needed a break from all the crazy people."

"So, Mom, Dad, Grandpa, Aunt Jean, Aunt Berry, Uncle Foster…" I trailed off.

"All of those people."

Mark grunted. "If you're not out here in five minutes, I'm sending your grandpa to the nearest microphone."

"No problem!" Rosie grabbed me. "Make me

human," she whispered, begging me. "Please."

"I'm no miracle worker, but let's see what we have here." I looked around. "Oh, great. A tap and paper towels. That'll turn you into Scarlet Johansson."

Rosie picked up the purse she'd dumped, then unzipped it. "Clutch. Makeup here. Make me look human and I won't tell anyone your boyfriend is a big fat fake."

"I love you, but you're a bitch." I picked up the concealer stick.

"Eh. Nobody would believe me."

"What does that mean?" I turned her face to look at me.

Her eyes searched mine. "Nothing. Just that you're doing a really good job at pretending you're into each other."

I glared at her, but hmphed and got on with it.

After all, it was her weekend.

She could believe what she liked.

CHAPTER THIRTEEN
POPPY

Bad Ideas and Balconies

I groaned, slumping against the door of our room.

Adam laughed, undoing the buttons on his shirt. "At least we got Rosie to bed in one piece?"

"Oh, please. She wasn't drunk." I bent and pulled off my shoes, tossing them to the side. "She was pretending to be drunk to escape the hell that is our family."

He paused. "Well, then, she did a good job at pretending."

"Of course she did. She spent long enough as a teen pretending she was sober. She knows exactly how to be drunk." I pushed off the door, making sure it had locked.

"I'm sure that was just her."

"I would like to invoke my right to remain silent." I crossed to the mini-fridge and pulled out a bottle of water. "My teen years also have the right to remain silent."

"By silent, you mean forgotten and ignored."

"You don't know my life, hockey boy."

He laughed, grabbing a half-sized bottle of champagne. "The sun is still going down. Want to join me on the world's tiniest balcony?"

Yes.

No.

Yes.

No.

You're doing a really good job at pretending you're into each other.

I hated my sister for planting that in my head.

"Sure. Why not?" I pulled the bobby pins out of the side of my head one by one and tossed them onto the coffee table.

My shoulders were tight. I could feel the horrible squeezing of my muscles as I took two champagne glasses from the top of the mini fridge. Tonight had been close to disaster—not that I actually believed my sister would elope—but we almost didn't pass it off well enough.

Shark week had been our excuse, and if my mom asked, Rosie thought her period had started and needed me to get lady supplies.

Yeah.

It wasn't the best, but it was about the only time I'd ever thanked Mother Nature for periods in my life.

I stepped out onto the balcony with Adam. A gentle sea breeze caught my hair, and I was thankful for the soft chill it brought with it. The ballroom had been hot, and the stress of my family had made me feel even hotter with all the fuss they'd made over just about everything.

I tugged up my dress and sat down on the floor next to Adam. "They could have given us chairs."

"Where would they put them? Inside?" He chuckled, pulling the tab on the champagne to remove the foil.

"Seriously, though. That huge suite and we can barely sit our asses on this balcony."

"Never mind our asses—I can barely cross my legs."

"Well, they are about five feet long," I said,

shifting so there was enough room between us to put the champagne glasses.

Adam shifted, bracing himself to pop the cork. "Ready?"

"Yes. Just don't pop it over the—"

Pop.

"Balcony," I finished, watching as the cork sailed over the top of the balcony and smoke swirled out of the bottle.

Adam turned to me, looking innocent. "Where else was I supposed to pop it? Into you?"

"No. That would be dumb." And painful. "I was just thinking that if someone was under the balcony…"

"I didn't hear anyone scream." He shrugged and picked up the first glass, tilting it to fill it without a ton of bubbles. He passed it to me when he was done. "We can look for it tomorrow."

"There's wedding tomorrow."

"At six-thirty in the evening," he replied. "I think we'll have time."

"Did you see my mother today?"

Adam stilled. "I did, and I think that's exactly why you need to be nowhere near her."

He wasn't exactly wrong, was he?

"I know, but I have things to do. The wedding planner will handle most of it, but there are little things that are my responsibility."

"Like making sure your sister doesn't need to be drugged again."

"Exactly that." I tilted my glass in his direction. "I don't know how much spare time I'll have."

"Well." Adam put the champagne bottle down to the side and rested his head against the wall.

While the balcony was thin, it was long. I'd have

preferred short and fat to stretch my legs out, but I wasn't paying for this room, so I couldn't really complain, could I?

Hell, I could barely afford a fucking sandwich in this place.

"Well?" I said, urging him to pick up where he'd left off.

"How long does it take to get ready for a wedding?"

"How long is a piece of string?"

"Ah. It's like that."

"Have you ever been with women getting ready for a wedding?"

"No," Adam drawled. "Funnily enough, Red, it's frowned upon for a man to be in a room with a bunch of half-naked women."

I sipped my champagne and side-eyed him. "Wow. You need to watch more porn."

He choked on his champagne, smacking his fist against his chest. I bit back a laugh as his eyes watered the tiniest amount and he looked at me.

"What?" I asked. "It's true. It's not always frowned upon. Sometimes it's celebrated."

"Yes, but I think that's mostly relegated to the lifestyles of those who like that kind of thing. Or get paid for it."

"Are you judging?"

"Do you swing?"

"Only when people swing at me first."

This time, his choke was a laugh. "Not punch-swinging. Sex swinging."

I blinked at him. "Before you, my last sexual encounter was with my right hand, so no, I'm not a swinger."

"Good to know."

"Did you even need to clarify that?"

"No, but I just enjoyed making you uncomfortable for a minute there."

"You're a sick man."

He laughed, turning his head to meet my eyes. "Why? Because it's fun to see you pull back your mask of confidence once in a while?"

"What mask?"

"See; you don't even know you do it."

I shifted, turning toward him and tucking my legs to the side. "Do what?"

"You're a self-proclaimed disaster, but all I've seen this weekend is you pulling the strings and holding everything together. You controlled your sister during her freak outs. You managed to get your mom out of the way—"

I held up a finger and shook it side to side. "That only worked because she wanted to feel our relationship out."

"And we convinced her. Somehow, you managed to not freak and tell her everything. You corralled your grandpa into leaving a strip club—"

"How do you know that?"

"I talked to Mark. Obviously." He quirked a brow. "Stop interrupting me."

"But it's more fun when I do. You make a lot less sense when it's interspersed with my bullshit." I smiled as I sipped.

Adam shook his head, sipping, too. "I'm just saying. You're more put together than you give yourself credit for."

"Except for when I slipped on the bathroom floor."

"Except for when you slipped on the bathroom floor," he agreed, shooting me a glance out of the side of his eye. His lips twitched, tugging up to one side in a smile that matched the spark in his eyes.

I looked down, breaking the connection of our gaze. My cheeks were burning, and butterflies were going crazy in my tummy. I couldn't even blame the shiver that ran over my arms on the breeze—it wasn't strong enough to get me while I was protected by the strong glass fencing.

It was him.

All him.

And once again, Rosie's words came back to haunt me.

"You're doing a really good job of pretending you're into each other."

I fucking wished I was pretending. I fucking wished I didn't get butterflies when he looked at me or shivers when he touched me. I wished I hadn't had that fairytale-style kiss with him in the parking lot.

I wished I wasn't sitting next to him right now, wishing we could close the gap between us so I could tuck myself into his side.

More than anything, I wished I wasn't even in this position.

Why hadn't I just walked away when I'd woken up in his bedroom? Why had my awkward ass asked him to be my date? I should have known better. Hadn't I seen a hundred romcom movies about this?

And if not, why not? Someone needed to make a few.

Warning: Take a fake date, and it might not be so fake.

I hated thinking that. We were different worlds.

Not in terms of money or status or stature, but sports was not my thing. I was not the girl who could ever stand in sidelines and pretend I cared about what the hell I was watching.

I also highly doubted I was the kind of girl who could ever sit and learn the rules of any kind of sport that wasn't beer pong.

Was that even a legit sport? Or had I just wasted my teen years on a mindless game that did nothing but make me a master beer drinker by high school graduation?

Eh. Either way, I was good with it. I was holding my gold medal high and proud.

"Poppy? Are you all right?" Adam reached over and pushed hair away from my eyes.

"Thinking," I said softly. "About something Rosie said earlier."

"Care to share with the class?"

Smirking, I elbowed him. "She knows this isn't real."

"Shock horror," he muttered.

Another elbow headed his way before I drew into myself. I twirled the champagne glass by its stem, my fingers drawing lines in the condensation of the glass as the warmth of my fingertips beat the coldness of the alcohol.

"What else did she say?"

"What do you mean?" I tilted my head to look at him.

He shrugged, looking out at the ocean that was barely-lit by the lights that illuminated the paths of the resort. "You haven't been right since you eloped to the bathroom. I know she said something to you. And before you argue—I have four sisters. I know when a woman is pissed off. I grew up with an almost constant rotation of periods."

I laughed into my hand, setting my empty glass down on the balcony between us. Now, I was glad for the space. I'd wished just moments ago for it to be closed, but I was happy for it.

"She just...She said something that got to me, that's all," I said.

Adam picked up my glass and the bottle and refilled it halfway, just leaving enough for his. "What did she say?"

"It's stupid."

"Not that stupid if you've got your panties all up in a twist about it, Red."

Yeah, well, that was his opinion. "I get my panties up in a twist about a lot of stupid things. Not having enough butter for my toast. Cliffhangers 0n TV shows when I'll get the next episode the following day. My neighbor's cat scratching at me—"

"Point well taken," he said, touching his finger to my lips to make me shush. "But that doesn't cover what your sister said."

I wasn't getting out of this, was I? No, because I'd gotten myself into it in the first damn place.

I sighed. "She said we're doing a really good job at pretending not to be into each other."

Adam jerked his head to the side, eyes finding mine quickly. He stared at me for a second with a flat expression. My stomach tied in knots—what if he agreed? What if I was more into this fake relationship than he was?

Why did I even care?

Then, he laughed.

Burst into laughter, actually. His entire body

shook as his deep chuckles sent tingles across my arms.

"I'm glad it's so amusing to you," I muttered, putting the glass down out of reach and getting up.

"Where are you going?"

"To bed."

"Come here." He reached over and grabbed my hand.

Stopping, I looked down at him. The sun had finally gone down, but the sky was still painted with golden hues—hues that danced across his features and made his eyes seem ten times brighter than normal.

I swallowed. "What?"

"Sit." He tugged on my hand.

I didn't move.

"I swear, Red, if you don't sit, I'll stand up and make you."

I took my hand from his and crossed my arms. Was I being petulant? Yes. Petty? Yes. Immature? Probably.

At least I could admit my faults.

The one thing I couldn't admit was that the idea of him not being into me bugged me more than I thought it would.

Adam jumped to his feet.

Oh shit.

He was serious.

"No! No! I'll sit!"

He grabbed me, picking me up with one sweeping movement. A tiny scream escaped me as he did that, one arm around my back and the other behind my knees.

Oh god, there wasn't enough room on this balcony for this.

"Put me down!" I squeaked.

"No. I warned you." Slowly, he sat down, taking me down with him. I didn't know what I was more impressed with—the fact he'd swept me up like I was freaking Cinderella or that he hadn't dropped me.

He set me down between his legs and leaned back against the wall. My back was against his stomach, and he pulled me back so we were sitting together. His legs were bent at the knees, caging me in, and my own were pulled up thanks to minimal room.

My heart fluttered in my chest as he tilted his head so his breath skirted over my cheek. It was warm and smelled like whiskey.

His fingers trailed up and down my forearms, lightly tickling me. It was weirdly soothing, such a tiny touch that I didn't want him to stop.

It was comfortable.

Too comfortable.

"I'm not pretending I'm into you, Red," he said softly into my ear. His lips brushed my earlobe, his fingers still trailing up and down my arms.

It was a dangerous mix of sensations.

"I'm into you. Don't think I'm not. Pretending to be your boyfriend is the easiest thing I've ever done." His voice was low and warm and…honest.

I didn't know honesty had a sound, but here I was, hearing it.

"You don't have to like it, but I can't help it." He shifted to the side slightly, reaching to cup the side of my face. He moved me until our eyes met. "I know this is fake, all right? I know that we'll probably never see each other after Monday. But that doesn't mean that my attraction to you right now isn't very, very fucking real."

I swallowed.

"I mean, you're crazy, aren't you?" His lips

twitched, eyes dancing with mirth. "You're a complete antagonist to your family, but you're also the cog that seems to keep them all turning. The strawberries, the drugging—while a questionable means of showing your love, still works."

I covered my mouth, biting back a laugh, looking away.

Adam hooked a finger beneath my chin and tilted it back up. "You have a smarter mouth than anyone I've ever met, and I'm fucked if I know why that's so attractive to me, but there you go." He trailed his finger along my cheek and pushed hair from my eyes. "That's just a couple things I like about you, Poppy. If you were worried I wasn't into you, then don't be. And if you were worried that I was, then tough shit."

I laughed, leaning against him and resting my head against his chest. He was laughing too, and for a moment, that was all there was.

Me and a guy who was into me, cuddled on a balcony, laughing.

And a part of me really wished this didn't have to be fake. But it was one thing to feel comfortable in a private setting—a public one was something else altogether.

And that was ultimately why we really did only have four days.

Adam tucked his hand under my chin again and lifted it. This time, it wasn't his eyes that found mine. It was our lips, coming together in a kiss that I felt from head to toe.

I wanted it to go on forever.

"Come on. Bedtime." Releasing me, he motioned for me to get up first.

I did, using his thigh for leverage. He "umphed,"

and I snorted. "That's what you get for picking me up on a balcony made for toddlers and putting the fear of God into me."

"Fear of God? Don't you mean the fear of your mother?"

"I told you not to confuse Satan and God. Satan doesn't like it." I flashed him a grin over my shoulder as I left him to lock the doors.

I walked into the bathroom and grabbed my makeup wipes. By the time Adam joined me in there, I was makeup free and struggling to bend my arm behind me to undo my zip.

He leaned against the doorframe, eyes skirting over me. "What are you doing?"

I stopped hopping. "A performance for leprechauns."

He looked around. "You don't seem to have much of an audience."

"Ha. Ha. Ha." I dropped my arm before I dislocated my shoulder. "I can't reach my zip. Can you help?"

"Can I help you undress? Oh, shit, what a hard decision," he replied dryly, walking over to me. Gently, he turned me around to face the mirror once more and swept my hair to one side.

His fingers brushed over the small area of bare skin at the top of my back as he grabbed the zip. Slowly, carefully, he pulled it down. Shivers followed the trial of the zip as it lowered and finally stopped just above the curve of my ass.

Adam lifted his gaze to meet mine in the reflection of the mirror. "Done."

"Thank you." It came out a little scratchier than I'd intended, and I quickly darted away into the bedroom. His low chuckle followed me, so I shut myself in the walk-in closet.

It was pitch black. I couldn't see my hand in front of my face, and for a second, that was a good thing. It allowed me to lean back against the wall and catch a breath.

My heart was pounding crazy fast. I could be running from a murderer and it couldn't beat any faster. My mouth was dry, and I couldn't put into a box what had just happened.

All I knew was that it was something very real, and I needed to stop it before my hare-brained heart got any stupid ideas about keeping in contact with Adam after this wedding was done.

The door opened, and I winced at the bright light from the bedroom.

"Red? What are you doing?"

He was asking me that a lot tonight.

Losing my mind? That was a good answer.

"I was looking for a tank top," I replied dumbly. "To sleep in."

He reached inside the door and flicked on the light. "That'll be a lot easier with the light on."

I nodded.

He smirked. "I have nieces who can lie better than you. They're three."

"Fuck off," I muttered, yanking open the drawer that held my clothes. I pulled out a baggy top I liked to sleep in that said, *If you can read this, fuck off*" and stepped out of my dress. Quickly removing my bra, I tugged the shirt over my head and went back into the bedroom, turning off the closet light.

Adam had already turned off the main light and had the one on the nightstand turned on. As I climbed onto my side of the bed, he reached behind him and turned it off.

He pulled me against him so we were spooning. His breath fluttered my hair, and his fingers splayed across my stomach beneath my shirt. Our legs tangled, and it was fucking horrible.

"I hate being touched when I sleep," I grumbled.

"I know. But I'm sure you can manage two more nights." He yawned, wriggling even closer.

"You didn't read my shirt, did you?"

"No. But judging by your mood, it's telling me to fuck off."

I snorted because he was right. "Exactly."

"My shirt says I don't give a shit what yours says."

"You're not wearing a shirt."

"I know. Aren't you lucky? You can feel these abs all day long."

I rolled my eyes as he stifled his own laughter behind me. "Wow. Someone thinks he's funny."

"Someone's in a mood."

"You're touching me. I want to sleep. This is like torture."

"All right. Fine." He released me, untwining our legs, moving his hand from my stomach, and yanking his arm out from under my neck.

"Ow," I muttered, shifting so not a single part of our bodies were touching.

That was better.

"Night, Red."

"Night." I moved, trying to get comfortable.

On my side.

On my back.

One arm over my head.

One foot out of the covers.

One leg out.

Both feet out.

On my other side.

Dammit.

"Stop wriggling," Adam mumbled after a few minutes.

"I can't get comfy." I huffed and flopped onto my back, letting my arms fall like dead weights onto the bed.

Adam rolled onto his back. "You wanna cuddle?"

Yes.

"No," I replied, rolling onto my side and against his.

He laughed, raising one arm and wrapping it around me as I nestled my head against his chest and hooked one leg over his. "Yeah. Feels like it."

"I don't want to." I rested one arm over his toned stomach. "Just because I am cuddling you doesn't mean I want to."

"I'm sure it doesn't," he said dryly. "You'll be asleep in minutes."

I yawned. "No, I won't."

He laughed quietly, shoulders shaking, but didn't say anything else to me.

"Adam?"

"Yeah?" His lips moved against the top of my head.

"I'm kind of into you, too," I murmured, eyes heavy with sleep.

Gently, he squeezed me. "I know. I know."

CHAPTER FOURTEEN
ADAM

Mimosas and Moms

We woke the same way we'd fallen asleep. Together, although we'd both been on our sides. Poppy's ass had been nestled against my cock, and if we hadn't been woken by the shrieking of her phone ringing, there was no doubt how the morning would have started.

Morning sex.

Damn her mom.

I was starting to see her point about her being Satan. My cock definitely was, and he'd protested the entire time I'd been in the shower.

I refused to jack off while she was in the next room. It felt weird and not…right.

I walked into the bedroom where Poppy was still grumbling to herself about seven a.m. wake-ups.

"You're really not a morning person, are you?" I asked, rubbing my hair with a towel.

She shot me a look so fierce I think my balls receded back up into my body. "Do I look like a fucking morning person?"

"You look like you should be the killer in a horror movie."

She turned, her gaze never softening. Her shirt summed up her mood perfectly. *"The early bird can have the worm. Because worms are gross and mornings are stupid."*

I couldn't bite back the laugh that bubbled out of me. "Interesting shirt."

Another flat stare at me. "Do you want to die?"

"In another seventy or so years," I replied, tossing the towel onto the bed

"Can you put some clothes on?"

"You know something, Red? Where you're concerned today, I've had brighter bouts of the stomach flu."

She flipped me the bird. "It's too early for this stuff. Seven in the morning and my mother is on the damn phone freaking about napkins. I told her to ask Rosie and she said she isn't even awake yet!" She slammed her mascara down on the side as I tugged my boxers up over my ass. "She doesn't get married until tonight! Can't we all have a little lie-in to make up for a late evening wedding? Nooo, Commander-in-Chief Mom requires us all up and at it like I give a shit about napkins."

I wanted to ask her if she was going to start her period, but I'd done that once with my sister and I never wanted to do it again. I still had the scar on my knee from her throwing a book at me.

It was a hardback and the corner had broken the skin.

That, and I'd been an irritating teen who picked the scab.

We all had our faults. I was a picker. That was mine. Everything but the nose.

So, I went for the safe route: "Do you want to go and get coffee?"

"Do I?" she asked, looking over at me. "What do you think?"

"I think *I* need coffee if this conversation is going to last much longer," I said honestly, grabbing a t-shirt and shorts from my drawer.

She poked her tongue out at me and grabbed her

hairbrush. Snapping a hairband onto her wrist, she pulled her hair up into a messy knot on top of her head. Wispy bits fell down over her pale neck and ears, and she pulled a bobby pin from her makeup bag to secure the neck bits.

She glanced over and saw me watching her. "What? Some girls can pull off a super messy bun. I'm not one of them. I look like I'm on the run from the police when I do it."

"I think you look cute."

"Now you're just trying to placate me."

"Is it working?"

"Are you a cup of coffee?"

"No. But I am capable of another kind of wake-up if you want to piss your mom off a little more." I grinned.

She fought a smile. "Normally, I'd be all over that. Today, however, I'm going to try to keep the peace."

"Right." I ran a bit of wax through my damp hair. "Let me wash my hair and we'll get coffee to attempt that peace-keeping thing."

"You don't think I can be nice for an entire day?"

"I know you can't." I dried my hands on a towel and grabbed my phone and the room key. "Come on, Red, let's make you semi-human again."

It was amazing, really.

Just twenty minutes ago she'd been rabid. Kill-you-with-my-eyes angry. Nobody-touch-me pissed off.

And now? Now, she was fucking smiling.

It was her second cup of coffee and she did have

a mimosa—at my order—so maybe that was why.

"Stop looking at me like I'm a weirdo you can't make sense of." She grabbed a croissant and tore it in two.

"You are a weirdo I can't make sense of," I replied, hugging my cup of coffee with my hands. "It's not my fault if you just went from one hundred to zero on the bad mood scale."

"I was woken up when I was having a very nice dream, thank you very much. It's not every day Chris Hemsworth comes into my dreams and wants to have sex with me."

"Nice. So you were in bed with me having dirty dreams about Thor."

She paused, cheeks turning pink. "Pretty much."

"Now say it without blushing," I smirked. "And I'll believe it was about Thor."

She opened her mouth, then clamped her jaw tight shut.

"I wasn't asleep. You said my name." I shrugged a shoulder.

Now, she blushed like hell.

I was lying through my teeth, but boy, this was fun.

"Just admit it, Red. You were dreaming about having sex with me. That's okay. I don't mind. I'm flattered, actually."

"I have the right to remain silent." She sipped her mimosa.

"You do. But your cheeks give you away." I grinned.

"I hate you," she muttered, going back to picking at her pastry.

I laughed. "Fine lines and all that. You'll love me

later when—"

"When what?" Her mom's voice cut into what I was going to say.

Which would not be mom-approved.

"I'm there to help her practice her speech for the reception," I said without missing a beat. I stood up and kissed her cheek. "Good morning, Miranda."

Poppy rolled her eyes.

"It most certainly is not. Poppy," she said, turning to her as she stuffed croissant into her mouth. "You were supposed to find me immediately."

"Mom. You woke me up. I needed to eat something." Poppy waved the croissant.

"You can eat later."

"No, I can't. You'll be on at me all morning to do this and do that and do the hokey cokey for the guests," she replied. "So I'm eating now. The napkins will still be there in half an hour."

"Mmm." Miranda's calculating gaze swept the table. "Mimosa? Poppy."

This time, she didn't hide her irritation. "Mom, if you want me to be a nice person today, I'm having a mimosa."

"You're never a nice person."

"All right, so if you want me to *pretend* to be a nice person today, I'm having a mimosa." Poppy shrugged.

"Why isn't Adam eating?"

"I can't eat this early," I interjected. Jesus, this was hard work. "I usually get up and work out before I eat. I'm just here to make sure the devil's minion doesn't murder anyone."

Poppy glared at me, shaking her head.

I grinned.

Miranda looked between us and blinked. "I don't understand you two."

"Neither do I," I replied.

Poppy kicked me under the table.

I jumped, and Miranda looked at me funny. "Cramp," I said, pretending to be in pain and reaching down. "Stretched it wrong."

Poppy grabbed another croissant and stuffed more in her mouth to hide her laugh.

"His pain is funny to you?" Miranda asked her.

"Yes," she replied with a mouth full of food.

Another look between us and Miranda threw up her hands. "Poppy, find me when you're ready to be reasonable and help." And then she left.

"Well, that'll be some time in the next century," I grumbled, rubbing my shin.

Poppy pointed the croissant at me. "You're pissing me off."

"Surely not," I drawled.

"You don't want me to be angry. I'm not nice when I'm angry."

"Are you telling me this morning was you being a delight?"

"I'm always a delight."

"I'm gonna buy you a dictionary, Red."

"Excellent. I can hit you with it when you piss me off."

I don't know why I laughed, but I did. It just escaped me, and I covered my eyes with my hand. I knew she'd be glaring at me, but I couldn't help it. All I could fucking picture was this crazy, angry redhead chasing me with a dictionary, attempting to hurt me.

Poppy's phone beeped on the table. She picked it up, and for the first time this morning, actually smiled.

"Did the Underworld call your mom back for duty?" I asked.

She snorted. "No. My best friend is finally here. She was supposed to come last night but had to work late. She drove halfway last night and woke up early. She's checking in now." Her fingers flew across the touchscreen as she replied. "I told her to come down here and meet us."

"Is she anything like you?"

"Total opposite, actually. I don't know how we live together."

"You live together?"

Poppy looked up with her brown eyes wide. "I didn't mention that?"

"Not once," I said.

"Crap. Okay, yeah, I live with Avery. Ever since we went to college. And the thing you should know is that it's a good thing that she's here, because my mom adores Aves. Literally wishes she could swap us and have her be her daughter instead."

"Why is that a good thing?"

"Because she distracts her. She's like a buffer between us." She shrugged a shoulder. "It'll make today way more bearable, that's for sure."

"Something has to."

"What happened to the nice guy from last night?"

"I can go around telling everyone how much I love you, if you want." I grinned.

She wrinkled her nose. "Stop swearing at me. I'll never get out of this alive if you tell people you're in love with me. I'm too prickly to fall in love with."

"You know, I do sometimes mistake you for a cactus."

"Ha, ha, funny man." She stuck her tongue out at

me again and sipped from her mimosa.

"Hiiiiiii!"

I turned to see a tired-looking brunette rushing toward our table.

"Aves!" Poppy jumped up and hugged her tight. "I thought you were checking in."

"I was. The porter is taking my things up because apparently I look like I need coffee." She shrugged.

"You do." Poppy sat down. "Avery, this is Adam. Adam, Avery."

"Hi!" Avery pulled out a chair and sat down, smiling brightly. "So. You're the boyfriend."

I glanced at Poppy.

"She's being a dick," she said. "She knows what's going on."

Avery rolled her eyes. "I am being a dick. She's always right. What does a girl have to get a coffee around here?"

Poppy pointed at me. "People pay attention to him."

"I don't alienate the bartenders by whistling," I reminded her.

"I did it once." She held up a finger. "And if people act like dogs, I'll treat them like ones."

"Sure. I need a coffee, too, so…" I picked up my empty mug and looked around for the waiter.

Avery tilted her head to the side as I did it, narrowing her eyes. I pretended like I hadn't noticed as I flagged a waiter down and motioned for two cups.

"How long are you here?" Poppy asked Avery.

"I have to leave early tomorrow," she replied. "Work starts at two. Amy quit, so we're all scrambling to cover her shifts."

"Where do you work?" I asked her.

Poppy raised an eyebrow at me.

"What? Since you live together, don't you think it'll be weird if I don't know anything about her?"

"Shit. I forgot that." She clicked her tongue.

Avery snorted. "Your master plan wasn't so smart after all, eh, Pops?"

Poppy rolled her eyes, picking up her coffee, but I caught the tiny smile she sent my way.

So did Avery.

"I work in a bar close to our apartment," she answered. "It's basically a restaurant during the day and a bar from dinner onward. We had someone quit last week, then another two days ago, so it's hectic." She paused. "I'm sorry, this is really bugging me, but I swear I know you from somewhere."

Of course. If Poppy hadn't known who I was, there was no reason Avery would.

Poppy was delayed from replying thanks to the arrival of our coffees. No sooner had I told the guy we were good for anything else right now than Avery gave a tiny gasp.

"You play for the Storms," she said in a hushed voice.

"What?" Poppy's jaw dropped. "You know who he is? Am I the only one who didn't?"

"You didn't know who he was?" Avery asked, then turned to me. "She didn't know who you were?"

I grinned. "And that's my cue to let you two catch up and go up to the gym." I wiped my mouth with a napkin and slid my coffee over to Poppy. "Here," I said, getting up. I walked around the table and grabbed the back of her chair. "You're gonna need that."

I straightened and caught sight of her dad, Mark, Celia, and Rory coming in the door.

Poppy caught my gaze and looked over. "Oh no."

I tapped her shoulder, then when she turned, bent down to kiss her. I cupped the side of her face and kissed her firmly, going back for one last one before I pulled away. She blushed, and Avery raised her eyebrows, lips tugging up.

"Morning," I said to her family. "You doing all right, Mark?"

"Not really sure," he answered with a laugh.

"Adam!" Rory ran around the table and barreled into my legs.

"Ooft!" I pretended to stagger back a few steps. "Have you been working out? You're stronger than yesterday!"

He nodded, pulling back. He lifted his sleeve and flexed his tiny muscles at me. "I did five press-ups this morning!"

"Five? Woah. Good job!" I held up one hand for a high-five, and he obliged, hitting my hand with great enthusiasm.

"Are you leaving?" Poppy's dad asked.

"Yeah. Avery just got here so I thought I'd leave them to it. I was gonna go work out."

Mark looked at the food on the table and wrinkled his face. "Mind if I grab a drink and meet you up there? I could use a workout."

"Sounds good to me. Always better with a friend." I patted him on the shoulder. "Pops, I'll text you when I'm done, all right?"

"Huh?" She looked over her shoulder at me, cheeks still pink.

I fought a smile. "I'll text you when we're done to see where you are. All right?"

"Oh. Yes. All right."

Avery snorted, and I winked.

She was losing her mind over this, and it was so fun.

CHAPTER FIFTEEN
POPPY

Napkins and Nonsense

Avery slammed the door to her room shut and stared at me. "You slept with Adam Winters and didn't know who he was?"

"I—well—you saw him in the bar and didn't tell me!"

Really. That was my argument? My god, I was lame.

"I didn't see him that clearly! You told me you were going home with him and I jumped in an Uber."

"So much for making sure I was safe."

She rolled her eyes. "I'd been talking to his friend all night. I knew he was safe. But stop deflecting! How the hell did you get away with that in your hockey-mad family?"

I told her what happened on Friday night. "So, yeah. Rosie saved my ass," I finished.

"Adam didn't think it was a good idea to tell you just in case?"

"No. He thought it was funny."

"He'd met your mom, right?"

"And she loves him," I muttered, dropping onto her bed. "This whole weekend is a hot mess, Aves. My family is obsessed with him—now personally, too—and soon, I'm going to have to break up with my fake boyfriend who happens to be the only boyfriend my family has ever liked."

"Well, you do run that risk," she said unhelpfully. "Without being that person, I told you this was a bad idea."

"I know. It was a bad idea. It is a bad idea." I fell backward and covered my eyes as I bounced on the mattress.

The bed dipped as she lay down next to me. "He seems nice, though. Very convincing."

I groaned rolling over onto my front and almost lying on top of her. "He is. He's lovely and perfect."

"Uh-oh," Avery said, shifting to sit up. She leaned against the headboard and tossed her shoes on the floor. "Lovely and perfect?"

Another groan and I buried my face into the covers. "Yes. And I hate that I like him."

"Like him, or *like* him?"

"I don't know, Aves." I turned my head to the side and rested my cheek on my arms. "I don't want to answer the question. Sure, he's hot as hell and he's a freaking magician in the bedroom, but we just…get along. It's so easy, you know? It's like we've known each other for years instead of hours."

"That's…I want to say it's cute, but I don't think you'll agree."

"No. Then last night Ro told me we were doing a really good job of pretending to be into each other, and—"

Avery barked a laugh. "Pretending my ass! That kiss after breakfast near damn turned me on!"

I cough-laughed. "Exactly. I told him it was bugging me and he told me he was into me. Ugh, Aves."

"So why are you freaking out?"

"I'm not freaking out."

"You're totally freaking out."

I shook my head. "Tomorrow this will all be over, so it doesn't matter, because—"

"Why does it have to be over?" She crossed her legs and hugged a pillow. "You're into each other. You both live in Orlando. Why not be honest and see if anything happens?"

"Because we're different people and our lives aren't compatible."

"You're like that heroine in romance novels who makes people want to throw their Kindles. You know, the ones where you sit and scream and go, 'HOW DO YOU EVEN KNOW THAT? YOU HAVEN'T TRIED!'"

I blinked at her. "In the middle of a book, huh?"

She blew out a long breath. "Angst central. Okay, but still, how do you know your lives aren't compatible?"

"Because he's famous and talented and rich and—"

"You're talented."

"It doesn't count. I paint for fun." I shifted to sit up and glanced away. "You're the only person who knows I still do that."

"So that makes it any less important? Pops, you're working as a waitress with a roommate in a slightly overpriced apartment. That's how most rich people start out."

I laughed. "In Hollywood and only if you're willing to sell your soul to the devil."

"Then you're fine, because you were birthed by the devil." She grinned. "I think you should try."

"Hmph. We'll see. For now, let's get through today. I'm ready for this wedding to be over and see my sister get married."

"All right, all right."

"Avery, did I tell you about that time in Amsterdam?" Grandpa said, leaning across the table with his eyes wide.

Avery hesitated. "Which time was that?"

Ding ding, wrong answer.

"The one with the British prostitute with tits like Jupiter."

"I'll get more place cards!" I scrambled up and ran to the other side of the room. While Avery may not have heard it, I'd heard it the night before, and I really didn't want to hear about it again.

He'd picked his topic of conversation for this family gathering, and when my mom found out, she was going to have steam come out of her ears.

Arms slid around my back and lips kissed the side of my jaw. "Hey."

"Hey," I said to Adam. "You can let go. Grandpa's too busy telling Avery about Jupiter to pay attention."

"Not her again."

"Yep."

"Your dad's probably coming, so I'll keep hold of you for now," he muttered. "We got interrogated in the gym by your mom."

I picked up a stack of name cards for the tables and spun in his arms, tilting back to meet his eyes. "I bet that was fun."

"Apparently Mark has to make sure all the suits for the groomsmen are correct and your dad needs to be here helping, and hell, since I was there too, I have to help."

"Ha!" I tapped his nose and passed him the cards. "They have to go in these little stands." Extracting myself from his arms, I picked up the box that had the cute little stands in.

"This is what she's got us doing?"

I nodded. "We've only done sixty. Not all the cards are cut to perfection, so we have to trim some. Grandpa is supposed to be helping, but..." I cut a look his way.

"He's drinking a Bloody Mary and telling stories about Amsterdam."

"Mhmm. We're hoping he'll fall asleep soon. We asked them to put an extra shot in this drink."

"I thought you were keeping him off alcohol."

"We were. Then we got tasked with this bullshit, so." I lifted the box with a grimace and headed back for the table.

"And let me tell you." Grandpa clutched his drink, slightly glassy-eyed. "She could ride a bull like a cowboy, if you know what I mean."

Avery nodded solemnly. "I do. I bet she was expensive."

"Worth every damn cent!" he cackled. "Adam, you ever been to Amsterdam?"

"Yes, sir," Adam said, putting the cards down. "I went when I was sixteen."

Grandpa leaned forward. "I'll take you one day! We'll have the best time!"

I sat on the table with a sigh, using a chair a footrest. Adam picked my shoeless foot up and sat down, resting it on his thigh instead with a wink at me.

I rolled my eyes.

I needed more Tylenol.

"Grandpa, you'd never make the journey," I reminded him. "Your doctor said no flights longer than three hours."

"He also said no Bloody Marys," he cackled

again. "And look what I have!"

"Don't shout so loud. As far as Mom knows, it's tomato juice to curb your addiction." I slid a card into the holder and set it to the side with the completed ones.

He went to say something, but he was interrupted by the slamming of the door.

We all jerked around.

Rosie was flat against the door, wearing yoga pants and a tank that had a slice of pizza on it and the words "Love Triangle."

"I'm gonna steal that shirt," I said, inserting another card. "Yours is backward," "I said to Adam. The little bird goes at the front."

He sighed. "My fingers are too big for this."

Avery snorted. "Only time a man will ever complain about being too big for something."

Grandpa did his signature cackle and hiccupped.

"I'm glad you're all having such fun," Rosie said tensely.

"Not really. I'm bored out my fucking min." I looked back up at her. "Why do you look like the police are after you?"

"They are!" she whispered. "The wedding police! Mom and the planner are on my back! I wanted to go to the gym because, hello, I get married today and I'm freaking out and panicking and I'm scared and I just want to let off steam, she's on my back about cupcakes and flowers and when do the bouquets arrive and am I sure about that table and is Grandpa seated too close to the bar?"

"I'll sit at it, petal, no problem." More cackling. "Drink?"

Rosie looked at the Bloody Mary and took it. She sipped, then winced, making face. "Jesus! How much is in that?"

"Sending him to sleep," Avery answered. "Then he can't get into trouble."

"Surprisingly, that makes sense," Rosie replied.

"Carry on about the wedding police." I grabbed my water bottle and uncapped it. "Are you hiding?"

"Yes." She sighed. "And you're not stealing my shirt."

"We'll see." I grinned. "This is probably one of the first places she'll come. She'll ask me if I've seen you."

A tiny snore came from Grandpa, and we all looked over in time to see him jerk awake. "Don't let the scoundrels get away, girls."

"You got it, Grandpa," I said.

Adam's face was buried in my thigh, and he was laughing hard.

Voices were outside the room, and Rosie's eyes opened wide. "They're here!"

"Under the table!" Avery hissed, lifting the cloth. Rosie darted under there and Avery dropped it just in time as the door opened.

"Can you pass more holders?" I said to Avery.

"Sure." She slid the box closer to me.

"There you are, Poppy," Mom said, walking into the room with the stuck-up planner on her heels.

I frowned at her. "You put us here with Grandpa and told me not to move until all the place settings were done. Where else would I be?"

"I don't know, that's why I'm surprised you're here."

Save me, God.

"Is he sleeping?" The planner asked.

"Yes," Avery said. "Old age. It even gets to the

ones who think they're twenty-one."

If that wasn't the most accurate description of Grandpa...

"Bloody Mary?"

"Aunt Blythe was here earlier looking for Dad," I improvised. "Left her glass. You know she's..." I mimed drinking and clicked my tongue.

Mom sighed. "This family feels like a meeting of alcoholics sometimes."

Truth.

"Have you seen your sister? There are last minute things for her to handle before she gets ready." Mom clasped her hands together in front of her stomach. "Anyone?"

Avery shook her head. "I haven't. Sorry."

"Adam?"

"I've been in the gym until you said to come here." He shrugged.

"Poppy?"

"When would I have seen her? I had breakfast, went up with Avery so she could change, then we found you." I finished another place setting. "But if it's about the damn seating plan, she'll kill you if you change that again. And she texted me this morning that the bouquets arrive at, crap, when was it?"

Three taps on my calf gave me the answer.

"Three," I said. "Pretty sure. The concierge is expecting the delivery to his desk."

That much I knew from the info she'd given me.

"If I see her, I'll tell her you're looking for her, though." I smiled at Mom and picked up another card. "Can we get on with this now?"

She sighed. "I suppose. We'll see the concierge now. Make sure you call if you see Rosie."

Crossing my fingers, I said, "Promise."

She nodded and left the room with the planner.

The door clicked shut, and we all breathed a sigh of relief. Jesus, that was like a fucking interrogation. No wonder Rosie was done with them.

She crawled out from under the table after a minute. "Is it safe?"

I nodded. "Come out."

"You can have my shirt as thanks," she laughed.

"I was having it anyway," I replied, grinning. "There. Done. Bought you some time. Although, right now, you're probably better staying here and helping us."

"Yeah, I'm useless at this," Adam said, dropping the stand.

I rolled my eyes and grabbed it. "You just sit there and look pretty," I said patting his head.

"I'll help. It's better than going crazy in the room by myself. The girls are all getting their nails done, but I already did that yesterday, so..." Rosie sighed. "Oh, these are cute."

"Shame they didn't come pre-made," I said.

We all lapsed into silence. Grandpa's intermittent snores was the only sound as we continued on making the place settings. Adam's hand trailed up and down the lower part of my leg, his thumb circling my ankle every time it came back.

Rosie side-eyed us before sharing a glance with Avery. I ignored them. I knew they were trying to rile me up, but whatever, I wasn't biting.

"Attack! The Armada is coming!" Grandpa snorted, jerking. "Shoot the bastards," he muttered, snoring one final time before lapsing into silence again.

We all shared a look before bursting into laughter, all of us trying to keep quiet so we didn't wake him.

Jesus.
You could always count on Grandpa.

CHAPTER SIXTEEN
POPPY

Pizza and Pizazz

"How long do we have?" Adam asked, linking his fingers through mine and dragging me through the hotel.

I could barely keep up—I was basically jogging behind him.

"Uh—thirty minutes," I replied. "Then I have to go and get ready. No arguments."

"None will happen. I told you I'd steal you before you had to get ready."

"I didn't think that meant you'd crash my shower!"

He laughed, finally slowing down as we approached the restaurant. "You needed to hurry up. You have hair stylists and makeup people up there. You didn't need to do yours for a date."

He was right, but still. "I almost fell over."

"Tell me something that won't surprise me." He grinned, letting go of my hand. "I called you half an hour ago," he said to the host. "Adam Winters."

The host nodded. "It's ready. One minute, Mr. Winters."

"What are you doing?" I grabbed his hand and tugged. "Tell me."

He was grinning as he shook his head. "I'm not telling you. It's a surprise."

I sighed. This wasn't fair. What had he planned?

"Here you go, sir." The host returned with a pizza box and a cloth bag bulging with things.

"Thank you." He nodded, shaking the guy's hand before he took the box. "Come on, Red."

I caught the host discreetly put his hand in his pocket. Had he just done that fancy handshake-tip thing? "Did you just him in your handshake?"

"You noticed."

"I notice everything."

"Sure you do. Come on. This will be the quickest date ever."

Following him outside, he took a sharp turn to the steps to the beach. "This is a date is it?" I asked.

"You bet. And we have to eat pizza, talk, and make out all in..." He glanced at his watch. "Twenty-five minutes."

I laughed. "You've got this all down, haven't you?"

"Planned to a T. Will you hold the pizza?"

"Sure." I slid my sunglasses down and took the box.

We walked a few feet onto the beach. Adam selected a spot close to a palm tree, giving us some shade from the hot sun. I stayed back as he put down the bag and pulled out a huge blanket, laying it on the sand in front of us.

He moved his arm in a sweeping motion, gesturing for me to sit with the pizza. My lips curved as I slid off my flip-flops and stepped onto the towel, making sure to set the pizza box down carefully.

Nobody wanted their pizza with a side of sand.

Adam pulled a half-sized bottle of wine out of the bag and two plastic glasses. "Voila," he said, setting the bag down and kicking off his shoes with expert balance.

If I tried that, I'd be dropping the wine. And I'm not gonna lie, my heart did have a little extra beat as I watched him do it.

Wine was important.

He sat down carefully on the blanket and handed me the glasses. I took them, watching him with a small smile as he pulled the cork from the wine and went to pour two small glasses. When he was done, he turned and carefully wedged the bottle into the sand.

"Now, we can eat." He grinned, taking his wine.

"This is perhaps the strangest date I've ever been on," I admitted. "But I think I like it."

"Of course you like it, Red. You've got pizza, wine, and a hot guy. It could be worse."

I snorted, and wine went up my nose. Adam laughed, and I couldn't even flip him the bird because fuck, my nose burned.

"I know it could. I've been on worse dates. I'm not single by accident, you know." I raised an eyebrow and reached to open the pizza box. The smell of the cheese and the sauce was making my stomach rumble, and I didn't even realize I was hungry.

Of course, it was mid-afternoon, and I hadn't eaten since that super-early breakfast, so it wasn't really a surprise. Not to mention I'd been running around like a headless chicken all freakin' day long.

I was more than ready to lie on a beach for twenty-five minutes and do nothing.

"I'm sure you're not," he said with a light chuckle. "Is everything done?"

I nodded, chewing. I swallowed and said, "Rosie's getting her hair done now. Her other bridesmaids are getting a bit of an ass-kicking from Mom for letting her out of their sight this afternoon, which was when I took my cue to leave."

"Why is your mom kicking their ass?"

"Honestly? I think she's one conversation away from losing her mind and having a breakdown, so we're letting her get on with it at this point." I shrugged and tore a bite of pizza off. "I ran away."

He laughed and licked sauce from his finger. "Do you think everything will go right tonight?"

"Absolutely not." I shook my head.

"Why not?"

"Because it's my family. I have full confidence in the ceremony, but after it? Not a chance. It's a miracle they managed to set it up without something going wrong."

Adam leaned to the side and looked down the beach. "That it? In front of the bar?"

I nodded.

"Nice. What are the lights?"

"Lanterns. They're positioned all down the aisle and around the arch. They're all over the bar, too, for the party after."

"It's all outside?"

Another nod from me. "Rosie had her choice of inside or out, and since the wedding is so late, there's no need for a sit-down meal. There will be speeches," I rolled my eyes, "But it'll all be informal."

"And you have to make a speech?" His eyes twinkled.

"If you laugh at me, I'm never having sex with you again."

He held up his hands. "I promise I won't laugh at you. Know what you're saying?"

"Yes, so I'll forget it when I stand up to give it. Not to mention I've been informed that my stage is a chair." That was asking for trouble.

Adam watched me for a second. "You don't look

happy about that."

"I'm not. I'm not allowed to switch light bulbs anymore. Avery banned me."

"Why?"

"Last time I tried, I slipped off the chair and broke the fixture because I took it with me." I grinned innocently. "It's not my fault it didn't hold my weight."

"Light fixtures aren't made to hold human weight, Red."

"I know that now, don't I? You don't need to be a pain about it."

He laughed and closed the pizza box. We'd gotten through a little more than half of it despite talking, and now, Adam pushed the box to the side of the blanket.

"Is this the part of the date where we make out like horny teens?" I asked, catching his gaze with mine.

"No, because if that happens, you won't be getting ready for anything except an orgasm." His lips twitched. "And then I'll be in trouble with your family."

"That could work in our favor. They need a reason to dislike you. It'll be easier when I tell them we've broken up."

Now it was his turn to roll his eyes as he lay down. "We'll come up with something. Maybe we drift apart once the season starts because I'm away a lot."

"And girls throw themselves at you and it makes me feel like crap."

"See? There. We nailed it." He held his hand up for a high five with a grin.

I slapped my hand against his, and he caught my fingers with his, tugging me to him. I fell forward, using his chest as my landing pad. He let out a harsh breath as I fell on top of him, but I could only laugh.

"That's what happens when you tug at me. I'm not a rope," I told him, moving and looking down at him. "I'm a dead weight."

"Oh, yes. All six-hundred pounds of you," he said dryly. "Like a rock falling on top of me."

"And you say I've got a mouth on me, hockey boy."

"You have. I'm quite fond of it." He grinned and flicked his thumb over my lower lip. "I never claimed I wasn't sarcastic myself. Actually, I think you bring it out in me. Is it infectious?"

"No. It's a language for smart people. It's how we confuse the idiots."

"Did you just call me smart?"

"You'd pull a compliment out of a toad, wouldn't you?"

"Especially if they gave me a veiled one." His laugh was the infectious thing. Especially when he threw his head back and closed his eyes, his whole body shaking with the power of it.

I buried my face in his chest and giggled myself. I didn't know why. Nothing was funny.

Except this entire situation, that was.

Adam trailed a hand up my back and swept all my hair to one side of my neck. His fingers sent shivers down my spine as they trailed over my skin. Slowly, I raised my head and looked at him.

His full lips were curved in a smile, his eyes shone with the laughter that lingered in his gaze, and the stubble over his jaw was tempting me into touching it.

His eyes caught mine.

I gently rubbed my thumb over his jaw, following the curve of it as the stubble prickled at me. It was weirdly…good. Like, it was the strangest sensation, and I couldn't believe that it was as enjoyable as it was.

Put "touching stubble" up there with stroking kittens.

I dropped my eyes to his mouth. His lips were there, and full, and smooth, and—

Under mine.

I kissed him softly, cupping the side of his face. It was so natural and gentle that my heartbeat picked up, and it pounded against my ribs in a fierce beat that was so against everything this kiss was.

Slow. Steady. Soft. It was a real kiss, one that made your feelings sit up and take notice, even if your mind wanted them to sit back down and shut up.

And that was what was happening to me right now. Feelings. I had feelings for Adam Winters, and they needed to shut up and get back in their box where they belonged.

Those thoughts were sent flying from my mind when Adam rolled me onto my back, diving his hand into my hair and kissing me deeper. His tongue teased mine, and I slid my hand around to the back of his neck.

He stretched his arm out, and the next thing I knew, I was getting splattered by a very cold liquid.

Wine.

"Oh my God!" I shoved him off me and grabbed the empty glass. "Adam!"

He clapped his hand over his mouth. "Shit. I'm sorry. I forgot it was there."

My hair was now covered in wine. "I have to shower again!"

"Just jump in the sea. That'll do it."

"I cannot go to my sister's wedding smelling like sea water and Sauvignon Blanc. I am not a drunk turtle."

He bent forward, shoulders shaking.

Oh no. I wasn't going to have that.

I grabbed the other full glass and tossed it over him.

He froze.

I did, too.

I bit my lower lip, holding it between my teeth to hide a smile as he slowly, so very fucking slowly, raised his head.

"You did not just throw wine at me," he said in a low voice.

"You did it to me first."

"That was an accident."

"So was that. I went to drink, then, whoops! My wrist flicked and it went all over you," I said, doing the motion with the glass in my hand.

"Poppy…" There was an edge of a warning to the way he said my name.

I had only one option.

Run.

I scrambled up from the blanket and with a shriek, hit the sand. He was right behind me, and I barely made it ten feet before he circled me with his arms and lifted me up.

"No, no, no!" I laughed, gripping onto his forearms.

"You didn't think you could outrun me, did you?" He spun, and I squealed.

"Yes!" I was still laughing. "It was worth a try."

"Silly girl. You can't outrun me." Now, he was laughing. "You did it on purpose."

"Fine! If I admit it, will you let me go?" My toes touched the sand.

"Yes."

"It was deliberate. I threw it on you on purpose

as payback."

"Right." His grip tightened on me and he lifted me again, this time spinning me several times, round and round.

"*Adaaaaaaam!*" I screamed. "Nooooo!"

Sure. I was screaming. But I was laughing, too. It was ridiculous, being spun around at twenty-four, but also weirdly fun.

It didn't hurt that I was being spun around by however many pounds of smoking hot muscle.

One more spin and he put me down. My feet touching the sand had never felt so good, and I laugh-wheezed when he released me. I'd barely caught my breath when he stepped in front of me, cupped my face, and planted a huge kiss on my lips.

"Go and shower before I do it again," he said in a low voice.

"You wouldn't dare."

He took one step toward me.

You know what?

I wasn't going to stay to find out, because I had a feeling he would.

The sound of his laughter following me up the beach as I ran away confirmed that.

———···———

"You're late!" My mother barked the second I walked into Rosie's suite.

"By five minutes. I had to shower." I pointed to the towel still on my head.

"No excuses."

"Mom, lay off her." Rosie appeared from the bathroom. Her hair was done, and so was her makeup.

Her makeup was flawless and natural, showing off the brightness of her eyes and the handful of freckles that were scattered over her nose. Her hair was pulled back at the front, two tiny French braids running along the sides of her head. The rest fell around her shoulders in loose curls. Tiny flowers dotted the braids, and one large one covered the place at the back of her head where the braids met.

"What?" she said, switching her attention to me.

"Nothing. You just look beautiful." I reached out and squeezed her hand.

"I know." She winked, and we both laughed. "Why are you late?"

"Adam threw wine on my hair."

She shrugged. "That happens when you make out on a beach."

I rolled my eyes. "Lay off me."

She grinned. "Come sit down. Lori will get your hair done."

I allowed myself to be guided toward a dining table that was littered with all manner of hair-things. Rosie sat me in one chair, nodded to a brunette, and that was that.

I sat for an hour being preened and primed. This had to have been how the Kardashians felt every morning. How did people cope with it? My head was tugged left and right. Brushes and wands and sponges and whatever else assaulted my face. I was on the verge of telling everyone I'd had enough when I was given the all-clear and told to get up.

I looked in the mirror.

Well, damn.

I looked good.

My makeup was the same natural style as my

sister's, and one side of my red hair had been pulled back and secured with a large white flower. The contrast of it against my hair was striking, and damn it, I felt pretty.

The bridesmaids all helped each other into our dresses. They were pale pink and flattering on all of our body shakes. The asymmetrical hems combined with a full but light lace skirts hid a multitude of sins, and the soft v-necks and spaghetti straps meant all our girls were supported even though we were all braless.

My sister had found wedding beach shoes that weren't shoes at all, but rather material that tied around our ankles and went down to loop over our second toes so we were essentially barefoot.

We were all sitting in various places putting on our special wedding shoes when the door to Rosie's bedroom opened.

I stilled as the other girls all gasped. Mom sniffed and reached for the tissues as she stepped out.

She was beautiful.

Her boho-chic dress hugged the top of her figure, with applique flowers perfectly positioned over it, before it flowed out at her waist into a loose silk chiffon skirt that made it look like the dress was made for her.

"Ro," I said softly. "You look amazing."

She swished the skirt side to side. "You think?"

"We know," Mom said, gently kissing her cheek. She checked her watch. "Right? Is everybody ready? Is Celia—"

"Yes," Celia said, pushing the door open. "Rory's here."

Rory stepped into the room, wearing a white shirt with a pale pink bow tie and gray shorts. "Mommy! You look like a princess!"

Rosie bent down and kissed him. "And you look

very handsome."

Mom checked her watch again. "Okay, girls, you need to head downstairs. The groomsmen will be waiting for you. Celia, you can go and take your seat, honey, thank you. Rosie, your father will be here any minute."

We all gave one last check in the mirror, and we all made our way to the door.

Rory held his tiny hand up to me. "Ready, Auntie Poppy?"

"I sure am, buddy." I took his hand in mine. "Ready to be the most handsome guy walking down the aisle?"

He nodded. "I'm ready."

I laughed and, after blowing my sister a kiss over my shoulder, took the most handsome little guy to walk down the aisle.

CHAPTER SEVENTEEN
ADAM

Rings and Reality

I couldn't stop staring at her. Not as she'd appeared at the end of the aisle clutching Rory's hand. Not as she walked past me, shooting me a shy smile. Not as she stood at the front, lined with the other bridesmaids as Rosie and Mark said "I do."

And, as Mark was told to kiss his bride, I still couldn't look away, especially when she glanced my way.

She looked so fucking beautiful it was almost painful. Everyone's eyes were on Rosie, but for me, Poppy stood out like a sore thumb. Her fiery hair was so much brighter than all the other bridesmaids.

Maybe it was because I was looking for her. Every time I tried to look away, my gaze gravitated back toward her.

And I think she knew it. She kept glancing at me, even when she was playing the perfect sister and bridesmaid.

It was magnetic. I had no control over how we looked at each other. I saw nobody but her, and it was fucking terrifying.

On paper, Poppy Dunn was nothing more than a beautiful stranger.

In reality, Poppy Dunn was a walking daydream with the allure of the devil.

Either way, I wasn't strong enough to resist her. Not while she was around me. Not while her mouth shut me down and her eyes captivated me and her laugh sent me wild.

I had feelings for that crazy redhead, and they were nothing but bullshit.

She'd made her position clear from day one, and I was willing to agree. This was a four day thing. A fling.

A four day fling.

Nothing more, nothing less.

I had nothing against that. Nothing except the feelings I was quickly collecting for the little spitfire, but those were easy to hide. How fucking attracted to her and how much I wanted her were another thing, but my emotions?

I built a career on hiding emotions. I didn't have the trophies and accolades to my name that I did by showing the opposition how I felt.

Poppy was, for all intents and purposes, the opposition.

Hiding how I felt about her was hard. I was attracted to her beyond belief. She was hot as fuck and sassy as hell—and everything else in between was so goddamn endearing I couldn't stop the things I felt for her.

Sure. I'd be a liar if I said I didn't want to clamp my hand over her mouth and shut her up every now and then. I'd be a liar if I said I didn't want to kiss her soft lips and shut her up that way.

I applauded as Rosie and Mark made their way back down the aisle, holding hands with huge grins on their faces. I was happy for them. It was always nice to see two people who loved each other get their happy ending, and there was no doubt in my mind that they were with the person they were supposed to be with.

Slowly, the guests all started moving from their seats, and the wedding party at the front began to disperse. People branched out into groups, friends greeting friends with hugs and family greeting family with kisses and shouts of "It's so great to see you!"

I slid out of the row of chairs when I was clear to do so, and I barely had a chance to do anything when I was stopped by two pre-teen boys. One was clearly nervous, shifting back and forth on his feet, but the other was markedly more confident.

"Excuse me," the non-nervous one said. "But, um, are you Adam Winters?"

I could have said no. That would have been the easiest thing to do, but hell, I was one of those boys once. Plus, the wedding was over, and I had nothing to do during the photos, so...

"You caught me." I grinned. "What are your names?"

"I'm Ross, and this is Ryan," the talker said. "We were wondering, if, uh, it wasn't a problem, if..." he trailed off, now just as nervous as the other boy who was now clearly his brother.

"If you could have a photo?" I finished for him.

They nodded shyly.

"Of course! One rule, though. You don't put them online until tomorrow when the wedding is done, all right?"

"We promise," they said together.

"All right then. Who's got the camera?"

Ross dug into his pocket and pulled out his phone. "Do you mind if we do one together and one alone?"

"You got it, buddy." I bent down as the boys came to either side of me. They did a few snaps of each shot and then alternated between having individual photos with me.

They were thanking me with enthusiasm when a familiar redhead came up behind them and ruffled their hair with her hands.

"What trouble are you causing now?" Poppy asked them. "You're not putting those on Twitter, are you? You know the rules of the wedding. No photos today."

Both boys' eyes widened. "We're not doing anything, Poppy," they said in unison.

I laughed. "They just wanted their photo. They know the rules. It's all good."

She grinned and hugged them both. "Your mom is looking for you. Go, quick, and I won't tell her about the time you pooped in the pool and blamed your sister."

They ran like their asses were on fire.

I quirked a brow at her.

"My cousins." She smirked. "They were six, and Ross accidentally pooped in the pool. He blamed Ryan, who blamed Ruby, and I'm the only one who knows the truth."

"You're going to blackmail them with that for eternity, aren't you?"

"You bet." Her smile widened. "I don't have a little brother, but if I did, I'd be the worst big sister ever."

"I can't imagine why."

She smacked me. "Mom wants you. Apparently, you're supposed to be in the photos."

I stilled. "Why?"

She sighed, throwing her hands out in a shrug. "Something about her thinking we're serious enough that you should be in some of the family shots."

I rubbed the back of my neck. "Do you think we

laid it on a little thick, then?"

"You think?" she said flatly. "Whatever. If anything, Mark and Rory get bragging rights that *the* Adam Winters was at this wedding. Just…tell them it's only been a few months and while you're happy to do a few, you don't think you should be in a lot, okay?"

There was an edge of frustration to her voice, and I wanted to remind her that this was her idea, but I got the feeling she'd simply tell me I didn't have to agree to be her date, but I had, so it was both of our faults.

And she'd be right.

She was right enough on her own without me literally inviting her to be right.

"All right. We can do this. It's only a few photos, right?"

"Yeah. Just a few, then Mark and Ro go off and do all their fancy lovey-dovey ones. It'll take ten minutes." She took my hand and pulled me through the people. "Promise."

Spoiler: it did not take ten minutes, and she lied.

"That was not ten minutes," I told her when she joined me at our table with drinks from the bar.

Poppy set a Coors Light in front of me and sat down with her pink margarita thing. "That's what they told me! I was passing on information. It's really not my fault if the photographer wanted every pose done ten times." She paused. "Also, it was cute when you posed with Rory. I'm pretty sure you made his entire life with that."

I shrugged, toying with the ice-cold bottle. "He's a great kid. That took so long because he talked my ear off between shots about how much he loves hockey and wants to be just like me."

Poppy's smile was small, and her brown eyes sparkled. "You have no idea. You know how teen girls are with people like Harry Styles?"

"Not Harry Styles in particular, but yes, I have four sisters. I know how crazy teen girls are."

"Well, that. You're his Justin Timberlake or whatever." She waved a hand dismissively. "I think he's going to be bragging about this for years. Actually, so is Mark."

I laughed, leaning back in the chair.

"Can I ask you something?"

"Other than the question you just asked?"

She pursed her lips.

I grinned. "Go ahead."

Poppy propped her chin up on her hand and tilted her head slightly. "Does it feel weird knowing that people look at you like you're some kind of God?"

Boy, that was a loaded question.

"Truthfully, yeah." I gave her a half-smile. "It feels weird. I'm not gonna lie. The only thing that makes it bearable is knowing that I was once Rory."

"I guess that makes sense."

"Haven't we had this conversation before?"

"I don't know. Maybe." She shrugged a shoulder. "I think we have, but it just made me think again. Seeing my cousins, then Rory, then all the others after the photos when they were practically lining up to take their turn…"

I chuckled and swigged my beer. "It can be overwhelming."

"And you smile at all of them. I can't even smile at myself most days."

"But you're not a people person," I reminded her. "You're barely a Poppy person."

"It's hard to argue with the facts." She snorted. "Are you a people person?"

"God, no, but I'm great at pretending I am."

She wrinkled her face up. She looked fucking cute. "I don't think I could pretend to be. I hate people that much."

"I never could have guessed."

"You're getting too sarcastic. I think I'm rubbing off on you."

"I can say with one hundred percent confidence that you can rub on me all you like."

She choked on her margarita. I bit back a laugh as she smacked her chest as she coughed.

"If you're laughing at me," she said scratchily, "I'm going to kill you."

I held my hands out at my sides. "Not laughing!"

"Mm." She gave me a fierce side-eye and took another sip of her drink. "Trying not to laugh is more like it."

Couldn't argue with the truth.

I gave her a playful grin and nodded when I saw her mom over her shoulder. "Your mom's coming."

She groaned, slapping her hand to her face.

"Poppy? It's time for the speeches," Miranda said, touching her shoulder. "Are you ready?"

"Sure. I'll be right there," Poppy said without looking at her.

I twisted my lips to the side as Miranda left. "You're not ready at all, are you?"

She shook her head, her curls flying. "Not in the slightest."

Reaching over the table, I squeezed her hand,

then brought it to my lips to kiss her fingers. "You'll be fine. As long as you don't fall off the chair."

She groaned as she stood up. "Great. Now I know I'm going to fall off the chair. Thanks."

"You're welcome, Red. You're welcome."

CHAPTER EIGHTEEN
POPPY

Sunsets and Speeches

My stomach rolled as Mark finished his speech. Everyone broke out into applause, and I caught Adam's eye in the crowd. He winked, giving me a small, reassuring smile.

It didn't work. I was nervous as hell. I hated speaking in front of people. I avoided it at all costs. The last time I'd done it, I'd tripped over my own feet on the way up to the stage and almost flashed everyone my underwear.

The only thing I had going for me for this one was the fact my dress was long enough to cover my ass if I fell over.

That, and I had alcohol. I'd drink my way through this if I had to.

I'd have to. I knew that.

"Your turn, sweetie," Dad said, holding his hand out for me.

Swallowing hard, I took his hand and stepped up onto the chair. My stomach literally flipped as I looked out at the hundred or so people turning in my direction.

"Her boobs look bigger. Did she get her boobs done?" My great-aunt Linda shouted. "Is she pregnant?"

I clicked my tongue and took the mic from Dad. "Not how I planned to start this speech, but, uh, Aunt Linda, no, I did not get my boobs done. And," I raised my glass, "Definitely not pregnant."

"Why?" she crowed. "Aren't you having sex?"

This was why I didn't do speeches.

"Moving on swiftly," I said, ignoring her. I caught Adam laughing into his hand and shot him a glare before focusing out on the crowd. "First, let me start this by saying the entire Dunn family should pat ourselves on the back. Why? Because we're all together, and nobody has gotten injured—"

"Yet!" Aunt Blythe yelled.

"Or drunk—"

"Yet!" she shouted again, holding up an empty Bloody Mary glass.

"Yet. Thanks, Aunt Blythe." I raised my glass in her direction, and she nodded, putting one wrinkled thumb in the air for me. "As I was saying. Nobody is injured, drunk, or fighting. Yet," I added before she could do it for me. "So, we're doing good. And as long as someone keeps an eye on Grandpa and Aunt Blythe near the bar, we should make it the whole night!"

Mild protests from Grandpa and Aunt Blythe rumbled through the laughter of everyone else.

"Anyway, to be serious, because apparently I have to do that, when Rosie asked me to be her maid of honor and she realized that meant I'd have to get up here and do this, she had three rules." I caught my sister's wide eyes. "The first was that I couldn't get up here and tell you about the time she accidentally dropped her curling iron on the cat, and that's why Sir Socks had a bald patch on his tail for the rest of his life."

Rosie covered her face.

"The second rule was that I was not allowed to mention the time she snuck out after curfew and ripped her pants on the window which was, to my delight, the reason she got caught. She'd gotten dressed in the dark and was wearing Mom's pants. After she tried to blame the rip on a honey badger, she had to 'fess up."

"I'm going to kill you!" Rosie shouted, wriggling against Mark's hold.

I grinned. "You knew better than to make me do this."

"What's the third?" Uncle Dave yelled.

"The third rule was that I was absolutely, one-hundred percent not allowed to tell you all that her obsession with N-SYNC was so extensive that when she was sixteen, she came home drunk and slept with her life-size cardboard cut-out of Justin Timberlake."

Now that drew laughs from everyone.

Everyone except my sister whose cheeks were the brightest shade of red I'd ever seen.

"And I was also told not to tell you there were rules, but I guess I really messed that one up," I smirked at her. "Sorry, Ro. But this is my revenge for that time you told Darren Fowler that the cold sore on my lip was herpes."

Rosie stopped, pursed her lips, then shrugged. "Fair enough."

I laughed. "Okay, but, seriously, I'm up here for a reason and that isn't to air all your secrets. I have to save some for your anniversaries, birthdays, and general sibling blackmail, after all."

Another light laugh went through the crowd.

"So, Ro, Mark..." I turned to them. "I can honestly say that I never once doubted this day would come. Of all the people I've ever seen fall in love, I don't think I've ever seen anyone love each other as much as the two of you do. So as much as I mess with you both, I know that nobody on this beach is happier for you than I am. You're a true fairytale, and if I'm ever loved with half the passion you love each other, I'll count myself very lucky. Congratulations, Mr. and Mrs. Perkins. May you be together forever. And, if not, I know how to hide a body. Lookin' at you, Mark."

I raised my glass to my brother-in-law and sister to toast them. They were both grinning, and Mark was laughing his ass off at me.

Well. That didn't go too badly.

I stepped off the chair to the sound of people toasting them and cheering.

I did it. And I was still alive. And I hadn't thrown up.

Bonus.

"Well, that wasn't too bad," Adam said, wrapping one arm around me and pulling me against his side. "You didn't slip, fall, or make a complete fool out of yourself."

"You could at least pretend to hide your surprise," I muttered, sliding an arm around his back.

"I could, but then you'd call me out for lying."

"Maybe. Maybe I would have pretended that I didn't notice." I shrugged and finished my drink.

"I think that's a lie."

I rolled my eyes because it totally was. There was no way I wouldn't call him out. Mostly because I, too, was surprised I'd done it without screwing it up.

Mom climbed up onto the chair, mic in hand, and waved her hand to get everyone's attention. "Hi, hi! Thank you, everyone. The beach has been cleared and the dance floor installed. It's time for the first dance, so if everyone could head back down, that'd be perfect. Thank you."

Adam took my glass and put it on the nearest table. "Come on. Your mom will have a cow if you aren't there at the front."

I watched as my dad guided my mom carefully down the dance floor. "I think the only thing my mom needs to have is a glass of water."

She slipped and giggled, gripping onto Dad's shirt.

Adam snorted. "That, too."

I bit my lip and buried my face in Adam's chest. His shoulders shook, and the rumble of his laugh in my ear sent chills down my spine.

"Really?" he asked. "You really hid a snake in her bed?"

"No, a snakeskin," I corrected him. "And that was only because she'd put a rabbit's foot in my bed."

"Why would you do that?"

I pulled back from him and shrugged. "I don't even remember how it started. I think it was with a dare that went wrong and we ended up trying to best the other."

"Who won?"

"Me, obviously." I rolled my eyes and rested my cheek against his chest.

The sun was almost completely set now. The sky was a mix of inky blue and deep red, but the beach and surrounding area was lit up by lanterns. The dance floor itself was alight, changing colors every few seconds. Adam and I had long given up trying to get onto it, so now we were on the outside of the dancing group, slowly swaying to the music.

"Want to go sit somewhere?" he asked me softly.

I nodded. I'd been able to ignore the fact this was our last night thanks to the hectic nature of getting to the wedding, and then the actual wedding itself, but now, dancing with him…I couldn't.

And there was this little hollow pit in my stomach that wouldn't let me forget it now, either.

Adam slipped his fingers between mine and led me down the beach. We walked until we could barely hear the music from the speakers at the bar and we were in almost total darkness. It was amazingly peaceful, and I was thankful for it. The low hum of the wedding in the background served as little more than white noise when it was combined with the gentle crashing of waves against the sand.

We dropped down to the sand, and I leaned back on my arms. Adam loosened his tie until he was able to pull it over his head and toss it to the side. Neither of us said a word for a minute, and when he leaned back on his arms, too, his fingers brushed mine.

"So you pranked each other all the time?" he asked.

I nodded, looking out at the ocean that was now starting to be illuminated by the almost-full moon. "As long as I can remember. They weren't cruel pranks—"

"I dunno. The snakeskin thing is pretty cruel."

"She did the rabbit foot first. When you up the stakes, don't be annoyed when someone else does the same." I shrug a shoulder. "It wasn't my fault I broke her curling iron."

"I feel like all the fights you had as teens were based on curling irons."

"Pretty much. Didn't your sisters fight over stuff like that?"

He tilted his head to the side. "I don't know. I ignored them for most of the time. They usually argued over clothes or boys or who used all the hot water in the shower. It took them two years to realize it was me, because while they were fighting over who got to use the main bathroom first, I was using it."

I laughed. "Been there, done that. Bathroom time is no joke. Once, I got in there before Rosie did when she had a date, so she turned the hot water off halfway through my shower. I had to get out with shampoo still in my hair because she refused to turn it on."

"Oh no. I think I know where this is going."

"She didn't count on the fact that, if she'd just let me finish in the shower, she'd have had hot water, too."

Adam shook his head. "How did you two survive your teen years? Seriously?"

"She moved out at eighteen to go to college." I snorted. "And I got the bathroom all to myself."

"How are you so close now?"

"We don't live anywhere near each other. It works. We talk all the time, and I always take Rory for weekends to go to Disney and Universal, but we don't actually see each other all the time." I turned my head to look at him. "Are you close to your sisters?"

"Yeah. I mean, it's kind of the same as you. They're scattered all over the country, so we make time to see each other if I'm in town for a game. That's about it, except for Christmas when the entire family drops back in at my parents' house and I end up with houseguests."

"Ouch. I'd hate it if my sister had to stay with me. Partly because I don't have a spare room, and partly because, well, I'd hate to share my apartment with her."

He laughed. "I don't mind it. I get to hang out with the kids and have fun. I don't get to do that often."

"Because you travel so much?"

He nodded. "It's hard. Why do you think I'm

single?"

"I dunno. I assumed you had a really bad habit. Like biting your toenails or something."

His lips twisted to the side.

"But the traveling thing does make more sense," I agreed.

It was also the perfect explanation for ending this, both in real life and in our fake relationship.

"Not everyone can deal with it. It's hard. If I'm in a city where one of my sisters lives, I might not go home for two or three weeks." He dropped back to his elbows and sighed. "My team is my family. Most women aren't ready to deal with what is, for a good seven months of the year, a long-distance relationship. The stress and the trust... Not everyone wants to find a way to cope with it."

The way he said it almost sounded like a warning. Like he wanted me to know just how hard it was, and while the idea that he was warning me made my heart skip, it also made my stomach sink.

I wasn't that person. I knew that. I was impatient, and I could be needy. I couldn't even have a long-distance relationship with my bed, never mind a human being I cared for.

And trust—he said that like he had experience with it. Like he'd either been hurt, or someone hadn't trusted him.

The sad thing was I doubted Adam would ever be a person to break trust.

It would be women around him.

Let's face it. I didn't trust women. Women were bitches. And, since I was a woman, I had that fact on very good authority.

"Do you ever get lonely?" I asked him, sitting up

and turning to face him.

"Lonely-lonely or…"

"Like, feelings. Relationship lonely."

"Sometimes. Some of the other guys are married, or their girlfriends or whatever fly out to see them. If we have a break where we can go home, it sucks sometimes knowing I'm going home to an empty house."

"Do you wish you could change it?"

"Sure. I wish there was someone who liked me for who I am and could deal with me being away as much as I am." His eyes met mine. "But that's harder to find than you'd think."

I swallowed, glancing away quickly. "I bet."

"It's not so bad. I tend to meet someone every now and then, but it never goes anywhere. I think of them like diamonds in the rough. Of course, I'm still looking for the diamond this summer, but…"

I smacked his leg, laughing. "You're a dick. Seriously."

He lay down flat on the sand and motioned for me to lie down with him. I did, resting my head on his chest. I could feel the beating of his heart beneath my cheek, and I briefly closed my eyes.

"Is it crazy," he said softly, "If I said that a part of me wished we didn't agree this was only for this weekend?"

"Absolutely," I said in a voice that was stronger than my own conviction.

No. It wasn't crazy.

A part of me damn well wished it, too.

"You think?"

"Yeah. It's all perfect here, isn't it? When there's structure to the days and things to do. Honestly, in real life, I'd probably bore you. My life is terribly unexciting."

"You. Poppy Dunn. Boring? I don't believe you."

"Seriously. I'd frustrate the crap out of you," I insisted. "I'm awful at going to bed at a decent hour thanks to a minor addiction to murder shows on Netflix. I have a long-standing battle with Avery's asshole cat whenever he decides to show up. I'm late for just about everything, including work, which is why I'm scheduled to start fifteen minutes before my actual shift does."

His upper body shook as he laughed quietly.

"I have a standing order to pay the rent to Avery the day after I get paid or I'd forget. I'm not allowed to touch the vacuum because I break them all the time. I don't even think I know how to use the dishwasher correctly. I just kind of jab at buttons and hope for the best."

More laughter.

"So, really, I'm a dreadful adult. That's why I'm single. I'm not the put-together girl everyone wants to take home to their mom. Suzy Homemaker I am not."

He tightened his arm around my waist, still laughing. "See, now it begs the question how I can be so damn attracted to someone who is, literally, my total opposite."

"Excuse me, Mr. Perfect."

"Hey, I have my faults, too. They just don't make me look anywhere near as cute as yours do."

"My faults don't make me cute."

"No, but the way you list them off as reasons not to like you makes you cute."

"Ugh. Whatever." I rolled my eyes. "What are your faults?"

"All right." He moved his hand and played with my hair. "I have to pay someone to do my laundry because I can never do it correctly. I can't remember anyone's birthdays, ever. My mom set up a Google calendar for me, so I'll get a notification three days before any birthday or anniversary."

I bit the inside of my cheek. *That* was cute.

"I work too much. I'm the first one in the gym and the last one out, even if it's supposed to be a day off. I worry too much about the other guys on my team. I don't know how to switch my brain off. I'm determined to be the best, even though one day it could cost me."

"See, the calendar thing? That's cute. I'd pay someone to do my laundry if I could." I tilted my head back. "And working hard isn't exactly a bad thing. Maybe you do need to slow down, but you'll do that when you're ready. You're determined, and that's not really a fault."

"Depends how you look at it. I wouldn't say having a long-standing feud with your roommate's cat is a fault, because, let's face it, cats are fucking assholes."

"And Spike is the biggest asshole of them all," I agreed. "I guess you're right. I don't see you being determined as a fault. I really don't. And you will slow down one day. You'll have to."

"Mm. Maybe I'll slow down when I find someone worth slowing down for." He kissed the top of my head. "You wanna go for a swim?"

"Now?"

"No, next week. Of course now."

"I don't have a suit with me."

"Do I look like I'm wearing swimming shorts under these pants?"

"Adam, I'm not even wearing a bra." I sat up and gave him a stern look. "Just panties."

"Red," he sighed, sitting up. "If you're trying to convince me that swimming in our underwear is a bad idea, you're failing miserably."

Jesus, Poppy. Live a little. Go swimming in your panties with the hot guy.

CHAPTER NINETEEN
POPPY

Seaweed and Sharkbait

I rolled my eyes. "Do you think they can see us?"

Adam looked over at the party. "I don't think they even know we disappeared."

"Aunt Blythe is probably halfway to hammered and dancing," I said, noticing a lot of people around the dance floor.

"Sorry to miss that."

"No, really, you're not," I assured him. "It's scarring. I'll never recover from the time she flashed everyone her thong."

"I take it back. I'm not sorry at all." Laughing, he undid the buttons of his shirt and shrugged it off his shoulders.

Carefully, I removed my beach shoes as he kicked his shiny ones off. I turned away from him and twisted my arm to undo the zip at the back of my dress.

Why were dresses made like this? Not only were we denied pockets, but you had to be a freaking contortionist to get the damn things off.

You wouldn't give a man a shirt with buttons on the back, would you?

No, you wouldn't.

Equality my ass.

Adam chuckled, stepping behind me. "I got it."

"Thanks." I pulled down the thin straps and immediately used my arm to cover my boobs.

Adam snorted, but he didn't say anything as he

took my free hand and led us down to the water. It didn't take us long to get down there, and I gasped as the water rolled over my feet. It wasn't cold, but it wasn't anywhere near as warm as I was expecting it to be.

"It's not cold," Adam said, stepping in front of me and dragging me into the water.

"Slow! Slow! Oh my God."

"It's not cold." He let go of me and walked farther back into the water. "It's nice."

Tentatively, I took a few steps forward.

"Stop being a wimp, or I'll throw you in the water," he threatened me.

"You wouldn't!" I pointed at him, clutching tighter at my boobs.

He simply looked at me as if to say I should try him. Given earlier when he'd picked me up and spun me around, I should have known better than to stop dead in ankle-deep water in protest.

A wave helped propel him forward to me, and he snatched me against his body before I could do anything. My arm was squished between us, but he didn't stop to let me move it as he walked backward in the water.

He dropped his lips to mine, stopping me from protesting as the water splashed higher and higher up over my thighs and, thanks to one adventurous wave, over my ass. I gasped into his mouth and felt his grin against me.

Right before he picked me up at the waist and tossed me into the water.

I was saved only by the fact the water wasn't really that deep at all. I still went under to my chin, meaning half of my hair was now soaking. "Asshole!"

He laughed.

Halfway to standing, a wave crashed into me, and

I went over again, this time getting fully covered by the water.

Oh. My. God.

I pushed the hair from my face and felt for the flower. It was still clipped in, thank God, but I couldn't damn well see.

Carefully, mindful of my mascara, I wiped under my eyes and touched my eyelashes. "I'm going to kill you!"

He laughed harder, and I took my chance. I jumped at him and pushed him. He lost his balance on the sand, and a wave full of karma dealt him the same hand I'd just been given.

I laughed so hard my stomach hurt. Karma was a bitch, but man, she was a beautiful one. It was hard to stay on my feet thanks to the rolling of the water and my inability to, well, stop fucking laughing and stand upright.

Adam wiped water from his face and pointed at me. "You—"

"No! It's fair! You pushed me first!"

"The water pushed you. I threw you."

"Whatever. I'm not arguing semantics in shark-infested waters."

He laughed. "I'm sure the nurse sharks would be delighted to eat you."

I slapped him. "They're nocturnal. Of course they're around."

"And they're not at *all* interested in eating a spunky redhead with a great ass."

"You think I have a great ass?"

"You got over the sharks pretty quickly." He slid his hands around to my ass, pulling me against him.

"Yeah, well, like you said, they aren't interested in

eating me." I wrapped my arms around his neck. My bare breasts were pressed against his chest, and my nipples hardened as they rubbed against the light smattering of dark hair on his skin. "Besides, I'm small and relatively scrappy. If anyone hungry comes along, there's much more meat on you."

He laughed, dipping his head. "Great. So I'm shark bait."

"No. You're dinner, just in case. That is the chivalrous thing to do. Sacrifice yourself to save me."

"Poppy, you're the last person on Earth who would need anyone to save them. You'd probably flip it around and end up saving your rescuer."

"I think that's a compliment," I murmured.

"It was." He laughed, brushing his lips over my cheek.

We both paused. I tilted my face, bringing my lips closer to his. My heart thumped in my chest. There was a lump in my throat that swallowing couldn't kill—a dryness in my mouth that wouldn't go away.

I wanted him to kiss me.

No.

I needed him to kiss me.

I needed one more moment to pretend this was real. That it was a real thing that wouldn't end tomorrow.

I needed one more moment to allow myself to feel the things I felt for him. To feel how he gave me butterflies and made my heart beat faster; how he gave me goosebumps and made me want to wrap myself around him like a clingy koala bear.

I needed to feel him, and I knew this was my last chance.

We were running out of time, and if this was the only moment I had to admit to myself that I had very real feelings for my very fake boyfriend, then I'd take it.

With both hands.

So, I kissed him instead. Lightly. Just a plain ghost of my lips over his. A tease, a little question. Asking him to kiss me back and kiss me harder.

He obliged.

His lips were soft but firm as he took my mouth with his. My fingers curled in the hair at the base of his neck, and he dug his fingers into my ass. I'd never pressed myself against anyone as hard as I did him, and I didn't hesitate to part my lips when he deepened the kiss.

His tongue stroked mine. Each time he kissed me, desire bolted through my veins. I kissed him harder and held him tighter, pressing my hips against him. His cock was getting harder and harder against me, and I was on the verge of telling him we needed to get back to our room when something touched my foot.

I squealed and jumped, using my arms around Adam's neck as leverage to wrap my legs around his waist. He staggered back a couple of steps before he grabbed my ass once again.

"What the hell?" he asked, looking at me.

"Something touched my foot!"

"So you screamed?"

"What was I supposed to do? Stand there and let it eat me?"

His lips twitched as his hard cock pressed between my legs.

This wasn't so smart...

"So you decided to jump and let me be eaten?"

"We already covered this! If there's something hungry in here, it's gonna eat you and not me. I'm too pretty to be eaten by a shark."

He clicked his tongue. "What am I? Chopped

liver?"

I touched his cheek. "Oh, no, you're very pretty, but it's every man for themselves out here."

"You know it was probably seaweed that touched you, right? And all you've achieved is making my cock so hard I'm tempted to pull your underwear to the side and fuck you right here on the beach?"

No. No, I did not know that.

The seaweed or the fucking on the beach.

His cock...I figured.

"Um," I said.

"Um. You kiss me like that then wrap your legs around my waist—where I know you can feel my cock— and you say 'Um.'"

"Um. Yeah."

He laughed and kissed me again. I hugged him hard as our lips moved together, and he slowly backed us into slightly deeper water. His teeth grazed my lower lip, and his fingers dug right into my ass cheeks again. My clit throbbed as his cock bounced against me, and—

"Fuck!"

We were underwater before I knew what was happening, and I sputtered as I found my footing and stood upright. "What the hell?"

Adam broke the surface, laughing, and wiped his face. "The sand dipped. I fell."

"Ass. That's what you get for going deeper in the water!" I huffed out a large breath. The water was chest-high for me now, and not gonna lie, I was not happy about having my nipples out in the ocean.

One creature was all it took and then—bam. No nipples.

I covered them with my arm again, and Adam grabbed my hand.

"Don't panic, but something just touched my foot," he muttered.

"Seaweed?" I squeaked.

"Nope. It was a tail."

I bit my cheek to stop screaming and grabbed it. I jumped onto his back, holding him tightly.

"That's right. Splash the water," he eked out. "That'll scare it off. Also, Red, you're strangling me."

"Sorry." I loosened my grip on his neck. "Is it gone?"

"I don't know. Stay still."

"I thought you said nurse sharks don't want to eat humans!"

"Okay, shit. For someone who grew up in Florida, you don't know a lot about the water, do you?"

"If you couldn't tell, it's not a place I go a lot." I wriggled on his back, trying to keep my feet out of the water.

"Stop splashing," he told me, tapping my thigh with his fingers. "We'll go slow."

"If I die because you wanted to swim in our underwear, I'm going to haunt you forever and make your life hell."

"Duly noted." Slowly, he began the trek back to the beach. His steps were slow and careful, and this was exactly why my mom always told me to stay out of the water at night. "Nothing like a potential shark to kill a boner."

"If it didn't, I'd be worried." I slid off his back to my feet and instantly winced. "Ow."

"What's up?" He looked at me, the concern on his face illuminated by the moon.

"My foot hurts." I put my weight on my right foot.

"Hold on. I have my phone in my pants pocket. I'll put my shirt out for you to sit on so I can look."

He moved before I could register that he was leaving me standing at the very edge of the water.

Wait—no.

"Adam!" I hopped on my right foot onto the sand. "Don't leave me with the shark."

"Jesus, Poppy." He laughed, running to me right before I fell over. "It's not gonna come up that high. Come on." He wrapped an arm around me and guided me over—still hopping—to where he'd laid his shirt on the beach.

He helped me down and got my dress, pulling it over my head to cover my boobs. He even did the zip up for me as I pulled my hair around and squeezed water out of it.

"Let me put my pants on." He did that quickly then pulled out his phone. Using the flashlight to get some light, he gently took my left foot in his hand and tilted it to see. "You're bleeding."

"Great. So I was the reason for the shark."

"Absolutely. It was entirely your fault we were almost eaten." He half-smiled. "I can't see anything in it. Does it sting or just hurt?"

"Just hurt."

"All right. Here." He rested my foot on his and, using the sleeve of his shirt, touched it to my foot.

"What are you doing?" I pulled away.

"Poppy, it's just a shirt. I need to stem the bleeding before I take you inside and get a Band-Aid or something, okay? It's right in the arch of your foot."

I sighed. "I bet that happened when I went down."

He nodded. "Probably when you fell the second

time. You wouldn't have felt it because you were too mad at me."

"So, it's all your fault instead."

"If that makes you feel better." He peered up at me, smiling, then checked my foot. "Okay. If I carry you, we can probably get there before it starts again."

I groaned. "Driving home tomorrow is going to suck so bad."

He gave me a sympathetic nod and stood up. Adam turned off the flashlight and tucked his phone back into his pocket, then bent to pick me up. I made sure to grab his shirt and both our shoes before he lifted me. He held me against his body with one arm behind my knees and the other around the top of my back.

"This isn't how I planned this night to end," I muttered grumpily as he carried me up the beach.

His laugh was light and low and oh-so-delicious. "You know what, Red? It wasn't my plan, either, but it makes total sense, don't you think?"

In a weird kind of way, he was right.

It did make sense.

CHAPTER TWENTY
POPPY

Goodbyes Are For Suckers

I felt sick.

I didn't want to say goodbye.

I shifted on my feet as Adam opened the trunk of his car. I'd been re-bandaged this morning and taken painkillers to make the drive home as easy as possible, but right now, knowing he was leaving, the pain in my foot didn't come close to comparing to the pain I felt in my heart.

And it was stupid pain. Not stupidly painful, but straight up stupid pain. I knew this would happen. It was written in the stars from the very beginning. This hadn't been a first date or a precursor to something longer or more serious.

Yet, I'd allowed myself to cross the line into falling for him. I know—four days. It sounded stupid, but we'd been together almost constantly. You put any two strangers with an attraction together and they were bound to feel things.

I just hoped I hadn't fallen too far and that I'd be over this in a week. That was all I was holding onto as Adam slammed the trunk and walked over to me.

He reached out, his fingers trailing across my skin as he pushed hair from my face and tucked it around my ear. "I had a really great time this weekend."

"Me, too," I said softly. "It was fun. You know. Apart from my foot getting cut open and Aunt Blythe stripping at breakfast."

She was still drunk... Or so she said.

"That did brighten the morning up," he said with a smirk. "I'm sorry I have to leave so early. I'd stay later if I could."

I shrugged. "It's fine. I won't be here much longer. I have to work the lunch shift tomorrow and I don't want to get in late."

"Did Avery already lave?"

"Yeah. She has to work tonight, so she left right after breakfast."

He nodded slowly. We stood for a moment, just looking at each other until I laughed and dipped my chin.

"What's so funny?" He hooked two fingers beneath my chin, so our eyes met.

"This is ridiculous." My hair came loose so I pushed it back again. "I mean—we'll see each other again. We don't live a million miles apart."

"I know your favorite bar. And where you work," he added.

"Exactly. This is dumb."

"Come here." He pulled me into his body, wrapping his arms around me tightly. I squeezed my eyes shut at the pang in my heart when he kissed the top of my head.

Jesus, I needed to pull myself together. We had feelings for each other, but we'd cleared it up last night. I wasn't the girl who could deal with him being away as much as he would be. Relationships were hard for him because of hockey, and that was fine.

Adam pulled back and kissed me, one hand around the back of my neck. I felt it right down to the tips of my toes—and when he pulled away, I pressed my face into his chest.

I didn't want him to see how deep that kiss had

tugged at me.

I squeezed him tight then pulled back. "Thank you for saving my ass this weekend."

"I'll save your ass anytime, Red." He smiled, then kissed me once more before he let me go.

I backed up, bumping into Rosie's car next to his. My foot stung, so I put weight on my toes instead of my whole foot and watched as he got into his car. He rolled the window down, and the rumble of the engine as it started made me want to climb on the roof so he couldn't go anywhere.

He winked, shooting me one of his sexy half-smiles before he backed up.

The last I saw of him was him raising his hand out of the window in a wave.

I held mine up lamely, swallowing back a thick lump in my throat.

It wasn't supposed to hurt this much.

Rosie came up next to me and wrapped an arm around me. "Come on, Hopalong. Let's sit." She guided me over to the stairs and we sat down, staring out at the parking lot.

Well, I stared at it. At the road out of it, to be honest.

She was looking at me with the kind of understanding only a sister could feel—like she felt the very same ache, I did knowing that he was gone.

"Tell me if I'm wrong, but that plan backfired, huh?"

That was one way to put it.

I shrugged and looked down at my painted toes. "Doesn't matter, does it? It was for one weekend only. I knew that. So did he."

"That's not the point, Pops," she said gently,

squeezing me into her side. "Does that really mean it has to be over?"

I opened my mouth, but nothing came out.

"He might be here to be your fake boyfriend, but you don't need to be a genius to see that you both developed very real feelings by the end of the weekend. Christ, Avery took one look at you and needed a hot shower."

I bit back a laugh and buried my face in my hands. "God, Ro. This was supposed to be easy. He wasn't supposed to make me laugh or anything like that. He was just supposed to be…there."

"Well, him being just "there" bombed the second you brought a hockey player into a hockey-mad family."

"All right, fine, I get it. Next time, I'll check that my fake date isn't famous in any way."

She shook her head slowly. "Admit it. You like him. A lot."

"No."

"Why not?"

"Because," I said softly, looking at her. "If I say it out loud, then I can't deny it anymore, can I?"

She smiled, but it was full of sadness.

Instead of arguing with me like I thought she would, she pulled me into her, and I rested my head on her shoulder.

I knew two things for sure.

I needed to get back to my real life, but there was one glaring problem with that.

My life would never be the same after Adam Winters.

CHAPTER TWENTY-ONE
POPPY

Flowers and Fuck This

Last night, I'd stumbled through the door—quite literally, thanks to my foot—and beelined for the freezer. Avery had texted me that she'd bought ice cream and wine and that it was all mine.

That was true friendship.

I'd allowed myself to whine at Netflix and get lost in a documentary while I ate my weight in ice cream, then went to bed. All right, so I fell asleep on the sofa with the empty carton in my hand and Avery had dragged me to bed, but don't judge me.

I was sad.

Now, I was feeling human again. A hot shower, a half-assed run, and a shift at work had pulled me out of the magic of my sister's wedding and into my real life. Even if work had put me behind the bar because I had no business running food when I could barely walk, according to my manager.

I wasn't going to argue with her. I liked serving drunk people drinks to get them even more drunk. If I could write a book, I'd have some real stories to tell.

Diary of a Cocktail Waitress. I'd nail it. With some elaboration, of course. I was no glamor puss serving cocktails in fancy restaurants, after all.

I closed the apartment door behind me and tossed my purse on the sofa. "Aves, I'm home!"

"Hey!" She poked her head out of her bedroom door. "How are you feeling today?"

"Human. I figured I'd get changed, order pizza, and paint." I stood by my door. "Do you have work?"

Yawning, she covered her mouth and nodded. "'Til eleven. I'm so freakin' tired."

"You have time to eat before you go?"

She looked over her shoulder. "If you order pizza now, probably."

"'Kay. I'll do it on the app." I ran back into the living room to get my phone, then went into my room to change. In seconds, I'd ordered the pizza and had tossed my phone onto the bed.

The knock at our door came when I was half naked with my head stuck in my closet.

"Want me to get that?" Avery yelled.

"Please! I'm half-naked!"

"Thanks for that!"

She was welcome.

I pulled out some yoga pants and a tank top emblazoned with, "I like to party, and by party, I mean read books." The click of the front door came right as I pulled up my pants and grabbed my shirt.

"Pops? There's something here for you."

Frowning, I tugged the shirt down over my boobs and walked into the main room. On our small dining table that was currently covered in my paints, was a massive bouquet of poppies. The blood-red color was a bright pop in our kitchen, and I stopped dead as reality hit me.

Only one person I knew would have the balls to send me my namesake flowers.

Avery picked at the card. "He's brave. The last boy who tried to give you a poppy got a punch in the nose."

"I was eight, and he was a dick." I took the card

from her, fingering the edge of one of the petals. I didn't think I wanted to read this, but I didn't have a choice, so I opened the small card.

Thank you for reminding me how to have fun this weekend, Red.
Don't kill me for this.

I smiled, closing the card. The flowers were even in a red vase that matched the poppies perfectly. I trailed my finger over one of the flowers and down the side of the shiny vase, my stomach flipping as I put the card down next to it.

Avery sighed and shook her head. "I don't get you."

"Don't start, Aves." I slid into my chair and pushed the tabletop easel to the side. "I don't want to hear it, okay?"

She slammed her hands on the table. "You hate poppies."

"I don't hate poppies. I think they're an easy cop-out and only an idiot would assume they're my favorite flower just because of my name."

With attitude, she motioned to the flowers.

"They're not—" I stopped and sighed. "Red. His nickname for me. It started the morning after we, you know."

"Fucked."

"Slept together," I said dryly. "I asked him why he called me red, and he said it was partly because of my hair, and partly because my name is Poppy, and poppies are red. I think this is him throwing back to that conversation."

"That's a ridiculous reason for a nickname."

"I know. Why do you think he told me not to kill him?"

Avery pinched the bridge of her nose and laughed. "You two so obviously have feelings for each other."

I held up my finger. "I told you not to start."

"I'm doing this because I'm your best friend and I care about you. You're so damn stubborn you can't see that you're hurting yourself because you're too afraid of telling him how you feel."

"No, Aves, you're wrong. I know I'm hurting myself, but it's not so simple. He's not here most of the time. He travels for most of the season. He admitted that relationships are a struggle because of it. Would you rather I get over this little crush now, or try a relationship that I already know isn't going to work just because we spent one weekend together?"

She went to say something, then stopped.

"If I spend more time with Adam, I can tell you right now, one hundred percent, I'm going to fall in love with him."

"Oh," she said in a small voice.

"And if I fall in love with him, that'll be it for me. I'm not afraid to tell him how I feel. I'm afraid to fall in love and get my heart broken."

"So is everyone else, but it doesn't mean it stops them from doing it." She smiled at me sadly and put her phone in her purse. "I'm gonna get to work. I think you need to be alone to think about this."

I agreed with her. As much as I didn't want to. I didn't want to think about this. My mind was made up, and he'd all but agreed. He hadn't exactly told me we should take it further.

Sure, he'd said that a part of him wished we'd

never said it was just the weekend, but that didn't equal "Let's see each other in real life."

Maybe I was beating a dead horse to make myself feel better, but whatever. I had to do what I had to do to convince myself this was the right choice.

No, you know what? I didn't need to convince myself because I already knew it was, and I didn't need to justify myself to anyone else either.

There.

I pulled my sketchbook over in front of me and pulled out a pencil.

I couldn't keep Adam, but I could keep one of his poppies.

CHAPTER TWENTY-TWO
POPPY

Time Heals Cuts, Not Hearts

"Will you please turn that off?"

Avery looked over her shoulder at me.

"What?" she asked, eyes fluttering innocently.

I looked at the screen. Adam Winters sat on my TV in all his handsome glory, doing a press conference for some sponsorship deal he'd just signed.

It was cool. It was fine. It'd been three weeks. I was so over it.

"You know exactly what," I said to her, sitting at the table. "Do you have to watch him?"

"I like hockey."

"You haven't watched hockey the entire time we've lived together, and this isn't even hockey. You're trying to make a point." I picked up my paintbrush and dipped it in the red paint I'd mixed earlier that day. I'd been trying to finish the poppy for weeks, and now all I had was a photo I'd had to take.

Avery sighed and muted the TV. "I don't get it. It's been three weeks. This shouldn't bother you, and if it does, you need to call him."

"I think he's doing just fine without the random redhead he spent a weekend with," I retorted. Especially if the figures the media were throwing around were correct.

"Poppy. You've started following the news on the Storms and you actually Googled him last week."

"I'm not following anything. It's that freaky thing the internet does when it gives you ads about things you've never Googled."

"Okay, so what about Googling him?"

"I don't have to justify my Google searches to you. I didn't make you explain when you searched for lesbian porn."

She shrugged. "Totally straight, but it's hot."

"Your porn is your porn. He's my porn, and I had a moment of weakness." I added a smidge of detail to a petal. "It didn't mean anything."

"It didn't mean anything? I think you miss him, or you wouldn't care so much that he's on TV."

"I don't know him enough to miss him."

"You know him plenty!"

"I'm trying to concentrate over here, Aves."

She shook her head and put the volume back on.

All right, so I wasn't over it. It bugged me. I didn't want to see his face if I couldn't kiss it and I didn't want to hear his voice unless it was in my ear.

Three weeks. It'd been three weeks and I'd thought about him every day. I'd drafted texts I'd never sent and hovered on the call button way too many times, but I'd never been able to do it. How lame was I?

"Can you at least turn it down if you won't turn it off?" I asked Avery.

"Nope."

That was that, I guess.

I did my best to block out everything that was coming from that direction to focus on adding the finer details to my poppy. The seeds, the shadowing, the tiny things that would preoccupy my brain and stop me paying attention to him on the TV.

I even hummed. Hum, hum, hum. A tune I didn't even know, but one that was designed to make me not listen.

"Oh my God call him!" Avery yelled, throwing the remote in my direction.

I ducked, and it hit the fridge behind me, falling to the door. The back popped off on contact, meaning the batteries went scattering across the floor.

"If that still works, you're gonna be so lucky," I told her.

"Poppy."

"No."

"Poppy."

"Go away."

"Poppy!"

"No!" I was about to throw something of my own when my phone rang. I pushed the chair back and glanced at the screen. "It's my dad," I told her expectant face.

She sulked and went back to watching Adam.

"Hey Dad," I said, answering. "What's up?"

"Your mother wants to have dinner this weekend," he said without even greeting me.

"Can't wait."

"And she wants Adam there."

I froze. "What—what does she want him there for?"

"She said she didn't get to speak to him as much as she'd liked at the wedding, and since we're coming for a meeting, if he's in town, she'd like to see him."

Shit.

Fuck.

Ass.

Assfuck.

I was in trouble.

Again.

"Oh, right, well, um." I turned away from Avery's flapping hands. "When is it? Saturday?"

"Yes. At six. She booked a table already."

"At least I don't have a cook," I said. "I can see if he's free. He's pretty busy at the minute."

"I saw his new deal. Cool, huh?"

"Yep. Very cool." *Please stop talking.*

As if he knew what I'd been thinking, Dad coughed. "Right, I should be off. Have a conference call coming. Just thought I'd give you the heads up."

"Thanks, Dad. Appreciate it."

"Love you, Pops."

"Love you. See you Saturday. Bye." I hung up and put my phone on the table, clapping my hand over my mouth.

Avery got up and walked over to me. "What's wrong?"

"My parents are coming into town for dinner on Saturday."

"Oh no."

"And they want Adam there."

"Oh no."

"Oh yes." I slumped into my chair and buried my face in my hands.

"Well," she said, opening the fridge. "I guess you have to call him after all."

I flipped her the bird. "I need to think." I got up and walked to my room, shutting the door behind me.

Then, I flopped face-first onto my bed and screamed into my pillow.

Fuck.

I pocketed the tip from the not-so-generous table and tossed the ticket in the bin. Today had sucked—work had been good, but my mind wasn't fully focused. I couldn't stop thinking about that stupid dinner.

I hated past me. She was an idiot.

"Hey, Poppy? You have a new table. He's been there a few minutes." My curvaceous co-worker Yvonne slipped behind me, rubbing her sizeable bosom against my back, to get to the register.

I looked up. "Oh, thanks. I'll head over there now." I pulled my pad out of my purse and clicked my pen as I approached the table. "Hi, I'm Poppy and I'll be your server this evening. What can I get you?"

"I'll have the bacon cheeseburger."

Oh no.

"With a lemonade."

Oh fuck.

"And a conversation?" Adam Winters dropped the menu and looked at me with a smile that sent my heart skipping through the roof.

My lips parted, but no sound came out. I was completely frozen in place, except for my heart. Holy hell, that thing was beating.

Me? I was dying.

"Well, I was expecting shock, but not total horror," he quipped.

I brought my hand to my mouth and stifled a small laugh. "I'm sorry. I just—yeah. I didn't expect you to be hiding behind that menu."

"Surprise." He smirked. "I wanted to talk to you."

"Uh...I have to finish my shift." I moved uncomfortably. "It's like thirty minutes. Can you wait?"

"I didn't order a burger to sit and stare at it, Red."

A shiver went down my spine at the nickname. "Oh—you, you actually want the food?"

He scratched at his jaw, grinning. "Yeah. If I'm coming in here, I'm breaking my diet."

Of course. Of course he wanted food. Ugh, I was an idiot.

"Okay. Sure. What burger was it?" I swallowed.

"Bacon cheeseburger."

"And a drink, was, uh..."

"Lemonade."

I scribbled it down. "Is that everything?"

"Do I get that conversation?"

I nodded.

"Then that's everything." His smile was lopsided.

I dipped my head to hide my own. "I'll be right back with that lemonade."

It took everything I had in me not to run back to the counter and punch the order through the kitchen on the machine. My co-worker was still standing there, and she looked at me with a twisted smile.

"Is that Adam Winters?"

I nodded.

"Do you know each other?"

I cleared my throat. "You could say that."

"You slept with him."

"That's neither here nor there," I replied.

"So, what's he here for? To deny his undying love for you? To profess his desire to have your babies?"

I coughed on my own spit. Seriously. "What are you smoking? No, here's not here for that!"

She raised her eyebrows. "Girl, how do you know?"

"Because it's not like that."

"Yeah? Is that why he can't stop lookin' at you like you gonna be his dessert?"

I glanced over at him, and Yvonne was right. He was staring at me, a smile on his lips.

"Oh God," I moaned, my cheeks flushing bright red.

"Mhmm," she said, looking at me. "This more than a booty call, huh?"

"I get it from Avery at home. You stop it." I tapped her with my pen and walked out of our station. "Don't you have customers to serve?"

She glanced over at Adam appreciatively. "I'd like to serve yours," she said with a wriggle of her huge bosom.

"Oh sweet Jesus," I muttered. "Well, he wants a lemonade. You're free to handle that."

She tugged down her shirt and adjusted her boobs. "I got you, baby girl."

I walked off, shaking my head and smiling. Lord, she was something else.

—•••—

"Whatever Yvonne said to you, ignore it," I said as Adam pushed open the door to the restaurant and held it open for me.

He half-grinned. "She's a character."

"You literally don't know the half of it." I shook my head and pulled my purse up onto my shoulder. "Where do you want to go?"

"I figured we could go to the park. I doubt you

want to go all the way to my place, and I guess Avery isn't at work?"

"She's home." *And she'd have a field day if I took you with me...*

"Park it is."

We fell into step beside each other. My fingers twitched, and it felt weird to not reach for his hand. It'd happened so naturally when we were in Key West. Our hands had simply gravitated toward each other.

Adam stuffed his hands in the pockets of his shorts. Did he feel the same? I knew I felt weird. I couldn't believe he was actually in front of me—or next to me, whatever. It was all the same.

And I was not over him. Not even a little bit.

Damn it.

We turned to the park, and I let him lead me to a private spot where nobody would see us. I was grateful for that—I didn't fancy my face plastered over sports pages or whatever.

I sat on the grass and put my purse down next to me. Adam sat opposite me, leaning back on his hands and stretching his legs out while I leaned back against a tree trunk.

"How are you doing?" he asked, looking at me with his bright blue eyes.

"I'm good," I said, somewhat evasively. "You?"

"I'm good. Training. Working."

"Yeah, Avery was watching you on TV yesterday. Something about a sponsorship deal?"

His eyebrow quirked. "You didn't watch?"

"I have no interest in sports," I reminded him. "Why would I watch?"

"I'm pretty interesting."

"Depends who you ask and whether or not it's

dark and there are sharks around."

He choked back a laugh. "How's your foot?"

"Healed. I saw a doctor when I got back just in case. Just a slightly deep cut from a stone, so you were right." I shrugged. "But it solidified I'm never getting in the ocean in the dark again."

"I'm right there with you on that, Red."

Why did that once-hated nickname now give me chills? Damn damn damn it.

"So. Why'd you come find me at work?"

His eyebrow went up again.

"That came out a little blunt." I bit the side of my bottom lip. "I mean. Shit."

Adam laughed, dropping his head back slightly. "I get it. I should have called you. Sorry."

"Eh, it's all right. I needed to call you anyway."

"You did?"

"Don't even think about it. I asked you first." I pointed at him.

He held up a hand with another laugh. "Okay, okay. Your dad called me this morning."

Oh no.

"Oh no."

Adam looked at me with a wry smile.

"Wait—how does my dad have your number?" I frowned. What sense did that even make?

"He...kind of asked me for it at the wedding. I didn't see how I could say no. I didn't think he'd ever actually call me."

I rubbed my temples. "Sweet baby Jesus on drugs. I bet I know why he called."

"Dinner. Saturday night."

"Yep. He called me yesterday and told me Mom wants to see you. I was growing a pair so I could call you and ask you, but I guess Dad beat me to it."

"He called and invited me. I didn't want to just show up, and I had today off training, so I thought I'd come see you in person."

I pushed hair behind my ear. "You could have called."

"I could have called," he said, tilting his head to the side. "But, Red, I wouldn't have gotten to see you then, would I?"

I blushed lightly. "I don't suppose you would have." I paused and played with the hem of my shirt. "Look, you don't have to. I told him you were busy so probably couldn't come. It's fine."

"Do you want me to come?"

"You're busy. You have a million other things you need to do—"

"That's not what I asked, Red." He shifted so he was closer to me and I could all but feel his leg as it got close to mine. "I asked you if you want me to come."

I took a deep breath and looked away for a minute. "Do you want to come?"

His lips pulled to one side. "Well, I don't particularly want to have dinner with your mother, no. I feel like there'll be all sorts of questions I don't want to answer."

That was the story of my life.

"It's fine," I said. "I'll just—"

"But I want to have dinner with you," he added softly, his eyes capturing mine. "And if that means your parents are there, too, then that's perfectly fine with me. And pretending to be your boyfriend for a few more hours isn't such a hardship, either."

"I…" I trailed off.

This didn't help. This was a step backward. I was

trying to get over him—and failing, but whatever—and this wasn't going to do that.

But, fucking hell, I missed him.

And that was crazy. I knew it was crazy. How could you miss someone after only a few days? It was meant to be a fling, nothing more and nothing less. Yet here I was, three weeks after said fling, with a severe case of feelings-itis.

"If you don't want me to, say the word and I won't. I can be busy. It's not a problem," Adam said. "That's why I asked you."

"No, I..." I sighed. "Do you think it's a good idea?"

"No. Absolutely not. But I think we should do it anyway."

"Okay," I said quietly. "Pick me up at five-thirty."

"You got it."

CHAPTER TWENTY-THREE
ADAM

A Series of Bad Ideas

"You've lost your mind," Warren said, shaking his head. "One weekend was bad enough."

"He ain't wrong," Kyle piped in, putting down the weight he'd been using.

I stared at them both. "I like her, all right?"

"We know. You've been a miserable bastard ever since you got back from that wedding. I told you to just fucking call her." Warren snorted.

"I didn't want to. She made it perfectly clear that what we do, all the traveling, all that shit, isn't for her," I said.

"Then why the fuck are you having dinner with her family on Saturday?" Kyle sat on the weights bench in front of me and leaned forward, elbows on his knees. "Just...why?"

"If you had the chance to see Keisha one more time, would you?" I said, referring to his girlfriend. "Poppy was pretty clear that she's not the kind of woman who can hack what we do. That's fine. But I didn't exactly tell her that I wanted to try it."

"So that's what you're gonna do? Pretend to be her damn boyfriend and tell her how you really feel?"

"Maybe. I don't know." I hadn't thought that far ahead. I just wanted to see her again, 'cause fuck me, I missed her. I missed her mouth and her laugh and her sass. I missed fucking everything about the feisty redhead who'd barreled into my life like a tornado.

Warren smacked his lips. "It makes sense, but only if you're gonna be honest with her. You have to get closure on this chick, because she's been distracting you since you got back."

And wasn't that the truth. Poppy Dunn had consumed my mind. I'd thought about her every single day, and it'd done nothing but piss me off that I hadn't had the balls to call her.

It was easier to walk into her damn restaurant and see her in person than it was to pick up the phone.

"Makes sense. I'll do dinner, then after, we'll get a drink and I'll tell her how I feel. If she tells me no, fine. She can leave without being under pressure." I rubbed the back of my neck. "If she tells me yes, we'll figure it all out."

"Okay, but you've never had a relationship with anyone since you got drafted," Kyle pointed out. "It's not like Keisha and me where we've been together since college. By the sounds of it, Poppy doesn't even like hockey."

"She didn't know who I was when we met," I reminded him. "Of course she doesn't like hockey."

"See, that's my favorite fuckin' thing about this," Warren said. "All the girls in the world throw themselves at Mr. Fuckin' Superstar over here, and he picks the one damn girl in the world who has no idea who he is."

"She's the most genuine one." Kyle shrugged and got up to adjust the weight of the machine. "She just saw the lovable asshole we're so fond of, not the mega-rich superstar."

"She didn't know, and she doesn't care." I leaned forward and rubbed my hands down my face.

"How do you deal with the fact you don't know how to have a relationship on the road? She has a life here, right? A job? An apartment?" Kyle sat back down. "It's a big change."

"I can make it work." I knew it. I knew we could if we tried. "I just never found anyone worth trying for until her."

My two closest friends on the team shared a look.

"Well, fuck," Warren said simply.

"You make it sound like I'm a playboy bachelor," I grumbled,

Kyle paused. "No. But you've always put hockey first. Not that it's a bad thing," he added quickly. "We all do it, but nobody as diligently as you, man. If you're willing to push it aside, even just a little, for a girl you've known less than a week in the total time you've spent together, she's gotta be somethin'."

Somethin'.

That was one way to describe Poppy Dunn.

And, weirdly, probably the most accurate.

Because she was. She was something.

I just wanted that "something" to be mine.

———

Issy: Did u buy her flowers?

Me: No. It's dinner with her parents.

Issy: U should always buy her flowers.

Me: I thought this trolling stopped when I moved out.

Issy: Not trolling. Just some sisterly advice. If a guy dates me, he better bring me flowers.

Me: If a guy dates you, he better bring security.

Issy: Ur a dick. Go or ur gonna be late. And take flowers.

I rolled my eyes at my little sister. She was the youngest, but fuck me, she was the most headstrong.

Flowers would do nothing in this situation. Despite her insistence that I had to, I liked to think I knew a thing or two more about dating than my twenty-year-old sister.

And, if not, I had issues.

I stuffed my phone into the pockets of my jeans and grabbed my keys and wallet. Poppy's dad had already insisted on buying dinner, but that didn't mean I wouldn't try to hijack that.

I locked the door behind me and headed for my car. I was nervous as fuck. Three weeks without seeing her properly—I didn't count a twenty-minute conversation two days ago as properly—and I felt like a teen boy on his way to the prom.

I just wanted to see her again. If this was the last time I got to see her, then fine. I'd accept it. I could accept it. It wasn't the end of the world—at least that's what I was telling myself.

At the end of it all, Poppy was a flame and she'd burn her own way. If she really believed we couldn't work because of what I did, then I could accept that. But that didn't mean I wouldn't try.

Four days. We spent four fucking days together, and the little pain in the ass had wormed her way under my skin so brilliantly she may as well have been a part of me.

Maybe it wasn't healthy to feel the way I did after so little time. Maybe it wasn't fucking normal that, three weeks later, I was still hung up on the little spitfire. Maybe this whole thing was fucking weird, but I was going to roll with it.

That last night in Key West, on the beach, before she cut her foot and attracted the local marine wildlife, I felt it.

Something took hold of me, and I knew the idea of a fling was fucked. It wouldn't be a fling. It was something more than we'd planned, and fuck, I was done.

I wanted her.

I wanted her then, and I wanted her now. Maybe more so. I should have forgotten about her by now, but I hadn't. Not even close. She consumed me like the fire she was.

I fought off any more thoughts of her as I headed across the city to her apartment. I knew Avery would be there, and I didn't know what to say to her. We hadn't spent a lot of time together at the wedding, at least not enough to know if she was for or against me and Poppy.

Fuck, was this what my life had become? Wondering if her best friend was on side for us being together?

Jesus fucking Christ. I needed to get ahold of myself. I was losing my goddamn mind.

After too many minutes, I pulled into the parking lot outside their apartment five minutes early. I killed the engine and smirked as Poppy's words ran through my mind—she was always late.

Would she be ready now? Probably not, knowing her tendency to piss off her mom at every turn.

I locked my car and headed for the building. Pressing the buzzer on the outside of the building, I waited for someone to let me in.

"Hello?" Avery's voice crackled through it.

"Hey. It's Adam."

"Oh!" Silence. "It's open!"

"Thanks, Avery." I pushed the door open and make my way up to the apartment. My shirt felt too tight and my goddamn stomach felt like it needed to roll like a ball going down a hill.

I still didn't know what I was doing, not even as I knocked at their door.

"It's open," Avery called.

Swallowing, I pushed the door open and stepped inside. "Hey," I said.

"Hey!" Avery bounded up off the sofa and hugged me. "How are you doing?"

"I'm good. How are you?" I returned the hug.

"I'm good, thanks. She's not ready yet. Make yourself at home. She's gonna be at least twenty minutes."

"I heard that!" Poppy yelled from somewhere in the apartment.

Avery rolled her eyes. "Seriously, Adam, sit. The girl is nowhere near ready. She's a mess."

"I heard that, too!" A door opened. "Shut your dirty mouth!"

I laughed into my hand.

Avery grinned. "She's so fun to piss off," she whispered. "Get dressed, for God's sake, or I'm calling your mother!" she shouted.

"I hate you!" A door slammed, and Avery's smile only got wider.

"So," she said in a hushed voice, perching on the edge of the sofa. "You gonna tell her you like her?"

"I'd love a drink, thanks, Avery. Do you mind if I use your bathroom? Training's going good. Thanks for asking," I said dryly.

She snorted. "Good to know. Kitchen's right there. Well, are you?"

"It's not that simple and you know it."

"Actually. I think you're both complicating it beyond belief," she said quietly. "But that's just my opinion, and opinions are like assholes. Everybody has one."

"And some people speak with theirs," I added.

"Nailed it." She winked. She stood up and went to the hall and banged on a door. "Poppy! Hurry up! You're gonna be late!"

"If my mother expects me to be on time she's a damn idiot!" she yelled through the door.

"She's a little tense," Avery whispered.

Something slammed on a door. "You are a bad whisperer and a terrible friend. Go to work, you heathen!"

I paused, trying not to laugh.

"Fine! I'm going!" Avery pounded on the door with a fist. "But your fake boyfriend is out here looking like a bar of chocolate during shark week—"

What the?

"—So you get your ass out here before I drag him to a street corner and start soliciting his services to the ladies to bump my bank account!" Avery winked at me.

"I swear to God—" Poppy snapped.

Avery grabbed her purse and stopped at the door. In an extra loud voice, she said, "You guys have fun! I'm working 'til one tonight, but Adam, I want her home by midnight, you hear?"

"You got it." It was so fucking hard not to laugh.

"And if you're still here tomorrow morning, I hear you make a mean omelet." She grinned, opening the door. "There are eggs, bacon, and mushrooms in the fridge. I won't be mad waking up to your fine ass making me breakfast in bed."

"*Avery!*"

"And now I'm leaving," she said with one final smile my way.

I rubbed my hand down my face, laughing.

Holy shit, Avery knew how to piss her off.

I sat back in the chair and waited for Poppy to come out. She was taking her sweet-ass time, and one glance at my watch told me we were going to be late.

Just as I settled in to watch TV, a door opened on the other side of the apartment. I turned my head in that direction, and Poppy stepped out into my view.

The black dress she wore hugged her figure to perfection, even as she muttered to herself and flattened it out across his hips. Her hair hung around her shoulders in her signature loose curls, and the hot-pink lipstick that coated her lips made me want to kiss her so fucking bad.

She stopped, looking up when she caught me staring at her. "You want a picture?"

"Yeah, actually." I smiled at her. "Got a problem with that?"

She blushed, tucking her hair behind her ear. "Let's go before I get my ass kicked. And, if we're late, it's traffic." She grabbed a purse off the kitchen table that was covered in painting things and shoved her phone in it. "Let's go."

"Hang on." I turned off the TV by the remote and got up, intercepting her before she reached the door. "I'm officially your fake boyfriend again, which means I get to do this."

Cupping the back of her neck, I kissed her. She melted into me, her hands instantly going to the sides of my shirt, and that told me all I needed—all I wanted—to know.

I wasn't the only one with feelings.

"Now we can go," I whispered against her lips.

Her throat bobbed, and she nodded. "Let's go."

CHAPTER TWENTY-FOUR
POPPY

Questions and Absolutely No Answers

Adam locked the car in the parking lot of the restaurant and immediately drew me into him. His arm snaked easily around my waist, and I tucked into his side as if I'd never left it.

It annoyed me how easy it was. How easy the kiss in the apartment had been. How right it felt to get into his car with him holding the door. How goddamn perfect it felt to be nestled into his side without a care in the world.

Except for my parents being inside, that was.

We were lead right to our table. Somewhere between the hostess' stand and the table, Adam had slipped his fingers through mine, and we moved so fluidly together.

That scared me. It was oh-so-natural, and while I was slowly accepting my feelings for him, I'd never really believed he felt anything serious for me.

The ease with which he accepted being my boyfriend yet again hit me hard.

He'd told me in Key West that pretending to be my boyfriend was the easiest thing he'd ever done.

Was that still true?

Because fuck me sideways with a suitcase, pretending to be Poppy, Adam's girlfriend, was so fucking easy it was scary.

Mom and Dad were sitting at the table as we approached. The greeting was easy and simple—hugs, kisses, handshakes. We all took our seats and Dad poured us all a glass of wine, which Adam rejected since he was driving.

Mom's eyebrows shot up at that, and I could tell she was impressed by that. He wasn't even willing to risk one small glass. Because my dad's idea of a glass of wine was not what people in a restaurant assumed to be a glass. There was a reason he always poured his own wine.

A glass of wine was just that—a glass.

If wine was meant to be half the size, the glasses would be smaller.

"So, Adam, we heard about your new sponsorship deal," Dad said. "We're thrilled for you. Tell us a little more."

Adam shifted, slightly uncomfortably. "It's the team sponsor. We agreed on a deal for a new line of sneakers and other sports equipment, mostly designed for helping children get into hockey. The value of it is mostly an investment—I don't need the money, so we agreed the deal on the basis that ninety-five percent of the agreed figure goes into junior hockey across the United States and Canada."

"Are the media figures accurate?" Mom asked.

"Mom!" I sputtered. "You can't ask that!"

"He doesn't have to answer," she said like I was stupid. "It's just a question."

"It's okay." Adam squeezed my thigh. "Yes, the figures are accurate. My team is trying to get out about the agreement, but it's proving important."

"Well, I imagine the media are more concerned about why hockey's highest-paid player needs a thirty-million-dollar sponsorship deal," Dad said matter-of-factly.

Jesus Christ.

Kill me.

"You're correct," Adam said. "They are. My team is working overtime, but most people don't want to know the truth. Even during the press conference, they were unconcerned about the real purpose."

"Get the sponsors to say it," I said, reaching for my wine. "They have a bigger platform than you do. Have them issue a statement to all media outlets regarding the terms. If they don't issue the statement, the sponsors remove all advertisement from their channels. It's not hard."

Slowly, Adam turned to me. "You're brilliant."

"I have something called common sense," I retorted. "The media likes money. Take the money, boom." I shrugged.

"I see studying marketing taught you something," Mom said, smiling almost proudly.

"Common sense," I repeated, taking another drink.

Dad chuckled. "She's right."

"You studied marketing?" Adam asked me.

"Can I get your order?" The waitress asked, interrupting us. We all quickly rattled off our orders, even though Adam and I had barely had a chance to look at the menu.

"It was a side subject," I said to Adam. "Not my major."

"You never discussed majors?" Dad asked.

"It didn't come up," I said tightly.

"What was your major?" Adam asked.

I took another drink, and Dad grabbed the wine bottle to top me up. I shot him a grateful look.

Mom sniffed. "Art."

"Now, Miranda, there's nothing wrong with art."

Dad put the bottle down. "You know she's talented."

Adam tilted his head and looked at me. "The painting stuff. On your table. That's yours."

Kill me.

Someone had to.

I'd take death by fork at this point.

"You didn't know?" Mom grasped her glass and looked at us with interest.

Seriously. Now. Stab me.

"It's just a hobby," I said tightly. "I paint for fun now."

"There you go," Dad said. "Problem solved."

"Will you show me some?" Adam asked. "Do you have any at your place?"

Yes. Your poppy.

"A few." I was deliberately evasive.

"You still paint?" Mom's eyebrows shot up.

"I need to use the bathroom." I pushed back from the table and headed the way of the bathroom.

More than anything, I needed to breathe. My feelings for Adam were going haywire, and the whole painting thing—yes, art was my damn major, but it was now just a passion—was driving me insane.

I couldn't take this anymore.

I locked myself in the cubicle in the women's bathroom, sat on top of the toilet seat, and took a deep breath. I took several, actually.

Why the hell had I agreed to this? Why had I done any of this? Fuck me, I was an idiot. A royal fucking idiot.

I took a few minutes to just sit and breathe and think about the hell that would ensue. I decided I was going to do a few things: I would be quiet and only speak when spoken to. And, if anyone asked, I was on my damn period.

I unlocked the cubicle door and stepped out in front of the mirror. I was still alone, so I washed my hands and dried them before stepping out.

Right into my father.

He held one finger up to his lips and pulled me farther down the hall and close to the staff-only room. "I know," he said quietly.

"You know what?" I asked, smoothing out my dress.

"I know about you and Adam."

I raised my eyebrows.

"I know that you had no damn idea who he was until you introduced him to us."

"I'm gonna kill Rosie," I hissed.

Dad held his hands up. "Listen to me, Pops. I know. She told me. But I also know you like each other. In around thirty minutes, I'm going to have an emergency call from my office and your mom and I have to leave immediately. We'll cover the bill, but—"

"You meddler!" I jabbed my finger into his arm. "Dad! What the hell?"

"I like him," Dad said simply. "I think he's perfect for you and I think you're a stubborn pain in the ass who won't admit that you love him."

"I don't love him."

"You're proving my point, Pops."

"You're a meddler," I repeated. "And I'm annoyed."

"Eh. It worked." He shrugged. "I have a flask of whiskey in my pocket. Want some?"

I held out my hand.

Without speaking, he put the flask in my hand, and I took a big mouthful. I was so annoyed—so freaking annoyed—but what could I do?

Kill my sister, for one. Although, I'd have to consider if that crime was worth the time.

Probably not.

"What do you expect me to do now?" I asked him.

"I expect you to tolerate your mother—who is being particularly difficult today—for thirty minutes. Smile. Nod. Eat. That's all you have to do."

"Mm. You owe me for this, Dad."

"Why? I'm doing you a favor."

"No, you're meddling. And making me have dinner with Mom for no real reason. You owe me."

He sighed. "Fine. What do I owe you?"

"I'll let you know when I figure it out," I said, walking back down the hall.

What was wrong with my family?

———···———

"I'm so sorry," Dad said, standing at the end of the table. "Miranda, sweetheart, we have to go. I've got a call at work—one of my clients is having an emergency I have to deal with."

I resisted the urge to roll my eyes. I was still annoyed, and I still wasn't on board with my father's plan.

I thought the whole thing was ridiculous. I was doing just fine until he'd stuck his nose in, and I'd texted my sister a few choice words, too.

They mostly consisted of "fuck" and "you" and "off," but still.

They were words.

"Oh, goodness. Of course." Mom dabbed at her

mouth with her napkin. "I'm so sorry. Honey, did you take care of the bill?"

"It's all handled. I'm sorry." Dad kissed me on the cheek then leaned over to shake Adam's hand. "Hopefully we can have dinner again soon."

Not on your nelly, Dad.

Mom kissed both our cheeks and scurried out to Dad saying, "I'll drop you back at the house, Miranda, then go to the office…"

My God. The little shit had it all planned out.

And yes, I would refer to him as a shit. He was a shit. I was mad.

I drank the rest of my wine in one go.

"That was weird," Adam said, turning around.

I peered at him out of the corner of my eye. "Not really."

"What do you mean?"

I sighed and put the empty glass down. How the hell was I supposed to say this? There was no way to say it that wasn't all weird.

Like, hey, my dad knows we're fake and wanted to set us up for real because he knows that I'm basically on the edge of falling in love with you.

No.

Jesus, no.

"Poppy."

I glanced at the wine. That's right. I finished it. Fuck this.

"Dad, uh…He knows," I said vaguely.

Adam stared at me to elaborate.

"He knows I didn't know who you were at the wedding," I said quietly, looking down. "He spoke to Rosie. She told him everything."

"Fucking traitor," he muttered.

I covered my mouth with my hand and laughed into my palm. Look—there was no arguing with the cold, hard truth. And that was the truth. My sister was a damn traitor.

"You know the British behead people for that," Adam added.

"Maybe two hundred years ago. Probably not so much now," I said. "But, yes. She told him. He set us up tonight."

Adam rubbed his chin. "So we sat through the stress of your mother to get set up? Couldn't he arrange that we all meet and then not come? If I was setting my son up, that's what I'd do."

"Your son? Why not your daughter?"

"Because any date of my daughter's, is getting greeted with the barrel of a shotgun," he replied.

"Well, any date of my son's is getting greeted the same way." I folded my arms. "That's how this works. You date my child, you get to sit your ass down and tell me about yourself before I agree."

Adam tilted his head. "Did your dad ever do that?"

"Does my dad look like he's the type to threaten dates with a gun?"

"No. Do I?"

"Only because you have muscles," I replied. "My hair makes me scary."

"Oh, yes. Look at those curls. They're terrifying."

"The temper," I reminded him. "Like a match."

He reached over and twirled a curl around his finger. "Is that why you've had a face like a smacked ass all night? Because you knew this was a set-up?"

"Mhmm." I met his eyes. "I'm not happy."

"There are worse guys you could be set up with."

"I'm not saying it's bad, I'm—"

"Your dad set us up for a reason, Poppy. It wasn't because we'd be a good ice-skating team."

It was because we like each other.

Those words hung between us. Unsaid. Neither of us wanted to admit it until the other did, so we were stuck in a loop of silence.

Adam sighed, releasing my hair. "You want me to take you home?"

I nodded, picking my purse up from my feet. "Please."

"All right, Red. Come on."

Adam pulled open my door. "I'll walk you up."

"You don't have to."

"I know. But I'm a gentleman, and that's what gentlemen do." He held the door for me to get out of the car. "Come on."

I got out, clutching my purse to me. I made it to the door before him and punched in the code, slipping through and trying to close the door before he made it there.

I failed.

Adam put his foot between the door and the frame. "Nice try, Red."

"Fuck it." I turned and went to the stairs, but he beat me there, too. Instead of letting me walk, he scooped me up in one movement, despite my protests, and threw me over his shoulder.

"Shut up," he said. "You'll disturb your neighbors."

"You're manhandling me!"

He took to the next flight of stairs. "Hardly. I'm giving you a helping hand."

He and I had different ideas of what a helping hand was. "Try offering me your arm next time, Fred Flintstone."

"Yes, Wilma."

"I can kick your balls from here."

"You won't do that."

"How do you know?"

"Because you like my balls."

"Wrong," I said. "I'm indifferent to balls in general. Footballs, basketballs, hockey balls—"

He coughed. "Pucks."

"What?"

"You play hockey with pucks. Not balls."

"Hockey is weird," I said matter-of-factly. "And so are you. Now put me down."

"Gladly." He slid me down his body. "Here's your apartment."

I rolled my eyes and pushed him away from me. "You're annoying me. This has been the most frustrating night ever." I dug in my purse for my keys and yanked them out from the bottom corner.

Why were they always in the bottom corner?

I jammed them in the door and twisted, unlocking it. The apartment was completely silent since Avery was at work, and I was looking forward to hiding in the bathroom.

That was how normal, rational people dealt with complete emotional upheaval, wasn't it?

I stepped inside and turned, catching Adam's eye. There was something rueful about his expression—a sadness that glinted in his gaze.

I put down my purse and hugged the door.

"Thanks for humoring my parents," I said softly. "Sorry it wasn't what we thought."

He shrugged one shoulder, lifting it to his ear before he dropped it down. "Hey—we got away with it for this long. It is what it is, right?"

"Right." My heart clenched.

Stupid heart.

"Now your dad is on your side when you have to explain why we didn't work," Adam continued. "Because that's how this goes, isn't it?"

No.

"Yeah. I mean... We wouldn't be here if it weren't for my dad, so... Yeah."

God, he was so beautiful.

This is why I didn't do this again. This is why I couldn't see him. I'd said goodbye once. I didn't want to have to do it a second time.

"Thank you," I said again.

Adam cupped the side of my face. "No, Red. Thank you."

He kissed me, his lips touching mine with an air of finality that forced a lump in my throat. Tingles ran over my skin, and I knew this was it.

This was goodbye.

This was where our crazy, fake romance ended.

And I wasn't okay with it.

He pulled back, running his thumb over my lower lip one last time. "See you, Red."

"See you." My voice was barely there, and I pushed the door shut so I didn't have to look at him.

It clicked, and I flattened my back against it, squeezing my eyes shut.

God, he was there. He was right fucking there.

Four fucking days. Four fucking days had me

twisted up like a freshly-knitted scarf.

Wood.

Wood was all that separated us.

What if I opened the door? Would he still be there? What if I pulled off my shoes and chased him?

Tonight, technically, we were still fake. Sure, my feelings were hella real, but he was right fucking there.

Could I let him leave without kissing him one more time? Like I meant it? If I kissed him hard enough, would I be able to tell him that I was falling for him?

That I was falling for him based on four days and those memories on loop.

Was that possible?

Would I hate myself if I tried?

Would I hate myself if I didn't?

Oh, fuck, man. Why did he have to be perfect? Why did he have to be everything? Why couldn't he be bad in bed or have one leg shorter than the other?

Why did he have to make me so completely obsessed with him?

And why did the thought of never seeing him again—ever—hurt me so fucking much?

I kicked off my shoes and kicked them right across the floor. My hands dove into my hair as I squeezed my eyes shut again.

This decision would change everything. It would either tell him how I wanted him, or it would put the nail of the coffin of what could have been.

I turned.

Took a deep breath.

Grabbed the handle.

And pulled out the stupidest game in the book— the quick answer game. The first thing that popped into my head would be the right thing to do.

Pink or purple?
Pink.
Tacos or pizza?
Pizza.
Wine or vodka?
Vodka.
Disney or Universal?
Disney.
Heels or flats?
Flats.
Open or closed?

CHAPTER TWENTY—SIX
POPPY

Repeat, Repeat, Repeat

I tugged the door open.

Adam was leaning against the wall opposite the door, one arm wrapped around his stomach and the other hand was in his hair.

He was standing there.

He looked up at me.

I opened my mouth, but nothing came out. I didn't know what to say to him. I didn't know what I could say to him.

But I'd opened this door for a reason, and I hope he knew it wasn't because of a spider in my bathtub or something.

He held my gaze for what felt like forever, the intensity in his eyes chilling in the best kind of way.

Slowly, I lifted one shoulder to my ear and dropped it again in a shrug.

He wasted no time closing the distance between us. He grasped the sides of my face and kissed me, staggering us into the apartment. He kicked the door shut with a bang behind us, and I grabbed his shirt.

The kiss was hot and heavy from the get-go, and it was interspersed with breaks to make sure we were heading to my room. Adam kicked the door to that shut, too, and we collapsed together on the bed.

There was a hastiness to our movements—a pure desperation as we clawed at each other's clothes and removed them. As I sat up to remove my dress, as he pulled back to shrug off his shirt and undo his pants.

It was hot and hard, neither of us willing to give anything less than all of us. We wasted no time getting to our underwear, and it was Adam's control under pressure as I was stripped to my bra and thong.

His hands explored my body as thoroughly as his mouth did, from unclasping my bra to tugging my panties down my legs so I was completely naked. He was fully in control as his mouth made its way from my neck to my nipples to my clit.

He was all in control as shivers and hot flushes simultaneously made their way across my skin. As he moved to remove his pants. To whisper into my ear that he trusted me, did I trust him, because he just wanted me.

Nothing else.

I answered simply, reaching between us and guiding his bare cock inside me. It was pure hunger and desire as he moved inside my wet pussy, and I wrapped my legs around his waist, tilting my hips so he could be deeper.

It was raw and hard, and I wanted it all. We kissed just as passionately as we fucked, and even as his fingers dug into my ass and my teeth scraped his lower lip, the sensations that rocketed through my body were insane.

The pain, the pleasure, the downright rawness of how I clenched around him as I came from his relentless fucking.

It was everything.

It was perfect.

It was the things fairytales were made of, because it wasn't romantic at all. It didn't have to be. It was real and uncontrolled, and it was the ultimate release of all the things I feared we'd both kept to ourselves over the past weeks.

And, as he kissed me hard, tongue fighting mine, his cock pressed hard me, I had the fleeting feeling that I had nothing to fear at all.

Because this was the most honest we'd ever been with each other, and neither of us had said a damn thing.

I guess actions really did speak louder than words.

Adam pulled out of me and rolled to the side, holding me against him for a second. He buried his face in my hair, and I let him curl his body around mine.

I hated being cuddled. Sleeping while cuddling was akin to torture for me, but with him—well, fuck. It was comfortable.

Mostly. I wasn't a light switch. I couldn't turn that shit on and off.

"Are you..." he murmured.

"If I wasn't, that wouldn't have happened," I said back just as quietly. "I didn't know who you were when I took you to my hockey-mad family. The last thing I need is a miniature you at family functions for the rest of my life."

Adam laughed, burying his face in my hair again. His breath danced over my shoulder, teasing goosebumps on my skin.

"Tell that to your dad."

"Please don't ever mention my dad after sex again."

"Does that mean we'll have sex again?"

"Not unless you swear you'll ever mention my dad," I said, swinging my legs out of bed and getting up with a groan.

"Can you bring me a towel?"

I looked over my shoulder at Adam. "Sure. You're the one who needs a towel. That's a bucketful of cum you've got inside you."

"I had it," he said nonchalantly. "Now you've got it."

I grabbed a stuffed bear from the dresser and tossed it at his head. "Shut your mouth." I left the room to the sound of his laughter.

I hated that I liked the sound.

Damn him.

I cleaned up in the bathroom and darted back into my room. Adam was lying on the bed on his back, one leg out of the covers, one arm resting on the pillow over his head.

I threw a towel at him. "I guess you're staying."

He moved the towel beneath the sheets to clean himself. "Are you protesting?"

No.

"No," I said, flicking off the main light. "I was just saying."

"Isn't it early to go to sleep?"

I pawed at the nightstand for the remote and turned on my TV. It immediately produced Netflix. "How do you feel about serial killers?" I asked, rolling over to curl into his side.

"You know," he said, "Pretty damn good."

———•••———

I wandered out of the bedroom to Avery sitting at the dining table and Adam at the stove. Avery was eating, her Kindle in one hand and a fork in the other.

Adam was cooking, humming to the playlist that was quietly beating from Avery's laptop in the living room.

"This is cozy," I muttered, going to the fridge.

Avery grunted, nose in a book.

Adam grabbed me, pulling me to him. "Morning, Red." His greeting was punctuated with a kiss to my lips. "How you doin'?"

I raised my eyebrows.

"We watched Friends while you slept," Avery added.

"Did I wake up in an alternate universe?" I asked, looking between them both. "Are you friends?"

Adam shrugged. "Sure. She's a decent girl. Why wouldn't we be?"

"She's decent? What is she? A pair of jeans?"

"Oh!" Avery snapped her fingers. "If I were, I'd be the pair that hugged your ass like a Care Bear."

I stared at her. "I need new friends."

She laughed as I turned to the coffee machine. Had I stepped into an alternate universe? Why the hell did this all feel so fucking normal? Why was Adam cooking Avery omelets while she read her latest book? Why was I so confused?

Was this my life?

Why didn't I know what was going on?

I sat at the table with my coffee mug. Adam presented me with a perfectly cooked omelet a-la our first morning together, and I stared at it.

I was so confused.

What was happening here?

Why would nobody tell me?

Adam kissed my cheek. "There you go. I have to get to training. Sorry Avery got hers first, but she was awake." He kissed the top of my head and walked to Avery before flicking her hair. "Thanks for the advice, Aves."

Aves?

275

Advice?

Had I slept through the fucking apocalypse?

I sat, dumbfounded, as Adam retreated into my room. Avery ignored me as she ate and read her books.

"Am I missing something?" I asked her.

Avery looked up at me. "I don't know. Are you?"

"I'm asking you, dumbass."

"Are you pissed he made me breakfast before you?"

"What? No." I stabbed my fork into the omelet. "At least, no. No."

"No biggie, then." She scooped another forkful of omelet into her mouth as Adam left my room.

He was wearing exactly what he had been last night. The shirt, the pants, the stubble...

I was still half-asleep. I was in the point of consciousness where nothing made sense. I could feel the sleep in my eyes for the love of fucking God.

Adam rounded the table to me. His hand cupped the back of my neck, and he kissed me. "Hey," he murmured. "I have a wedding to go to and I need a date. Call me."

I blinked at him as he left.

Avery watched the door shut and snorted her omelet across the table.

"Yum." I pushed mine away.

She laughed. "You don't get it, do you?"

I stared at her.

"He doesn't have a fucking wedding. He's playing you at your game. It's fun."

"You know, for my best friend, you take a lot of pleasure in my pain."

Aves shrugged, putting her plate in the sink. "Only when you're dumb about it."

CHAPTER TWENTY–SIX
POPPY

Truth and Tru Dat

I stared at my phone. It'd buzzed three times with Adam's name. I'd ignored it until now, but I finally gave in.

Adam: What's your zodiac sign?
Adam: When's your birthday?
Adam: What would you rate yourself out of ten on blow jobs?

I laughed and tossed my phone.

Fucking hell. We'd reached a new low. I wasn't going to reply to that. He was trying to push me into doing it. I wouldn't give in.

No. No, sir. No, madam. No.

Avery glanced at me. "Adam?"

"No." I went back to painting. I was so close to finishing the poppy. It was nothing more than details and accents.

I wanted to sit here in my corner, ignoring his texts, so I could add the last of my poppy seeds to the image.

"Ohhh-kay," Avery said. "I'm going to work."

"Have fun," I said, focused on the image.

The seeds were everything. The focus of the poppy. The core. I had to get them right.

Seed after seed I painted. All I wanted was the accuracy.

Until my phone rang.

Adam's name flashed on the screen.
I ignored it.
The text was immediate.

Adam: I know you're in there.

I said nothing.

Adam: It's like that, huh?

I finished my poppy seeds.

Adam: I have to talk to you.

I gave in.

Me: What?

His response was instant.

Adam: Open your door.

I wrinkled my face.

Me: No.

I put my phone to the side and wiped my
paintbrush on my arm. I just wanted to get this painting
done. Was it so hard? Was it too much to ask for?
There was a knock at the door.
Avery moved.
"Sit down!" I hissed.
She froze, eyes widening as she looked at me.
"Why?"

"I don't—it's Adam," I finished with a mutter.

"So why can't I let him in?"

"He wants to talk to me."

"Shock horror. A hot, rich guy wants to talk to you."

I flipped her the bird. "It's not that simple."

"I think you're a wimp," she said, getting up.

"I told you not to open the door!"

"I'm getting water!"

My phone buzzed again.

Adam: I know you're in there. I can hear you telling Avery not to answer the door.

Me: You could be guessing based on the fact I don't like people.

Adam: But you like me.

Me: I never said that.

"Hi, Adam!" Avery said brightly, opening the door.

I gasped. "Traitor!"

Adam grinned. "Can I come in?"

"No," I said.

"Sure!" Avery bounced to the side. "I was just on my way out."

"No, you weren't." I glared at her.

Adam stepped inside and put his hands in his pockets. "Going anywhere nice?"

She grabbed her purse and patted it. "Taking my book to get some cake."

"Do they do take-out?"

"You want cake?"

"Chocolate would be great. Thanks. Here. My treat." He pulled out his wallet and looked at me. "You want some cake?"

I stared between them both. "What is happening here?"

"I'll get her cake," Avery said, plucking the twenty-dollar bill from his hand. "You're not getting change on that, by the way."

"Didn't expect to." He chuckled. "Enjoy your cake!"

Seriously.

What was happening?

The door swung shut behind Avery.

I was so confused.

Had they set me up?

"Is this a set-up?" I asked, peering at Adam over the top of my canvas.

He had the decency to look sheepish when he raised one hand and pinched his finger and thumb together. "Little bit."

"Little bit? It's either a set-up or it isn't. I don't like it either way."

"I need to talk to you, and I know you won't let me do that. So I had to be creative."

"Creative? Seems like a blatant violation of my right to ignore you." I sniffed.

"You've been ignoring me all day long, Red."

"I haven't been ignoring you. I've been busy. It's my day off and I want to finish my painting."

"Can I see it?"

I sighed. "You're just gonna walk around the back of me if I say no, so you may as well."

He laughed. "You know me so well."

Scarily so, actually.

He walked around the back of me and gripped the back of the chair. "Whoa."

I hated showing people my paintings.

"Is that a good whoa or a bad one?"

Adam leaned down. "You can't see how amazing this is?"

"No. I'm an artist. I'm a self-deprecating disaster."

He laughed, dropping his head down. "This is incredible. Is it...one of the ones I sent you?"

I swallowed, dipping the brush in the black. "Yes."

"Why did you pick it?"

"Art has to come from the heart." I swallowed again. "That's what was in my heart that day."

"Poppy..."

I dropped the brush and got up, walking around the table. "No. I—I can't have this conversation with you, Adam."

"Then don't talk. I have no problem doing all that if you'll just listen to me."

"I don't want to listen," I said quietly, turning around and meeting his eyes. I hugged myself with my paint-streaked arms. "And it's not because I don't care. I do care. I care about what you want to say, but I also care that it's going to hurt to hear it."

"It doesn't have to hurt to hear it."

"It will, though. We both know—"

"Do you hear yourself?" He pushed off the chair and walked over to me. His hands framed my face, and he forced me to meet his eyes. "Do you hear how ridiculous you sound? No, Red. We don't know anything."

"I know that you could break my heart."

"And I know that you could break mine." He touched his forehead to mine for a second before his eyes locked on mine again. "And I don't care, Poppy. Four days. We had four days together, and three weeks later, I'm still out of my fucking mind thinking about you. You know the last thing I thought about three weeks later? Food."

I bit my bottom lip to stop myself smiling.

"Really great tacos by my mom's house," he went on. "Seriously. Give me all your reasons why we shouldn't try and make us work and I bet I have an answer for every single one."

"Fine." I stepped back out of his touch because I couldn't concentrate when my heart beat stupidly fast. "You're rich and famous."

"Okay, those are two reasons *to* be my girlfriend. Really great ones, actually." He grinned. "You're not starting this very well."

I pursed my lips and moved from hugging myself to folding my arms in annoyance. "You travel all the time."

"Only during the season which is October to April. Little longer if we make the Stanley Cup playoffs. The rest of the time, I'm pretty much right here. And the travel isn't that constant. I can come home or fly you out or we can Facetime."

"I have a Samsung."

"Okay, so we'll Skype every day. Next." He folded his arms, looking way too smug about this.

I was already running out of steam. "I have a job. I can't just drop it to fly out and see you."

"I get the games in advance. We can pick weekends and you can request them off."

Shit.

"Rory will expect you to be his personal coach and show up at all his birthday parties."

"I love Rory. I can cope with that."

"Is there anything you haven't thought of?"

Adam shook his head. "We already went through all the reasons we should fake break up, remember? And before you say it—I can handle the media. Just threaten to sue for harassment and they leave you alone for the most part."

I pursed my lips.

"Run out of reasons, Red?"

"No. I'm thinking." Think, Poppy, think. Damn it.

Ah-ha.

I had it.

"Aunt Blythe!" I pointed at him. "My family!"

He pinched the bridge of his nose and shook his head. "Wow. You really don't want to be with me, do you?"

I covered my face with my hands and laughed. "We don't know each other that well!"

"Bullshit. We talked forever. We know tons about each other. I even know all the things you don't like about yourself." He held his hands out to the sides. "Come on. Admit it. You can't think of one good reason why we shouldn't try this for real."

Man.

I hated it when other people were right. It really messed with my ability to argue with them.

He cupped my face again. "We're good together and you know it, Red. And I'm not just saying this, but seriously. I'm rich. I'm famous. I'm good in bed. I am one hell of a catch."

I closed my eyes and laughed. "I don't even know how to respond to that."

"You agree and say you'll be my girlfriend."

"This feels very high school."

Adam laughed and wrapped his arms around my shoulders. "Jesus, you're stubborn. Is that the hair or just a delightful trait you possess?"

"Probably a mixture of both," I said into his chest. "Mostly a trait though. I'm sure there are nice, non-stubborn gingers out there, but I'm just saying I haven't met one yet." I turned my face to the side. "Do we have to decide this right now? Can't we just see how it goes?"

"Yes, and no. I was explicitly told by Avery that if I leave this apartment and we aren't officially together, she's going to kill you in your sleep." He paused. "And implicate me so I go down with her because orange isn't her color."

"Orange isn't her color," I confirmed. "I would believe her on that."

"Noted."

I sighed and wrapped my arms around his waist. It felt right. Like I was supposed to be here with him. Like I was made to be here. "I'm scared, Adam."

"I know, Red." He kissed the top of my head. "I'm scared, too. I have no idea how to make a relationship work, but I know I want to make it work with you. I believe we can."

"Do you think we're crazy?"

"Absolutely." He laughed into my hair. "But you remember when we were talking on the beach on Sunday night?"

I nodded.

"I told you I'd slow down if I found the person worth slowing down for."

I nodded again.

"I'd already found her," he said softly. "She's

you."

I squeezed him tight, and he did the same to me before he nudged my chin up and kissed me.

"Is that a yes?" he asked against my lips.

I kissed him again. And again. And again.

"That's a yes."

EPILOGUE
POPPY

Happily Ever After

ONE YEAR LATER

"I don't like this," I grumbled as Adam tugged me along the hall with a blindfold over my eyes. "I can't see where I'm going."

"That is kind of the point, Red."

"Is this what living together will be like? If so, I want a refund."

"You can't. Avery already moved in with Warren and your apartment already has a tenant." He laughed.

Without the gift of sight, that laugh was spine-tinglingly delicious.

Damn it.

"I can find another apartment."

"On an artist's wage?"

He had a point. I, myself, was pretty broke. Mostly because I refused to touch the inheritance my parents had finally released to me when I'd made the choice a month ago to quit my job and paint full-time.

I thought I was taking the moral high road. Adam used it to blackmail me into living with him, because once Avery moved out, I couldn't afford the rent if I wouldn't touch it.

All right, so it wasn't blackmail, but it was a very well-thought out argument that I had nothing to counter with.

That was a habit he had. I didn't like it.

"Shut up," I said.

"Okay, stop."

I walked right into him.

"I said stop, Poppy."

"I stopped, Adam. Technically."

He sighed. "You're making this very hard work."

"You did not know what you got yourself in for when you decided to date me for real, did you?"

"I wish I could argue that point."

"I warned you and you didn't listen."

"Great. I'll make that a house rule. 'Listen to Poppy.'"

"Hey, that's valuable advice. Everyone coming here would do well to pay attention to it."

"Noted. Can you stop talking now so I can show you?"

"Show me what?"

"The thing I'm hiding from you," he said slowly.

"Is it food?"

"Why would it be food?"

I shrugged. "It's lunchtime. I'm hungry. Food is plausible."

"Poppy."

"Yes?"

"Shut. *Up.*"

I mimed zipping my lips.

Adam moved behind me and untied the blindfold. The light of the hall was a shock to my eyes, and I had to blink several times before they adjusted, and I no longer felt dizzy.

Focusing, I looked in front of me. "Uh, that's a door."

"You're on fire today," Adam quipped.

I shot him a look. "Why did you blindfold me if

the door is shut?"

He opened his mouth, then stopped.

I raised my eyebrows.

"Shut up and open the door," he muttered. "Damn it."

I laughed and reached forward for the door. The handle creaked as I pushed it down, and a bubble of nervous energy tickled my stomach as the door opened.

The first thing I noticed was the doors. Big, huge sliding doors made up the wall at the end of the room, flooding the space with natural light.

The next was the easel.

Then the tables.

The stools. The storage. The paints. The brushes. The pencils. The pens.

And the poppy I'd painted on the wall.

"What is this?" I whispered.

"This is your studio," Adam said, stepping up behind me and wrapping his arms around my waist. "As charming as it is to wake up to you painting in your underwear at the kitchen table, I figured you'd want a space where you can paint without pants on without scaring any guests."

"One time, Adam, and I didn't know anyone was going to be here."

He laughed. "But still. The doors give you all the natural light you need. All this paint stuff is yours, but there's a ton of storage for you to fill with everything. And all the space on the walls to display stuff. You can literally sell your paintings online right from here."

He'd even set a computer up in the corner.

"Oh wow," I whispered. "And there's a coffee machine!"

"For the times you forget to make coffee before

you come in here."

"Again, that was one time."

"Poppy, one time encountering you on a morning without coffee is one time too many."

I elbowed him, but it was true.

I spun in his arms and hugged him tight. Adam kissed the side of my neck as I whispered, "Thank you, thank you," over and over in his ear.

I broke out of his arms and darted around the room, taking in everything. Running my fingers over the new worktops for me to cover with paint. Brushing the stack of different sized canvases, looking at all the sketchbooks, both new and old. Staring out of the huge doors that opened onto the back patio and looked out at the greenery in the huge backyard.

It was perfect. It was everything I'd ever wanted in a studio—and I didn't even know I wanted one until I walked in here.

I turned to Adam and smiled.

His eyes sparkled. "Marry me."

I froze, blinking at him. "What?"

"Marry me." He walked toward me and cupped my face. "I mean it."

My lips parted.

Oh my God.

"I just saw you so happy. I want to see you here, in this room, happy all the time." There was no doubt in his eyes—just love. "I mean it, Poppy. I want you to marry me."

"Okay," I whispered.

"Okay?"

I nodded.

He kissed me hard. I grinned against his lips.

"I thought you'd put up a fight," he said.

"Nah. It's like you once said to me: you're rich, you're famous, and you're good in bed. You're a catch."

He laughed, hugging me into him. "That might be the most random thing I've ever done. Well, that and going to your sister's wedding with you."

"Notice how those things both involve me?"

"Yeah, well, I told you. You're worth slowing down for." He cupped the back of my neck and kissed me again. "Love you, Red."

"Love you, hockey boy."

And I did.

Who would have thought a four day fling could last forever?

I hadn't, but here I was.

With forever.

COMING SOON:

BEST SERVED COLD

Revenge is a dish best served cold.
Which is a real problem when the attraction runs red-hot.

Ice-cream store owner Raelynn Fortune has everything but her last name—fortune.

Despite living in a Floridian hotspot for tourists, she just can't get her business back off the ground. And she knows why.

Her rival store next door is run by nobody other than her ex, and with his fancy-schmancy concoctions, he's taking all the clients two generations of her family cultivated. Never mind that Raelynn taught him all he knows, and his revenge for her breaking up with him was putting her plans into reality—and her almost out of business.

But, she has a plan. The height of the season is just two weeks away, and she's tired of playing second fiddle to her ex. She's going to take back her crown as the queen of ice cream, even if it means getting close to Chase once again.

After all, all is fair in love and war, and you know what they say about keeping your enemies close...

Although maybe Chase is a little too close...

Releasing September 25th, BEST SERVED COLD is an all-new romantic comedy from Emma Hart. Bring your sweet tooth!

Now available for pre-order everywhere! Visit www.emmahart.org/best-served-cold

BOOKS BY EMMA HART

Standalones:
Blind Date
Being Brooke
Catching Carly
Casanova
Mixed Up
Miss Fix-It
Miss Mechanic
The Upside to Being Single
The Hook-Up Experiment
The Dating Experiment
Four Day Fling
Best Served Cold (coming September 25th)

The Vegas Nights series:
Sin
Lust

Stripped series:
Stripped Bare
Stripped Down

The Burke Brothers:
Dirty Secret
Dirty Past
Dirty Lies
Dirty Tricks
Dirty Little Rendezvous

The Holly Woods Files:
Twisted Bond
Tangled Bond
Tethered Bond
Tied Bond
Twirled Bond
Burning Bond
Twined Bond

By His Game series:
Blindsided
Sidelined
Intercepted

Call series:
Late Call
Final Call
His Call

Wild series:
Wild Attraction
Wild Temptation
Wild Addiction
Wild: The Complete Series

The Game series:
The Love Game
Playing for Keeps
The Right Moves
Worth the Risk

Memories series:
Never Forget
Always Remember

ABOUT THE AUTHOR

Emma Hart is the New York Times and USA TODAY bestselling author of over thirty novels and has been translated into several different languages.

She is a mother, wife, lover of wine, Pink Goddess, and valiant rescuer of wild baby hedgehogs.

Emma prides herself on her realistic, snarky smut, with comebacks that would make a PMS-ing teenage girl proud.

Yes, really. She's that sarcastic.

You can find her online at:
www.emmahart.org
www.facebook.com/emmahartbooks
www.instagram.com/EmmaHartAuthor
www.pinterest.com/authoremmahart

Alternatively, you can join her reader group at http://bit.ly/EmmaHartsHartbreakers.

You can also get all things Emma to your email inbox by signing up for Emma Alerts*. http://bit.ly/EmmaAlerts

*Emails sent for sales, new releases, pre-order availability, and cover reveals. Each cover reveal contains an exclusive excerpt.

CPSIA information can be obtained
at www.ICGtesting.com
Printed in the USA
FFHW01n1328210918
48532551-52404FF